BLOODTIES

ALSO BY GLORIA MURPHY

NIGHTSHADE

BLOOD-TIES

BY

GLORIA MURPHY

DONALD I. FINE, INC.
NEW YORK

Library of Congress Catalogue Card Number: 86-46383

ISBN: 1-55611-036-7

Library of Congress Cataloging-in-Publication Data

Murphy, Gloria.
    Bloodties.

    I. Title.
PS3563.U7297B5   1987   813'.54   86-46383
ISBN 1-55611-036-7

Manufactured in the United States of America
10 9 8 7 6 5 4 3 2 1

Thank you Rick Horgan, Alice Martell,
Billy and Julie Gitelman.

*For Joe, with lollipops, balloons,
barracudas, and love.*

PROLOGUE

"One, two, buckle my shoe; three, four, shut the door."

Mother and child sat on the ground, clapping their hands in time to the verse. "Excuse me," Chris said.

"Five, six, pick up sticks."

"Excuse me."

"Seven, eight, lay them—"

"PLEASE."

The mother looked up, squinting, her hand held like a visor against the sun. Chris got down next to her, the grass a welcome cool against her bare knees. She pulled the picture from her purse and held it up: blue eyes, blond bangs over his forehead; a crease in the photo running through the center of his well-defined lips.

"This is my little boy, Kevin," she said. "Have you seen him?"

The toddler stood up and sank into his mother's lap. The woman pulled him to her tightly—too tightly. She stared at Chris, at the picture, then back at her. Oh, no. Was she one of the ones Chris had already asked?

Finally the woman shook her head. "No, I'm sorry. Where was he last seen?"

"Here. In the park."

"Have you notified the police?"

"Oh yes, of course. They're looking too."

She shook her head back and forth, clicking her tongue, not finding the right words to say because there weren't any.

1

"If you do see him ... my name is Chris. Chris Mathews. I'm here every day." Standing, she lifted her hand and pointed across the street to the brownstone. "I live right there."

The woman's eyes followed Chris' finger, then came back again to her face.

"Of course. I'll keep a lookout. How long has he been missing?"

"Nine months today."

Chris heard the intake of breath, but she turned away. She couldn't bear to see the silent accusation in the woman's face—the same accusation she saw every day in Neil's face: how hard is it to keep your eye on one little boy?

The truth was she wanted Neil to say the words, just once. Somehow blame would be easier to take than silence. All he wanted was to forget that Kevin ever existed. That was what everyone wanted—everyone, that is, except her.

Chris had been searching the area for hours. Hot and tired, she sat on a bench and undid the top two buttons of her blouse. When she'd left that morning, the thermometer had already passed 85 degrees; her clothes stuck to her body now as if they'd been glued. She glanced around at the children busy playing or eating sandwiches or sipping lemonade. A towheaded little boy shared an ice cream cone with an Irish Setter whose sad eyes were at odds with his bushy tail waving delight in the air like a fan. Kevin loved animals; if he were here, he'd be fast friends with the pup.

She directed her eyes to the giant oak at the rim of the playground, remembering ...

"Look, mommy. Look!"

She had let the paperback fall to the blanket, then leaned against the tree trunk. Kevin was running up to her; a dog nearly twice his size was running at his side. *"Wow, he's a big guy. Where did you find him?"* she had asked, gesturing to Kevin's companion.

Kevin stopped in front of her, and the dog knelt. *"At the sandbox, and know what?"*

She had smiled. *"Nope, I don't know. You tell me."*

"I could keep him."

She leaned forward and scratched the dog's furry neck. *"Oh ... says who?"*

Kevin turned to the dog, nuzzling his nose into the dog's wet one and hugging him. *"Says him. He's my friend."*

"But he belongs to someone else, Kevin. Maybe another little boy. How do you suppose he'd feel if we took his dog home?"

Kevin swallowed hard, then looked at her, shaking his head. *"Not so good?"* he said finally.

Then she remembered thinking: when he got a little older, Neil and she would buy Kevin a dog ... Suddenly the one giant oak became a forest of trees, and it was another day and Kevin was somewhere in that forest! She raced around and around between the trees, but she couldn't find him! He was there, she knew he was there! Why couldn't she find him?

Now she jumped to her feet. She forced her eyes away from the oak tree and toward the pond. And that's when she saw him. Holding her breath, she stared at the little boy crouched down near the water's edge tossing popcorn to the ducks. She waited until his head turned in her direction, until she was sure. She would not remember running to the pond, but the next instant she was there, only inches away, her arms stretched out to him.

"Kevin," she said, her voice so calm she could hardly recognize it.

He looked at her but said nothing.

"It's mommy, Kevin!"

His blue eyes widened. Then, slowly dropping the bag of popcorn on the ground at his feet, he stood up.

"Darling, everything's all right now. Mommy's come to take you home."

One step backward.

"Kevin. Come here."

His mouth opened: shrill screams of terror. Chris couldn't move; her feet felt planted. Then, out of nowhere, a woman appeared and scooped Kevin up in her arms.

"Put him down!" she cried.

A crowd gathered—people rushing out from behind bushes and trees as if they had been there all along, waiting. They moved toward Chris, forming a huge circle with her in the center. Finally her feet pulled free and rushed toward the boy. A hundred arms seemed to reach out, grabbing her, holding her tighter and tighter as she fought to get free.

Two policemen pushed through the crowd. Chris shouted at them over the mounting noise, one word tumbling over another.

"Look at the picture!" She thrust her purse at them. One policeman opened the purse but pulled out her wallet instead, sifting through her cards and papers, not even noticing the photograph as it sailed to the ground. Jerking free, she dived for the picture, but the arms came after her again. This time, it was she who screamed.

Time passed, but no matter how hard she tried to keep track of minutes, she couldn't figure out where they were going. Suddenly a hush fell over the crowd and the people drew back. Then, through the opening they'd made, Neil came running toward her. He was crying. My God— why? She pointed toward the little boy.

"It's Kevin. I *found* him!"

Neil looked, but turned quickly away as if he couldn't bear to see his own son's face.

"Don't you understand? It's Kevin!"

He reached out, grabbed her by the shoulders and shook her.

"Chris, please. Don't do this. He's not coming back."

She swung her arms out, pounding her fists against his chest, raking her nails down his face. Drawing blood.

"You bastard! Lying bastard!"

He pushed her onto the ground and fell on top of her. One hand held her wrists together over her head; the other hand ran through her hair.

"Chris." His voice sounded choked, anguished. "Kevin is dead ... Kevin is dead ..."

He said the words over and over until the ambulance arrived.

CHAPTER ONE

The five-year-old boy knelt on the wooden floor next to the man and repeated after him, "Dear Lord, make Davie a better boy. Take the craziness from his head and bury it. Amen." Then the boy hopped into bed and pulled the covers up over himself. The man stood up, ran his nail-bitten fingers through his coarse red hair, and went to the door.

"Goodnight, Davie," he said.

Silence.

Again, "Goodnight, Davie."

The boy's fists gripped the edge of the scratchy woolen blanket. "Goodnight, Fletcher," he said finally, though he knew Davie wasn't really his name.

Then the door closed, and as always the boy welcomed the darkness and solitude. Now was the time he talked to *them*. He rolled over onto his belly, closed his eyes real tight and waited ...

Finally, he saw them, and he heard their voices saying hello. *"Where are you, Kevin?"* mommy said, *"I can't see you."*

"I'm here, mommy, here at Fletcher's house," he said quietly into the pillow. "Can you see me now?"

She smiled, that same smile that made all the scary thoughts run out of his mind.

"I miss you, Kevin, I love you."

"Me too," he said, then taking a deep breath and baring his teeth, *"Look, I brushed my teeth three times today."*

"You're a good boy, Kevin," she told him. He knew he wasn't really a good boy, but mommy never asked him about those bad things he did so he didn't tell her.

"Can I come home *now*, mommy, daddy? Please."

"*Soon, Kevin,*" daddy said. "*One days soon, you'll look out your bedroom window and there we'll be, right out on your front lawn.*"

He wanted to go home now! He could feel tears stinging beneath his closed lids, but he buried his face in his pillow so mommy wouldn't see. "Maybe tomorrow, daddy?" he asked.

"*Maybe tomorrow, Kevin.*"

"*Would you like to hear a story, Kevin?*" Mommy asked.

The boy nodded.

"*Okay, step up and take your pick of stories—funny or happy or adventurous or—*"

"Funny," he said.

"*Okay. First off—wiggle those arms and legs and fingers and toes. Let's get those big muscles nice and loose.*"

Kevin wiggled himself around the bed, giggling softly as he did.

Finally he stopped, and mommy began, "*Once upon a time, there was an owl named Oscar. Now Oscar did pretty much the same things as the rest of his friends—that is, except for one very outrageous thing. Oscar chewed bubble gum.*"

Kevin smiled—this wasn't a book story, this was going to be one of mommy's home-made stories. Just before he fell off to sleep, he heard mommy's same whisper in his ear, "*Be patient, Kevin. Soon you'll be home.*"

The next morning, Kevin rushed to the window, hoping, that today would be the day. But all that was on the front lawn was two of Fletcher's empty beer cans. He didn't understand why it was taking them so long to get here. Mommy kept saying to be patient, and he was trying to, he was ... But he would try longer.

Until he was seven years old, David carried those two people around in his head, and then one day, as though his brain had been rubbed with a giant eraser, the people disappeared. The strangest part of it all was that, after holding onto them as if they were the most important things in his whole life, he was the one who finally rubbed them away. If those people were his parents and his real name was Kevin, like the voices inside kept telling him, then he was dead.

It was ten years ago, but he could still remember the way Fletcher sat down next to him and held the *Boston Globe* newspaper photo in front of his eyes so he couldn't help but look.

"It's time I showed you this," he said, nodding at the photo. "Those the people?"

The boy stared at the two faces, transposed for the first time from his head onto paper, then followed their eyes—the saddest eyes he had ever seen—to a coffin being lowered into the ground.

"What does it say?" Fletcher asked, pointing to the story underneath. Though David had never been to school, he'd taught himself to read. Slowly, he made the small-print letters into words and read them aloud.

"Christine and Neil Mathews ..." He stopped to look again at the faces that, until now, had had no names.

"Go on," Fletcher said. "Read."

"... Bury son, Kevin, found dead after sixteen-month search. The three-year-old disappeared from Keeny Park in Brookline on November 8, 1971 ..." The rest of the story had been torn away. David looked up at Fletcher, wondering how he'd known that those were the faces always there inside him. Fletcher had always told him he could see right inside his head, but until that moment, the boy hadn't believed him.

"If these are your folks and your name is Kevin," he said, "then I guess you gotta be dead. Why ... this boy's been dead three years now."

David stood frozen for a moment as if weighing what Fletcher had said, then threw his arms around the man's neck, nuzzling his face against his wide, warm chest. His tears made a big wet spot on Fletcher's T-shirt, but he let him stay like that for a long time.

Finally the man pushed him away and his watery blue eyes looked right into his.

"Well, what's it gonna be, Davie? Whose little boy are you—mine or the Mathews' little dead boy?"

He didn't have to think long about it.

"Yours, Fletcher." It was the very first time he had said it, even though Fletcher had asked him the first part of the question dozens of times. "I'm your little boy."

"Now, you're sure of that, are you? If not, if you're gonna talk more foolishness, I can dig a big hole and—"

The man ran his hand through the boy's hair and smiled down at him.

"Now, that's more like it. Looks to me like we're gonna knock that craziness out of you once and for all. Yes sir, get you all better so maybe you can go to a real school like other kids."

Other kids were something David saw only on TV, in Fletcher's magazines, or through his bedroom window. The idea of going to school, being with real children, made him happy, but he tried not to show it, thinking that if Fletcher knew he might change his mind.

"Quick—go get the book," he said The boy jumped off the chair and raced to get the black photo album, then hurried back and placed it on Fletcher's lap. "I'm gonna put this picture right here in the album, Davie, to be a reminder of who you really are. Whenever you're not sure, you take a peek at this poor little dead boy being put in the ground. Understand?"

He watched as Fletcher's hand lifted the cover—a red, heartshaped birthmark darkened the inside of his wrist—then turned away as Fletcher leafed through the pages and mounted the picture. When the boy heard the heavy cover close, he took the book and put it in its special place on the shelf in the parlor.

Not too long after that, Fletcher, true to his word, enrolled him in the second grade at the Farley Wentworth Elementary School in Laconia, New Hampshire. David was true to his word, too. The day Fletcher showed him the newspaper article was the last time he ever thought about his name being Kevin or about not being Fletcher's little boy. It was even the last time he allowed those two faces to sneak into his head—until the day of high school graduation, when he opened the photo album and studied the now-yellowed picture. That was the day he made up his mind to go to Massachusetts. He had to go somewhere—after what he'd done to Fletcher—and Massachusetts seemed as good a place as any to hide from the police.

It wasn't until he crossed over the state boarder, that he began to wonder if Massachusetts had really been such a random pick after all. Or had he chosen it because *they* lived there—the parents of the dead kid who had mysteriously crawled inside him so long ago. Either way, it had nothing to do with him now ... not that he wouldn't mind just seeing them.

The idea churned through his mind: it wasn't like he had other plans ... besides what would it hurt? If anything at all, it might do him some good. Some instinct told him that if his phantoms were ever to be conquered, they would have to be met in the flesh.

It had been more than two months of watching, catching glimpses of the woman from his car as she came and went. A few times he spotted a girl coming out of the house, too, but he wasn't much interested in her. He didn't try to kid himself about what he was doing—it was spying, clear and simple. Not that he hung around the neighborhood all the time. He didn't. He couldn't chance the police stopping, asking him questions. Most of the time he'd just ride around town, pick up something to eat, maybe even see a movie. Then at night, he'd pull into a deserted lot or occasionaly the YMCA and stay the night. Always, though, some strange compulsion took him back here.

Today he saw a "For Rent" sign go up in their window, making him wonder if that weren't some bizarre invitation put there just for him. And once that idea caught in his mind, it wouldn't go away. He was like that—he couldn't let go of things easily.

Until then he had only seen her from a distance, but when he rang the bell and she opened the door for him, it seemed like a curtain in his mind had parted: he remembered her face as if it had never left him, even down to the small beauty mark at the right of her mouth. It took every ounce of willpower he had just to keep the recognition from showing.

She stared at him through the screen door, and for a second he thought maybe she knew his face too. But she just smiled and said, "Can I help you?"

"The sign," he said finally. "Room for rent."

She opened the door wider and stepped back. "Come in." He went inside. "I'm Chris Mathews," she said, extending her hand.

David brushed his sweaty hand against the side of his jacket, then took hold of hers. He had taken a room at the YMCA that morning just to shower and change, but still he didn't feel clean enough.

"David Crane," he said. It was funny: he half expected her to jump when she heard the name, but of course it meant nothing to her. She lead him from the foyer into the parlor. White draperies covered one whole wall; two pictures—one of a girl and one of a boy—stood alone on the fireplace mantel. And a grand piano, polished like a looking glass, dominated one end of the room. She gestured for him to sit.

"Do you play?"

He shook his head and sank down carefully onto the plush, brown, velour sofa cushion.

"Forgive me," she said. "but you look so young to be off on your own."

"I'm seventeen. A freshman—Boston University."

"Tell me something about yourself, David. Where are you from?"

"New Hampshire. Laconia." He stopped, trying to calm himself. It felt like the whole room had fallen away and though he knew she was sitting only a few feet from him, he might have been looking at her from the other end of a tunnel. She waited for him to go on, her soft brown eyes staring at him from a distance.

"My father died this past spring. There were just the two of us."

She leaned over—coming out of the tunnel, bringing the room back with her—and put her hand on top of his.

"I'm sorry," she said softly.

He took his hand back. "He left me insurance money. For my education."

"Wouldn't you rather live on campus, David? With people your own age?"

"Not really," he said. "I'd be more comfortable with a family."

"How did you learn of the vacancy? We're five miles from Boston."

He shrugged. "Just riding around, I spotted the sign. And then, when I looked at the house ..."

"Yes?"

"Did you ever dream up something in your head—imagine it so clear that it seemed almost real?"

"I guess many of us have had that experience," she said.

He hesitated, not sure if he should go on, but he could see she was waiting.

"That's kind of how it was with this house," he said finally. "Almost like I knew it, almost like it had been a part of a dream."

She took a deep breath, then let it out. "I'll be frank with you, David. I hadn't really planned on renting to a

young man. You see, my daughter and I are alone temporarily. My husband suffered a stroke a couple of months
ago." She paused, folding her hands in her lap. "I intend
to bring him home soon and he'll need some care. What
I really had in mind was a woman—an older woman,
someone who could help out a little once we do get him
home."

"But *I* could help," he said, louder than he intended.
He looked down at his sneakers. "I'm sorry. What I mean
is, I've done household chores ever since I was a kid. I
could take care of the yard, too. And I could help out
with your husband—lifting him, things like that."

She pursed her lips and studied his face, and he knew
she was wondering why it was so all-fired important for
him to rent this particular room. He had a feeling for the
house—so what? He was afraid he had scared her into
not wanting him around at all. But then she stood up,
and the tiny lines around her mouth smoothed into a
smile.

"All right, David, why don't we give it a try. I don't
think you'll find the room and board too steep—twenty
dollars a week and a few hours of chores."

"Thank you, Mrs. Mathews."

"Chris' will do," she said. "Now suppose I show you
your room."

David followed her up the winding staircase to the end
of the hall. She cupped her hand around the knob, hesitated a long moment, then opened the door, leading the
way in. The minute he laid eyes on the room, he knew it
had belonged to Kevin. It was the size of two kids' rooms.
Blue carpeting covered the floor, and white paneling ran
about five feet up the walls, topped by shelving along two
sides. Statues of Disney characters and children's books
neatly lined the shelves. The top half of the walls was covered with a blue plaid fabric that matched both the spread
and the curtains covering the double windows overlooking
the street. A fire engine red lantern hung by a thick brass

chain from the ceiling over the built-in white wood desk. Straight out of one of those "House Beautiful" magazines—not the kind Fletcher ever had around but the kind David sometimes leafed through at newsstands.

". . . A very special room."

He turned quickly toward her, suddenly realizing she had been talking.

"It's nice," he said, knowing he sounded dumb. Anyone could tell it was more than nice. It was probably the nicest bedroom in Massachusetts.

"I'll clear off the shelves for you, David."

For some strange reason he wanted it all left just like it was. Would she think him crazy for saying so? "Do you have to?" he said. "I like them fine the way they are."

Silence. Staring. Then, "No, I . . . I suppose that's okay." She walked over and opened the door to the walk-in closet, then another door. "You'll have your own bathroom."

He nodded, then turned toward the window. A white police car cruised up the street and passed the house. He looked across the street. "Nice view."

"That's Keeny Park," she said. "It's beautiful, particularly in the fall . . . When would you like to move in, David?"

He swallowed hard. "Now. I was thinking of now."

She laughed, a soft, light laugh that took away the tension. "You certainly don't drag your feet."

"Once I make up my mind to something, I can't see the sense in waiting."

She crossed her arms over her chest. "Well, David, how does Italian fare sound for tonight?"

"Pardon?"

"Food. You like Italian food?"

"Sure."

"Good. We eat at six. Why don't you bring your bags in and get settled while I see about dinner?" She headed for the door, then turned back. "Make yourself at home, David."

He watched her walk away, then plopped down on the bed, thoughts racing. It had all happened so fast. He had a room—not just anyone's room—Kevin's, the very same boy who had somehow managed to crawl into David's brain so many years ago. What would Chris think if she knew it wasn't the *house* he had dreamed up? It was *her.*

David washed, changed his shirt and sat on the edge of the bed, watching the bedside alarm clock. One hour till dinner. It hadn't taken him long to bring in his things and unpack. He had only two suitcases, a box, the camera, the developing equipment—and the black photo album. He hadn't exactly planned on taking the album along, but he couldn't just leave it behind. After all, it was a link to his past, all he had left to remind him who he really was ... He had stuffed it in back of the closet along with the empty suitcases, knowing he wasn't likely to open it often. He put the box there, too—more things he couldn't part with: an old bird's nest wrapped in cellophane, a squirrel's tooth he'd found and kept under his pillow for years, and a rusty dart. Fletcher's hunting knife he had left in the car.

At five to six, he went into the bathroom, frowning as he checked his reflection in the mirror. His eyes were bright blue—his best feature, he'd been told, but he knew they were *too* bright. His face was long, real skinny, making his misshapen nose—Fletcher had busted it once—look even bigger than it was. A Pinocchio nose, growing with each lie. He held up his fingers and counted the lies he'd told today: he wasn't in college, he didn't just happen by, there was no insurance money— only two hundred dollars in cash and a rundown 1976 Chevy Nova. That was three. And oh, yes—Fletcher didn't just up and die like he made it seem. Four.

He concentrated again on the mirror, then shut his eyes, trying to picture his own face. Weird how hard it was to do. Out of all the faces a person has stamped in his mind, his own—the one most important face—is the least familiar. Taken a step further: if all the mirrors in the world suddenly shattered, each person would become his own stranger, only to be glimpsed now and then in a photograph. Then it would make no difference to him what he looked like. More important would be: What does the next guy look like?

He opened his eyes, ran his hairbrush under the water faucet and flattened the dark clump of hair that always stuck up from his cowlick, then turned away from the mirror and headed downstairs, hoping the butterflies he felt in his gut would go away. That's all he needed: eat the dinner she fixed, then puke it all up.

She must have heard the footsteps coming down, because she called out to him even before he was there. The next thing he knew, he was looking over a big plate of ravioli at a little mouthful of white teeth encased in silver wires, and lips curved in a wide smile directed at him.

Chris gestured toward the girl—"This is my daughter, Erin"—then back to him. "And this is David, the young man who'll be staying with us."

David nodded and unfolded the cloth napkin onto his lap. "Hi, Erin."

Erin hooked her long, dark shiny hair behind her ears.

"My mom says you go to B.U.," she said. "What's your major?"

"I haven't decided yet."

"I want to be a lawyer, like my father."

"What grade you in?"

"Eighth."

"Guess you have a long ways to go."

"Maybe so, but at least I know what I want to do."

Chris looked at her daughter. "It's not unusual to begin college still unsure of what direction you're going in, Erin. For that matter, my dear, you may change your mind altogether by the time you get where David is."

"Never," she said.

Chris turned toward David and smiled. "Don't mind Erin. She's just one of those people who was born knowing what she wants to do with her life."

Erin put down her fork. "You make that sound like it's something bad."

"Not at all, honey. Only, nothing is as certain as you'd like to think. Plans change, circumstances change—lives change, sometimes without our having all that much to do with it."

"Now you're talking about dad."

"Maybe I am." Chris turned back to him. "What do you like to do, David? Any hobbies?"

"Photography. Mostly of animals, the countryside, things like that. My father was a photographer for the Laconia *Daily Sun*. He had his own darkroom in the house. He taught me a lot about it."

"Excellent," Erin said. "Would you teach me, David?"

"Well, I don't know . . . you need the right setup."

"If you'd like," Chris said, "we have what used to be a laundry room directly across from you. There's no reason you can't use that for a darkroom."

"I wouldn't want to put you out."

"Not at all. It's just sitting there, no one's using it."

"Well . . . I did bring my dad's equipment."

"Then it's settled. I'll hunt up the key tomorrow."

"Now will you teach me?" Erin asked again.

David looked at her, knowing he was trapped and knowing she knew it too. He nodded.

"And can I see some of your work?"

"What work?"

"Well, if you're a photographer, you must have some pictures. I mean taking pictures *is* what photographers do, isn't it?"

David picked up his water glass and took a sip, then carefully put it back beside his plate.

"I didn't take them with me," he said finally.

"Why not?"

"They weren't good enough. I wanted to start a new collection." Out of the corner of his eye, he could see Chris studying his face as if she were trying to read it.

"That was dumb," Erin said. "Why would you do a thing like that?"

Chris to the rescue—again. "David's father died recently. Sometimes it's hard to face the memories pictures bring. Besides, Erin, it's David's business, not ours."

He didn't agree or disagree, just sat there feeling like maybe he would puke after all.

"Sorry," Erin said in a small voice.

Chris stood up. "Why don't I bring in dessert?" David got up and lifted his plate, but she pulled it away from him. "That's all right, David. Let me take it. You two get time off this evening." She headed to the kitchen; he sat back down, looking away from Erin, toward the piano in the living room.

"I didn't mean anything, David. Don't be mad."

He didn't answer her.

"You know," she said, "You wouldn't be bad-looking if you cracked a smile once in a while. Ever try it?"

Now, he did look at her. "You know," he said, "you wouldn't be so bad yourself if you kept your mouth shut once in a while. Ever try that?"

Erin's face flushed, but she didn't look away.

Later that evening, David heard a tap on his bedroom door. He quickly pulled on his jeans and opened the door to find Erin standing in the hallway.

"What do you want?" he said.

She looked around the room, then at him.

"I just thought I ought to warn you. It's only fair."

"Now, what's *that* supposed to mean?"

"My mother planned to rent out the spare room on the third floor, but instead she went and gave you this room. No one's ever used it before now, not even me. It belonged to my brother and he's dead."

"So?"

"My mother seems to think there's something special about you. Personally, I just think you're strange. But I intend to find out all about you, David Crane. I just thought you ought to know that."

When David entered the kitchen the next morning, he immediately sensed that he had walked in on a conversation about himself. Lots of chatter, then sudden silence. Even Chris' usual poise seemed blown. She said "Good morning" real fast, then arranged a place setting for him even faster. Erin looked smug, as if amused at his discomfort and daring him to do something about it. Finally Chris gave Erin one of those looks that seem to warn without a word, and Erin's eyes turned back toward her plate where they belonged.

Chris lifted the platter from the center of the table and passed it to David. "Here, have some."

He took his fork, speared two pancakes and put them on his plate, all the while trying to think of something light and inconsequential to say—small talk, something he wasn't very good at. That's when Chris dug her hand into her bathrobe pocket and pulled out a straight-backed silver key.

"Before I forget," she said, "here's the key to the room upstairs. It ought to make a perfect darkroom. It has shelves, a washtub, running water—and no windows. Of course, the dust is yay thick." She held up two fingers spaced a couple of inches apart. "I warn you, it will need a good cleaning."

David wasn't used to people putting themselves out for him. Now that someone was, he didn't quite know what to say. But he chose his words carefully, not wanting her to think him ungrateful. "This will be great, really great. I'll pick up some chemicals today in Boston. Maybe I can get set up tonight."

"I'll help you," Erin said, putting her two cents in.

He ignored her.

"When do your classes begin, David?" Chris asked.

"Not till next week."

She nodded, lifted her coffee cup and walked to the sink, then turned toward Erin and smiled. "I'll be talking to Dr. Frank today. I think he'll be able to tell me what day your father can come home."

Erin's face broke into a wide grin, showing braces and a mouthful of half-chewed pancakes. David made a face, not too obvious—just enough so Erin would take offense. But this time, she ignored *him*. She jumped up, ran over and threw her arms around her mother. Both of them hugged each other and danced around the kitchen, caught up in what looked to David like some hokey Indian ritual, with Erin's one-hundred-decibel squeals for sound effects.

Chris finally pulled away, laughing. "You'll have to forgive us, David. It's seems like we've been waiting forever for this."

He nodded, again not quite knowing what to say. The truth was, he was as anxious as they were to see Neil. Of course, for different reasons. To him, Neil was simply the other face that had been in his thoughts for so long. As it was, he didn't have to say a word: Erin's mouth began to run as if its motor got stuck in high gear, asking one question after another until Chris' head must have hurt.

She put her finger to her daughter's lips. "The hospital bed will be delivered tomorrow. Yes, you can help me get the room fixed up. Yes, he will be home for good. Yes, he will continue therapy. And no, he will not be going back to work. Not yet. Now, did I answer everything to your satisfaction?" She lifted her finger and waited.

"I guess for now."

"In that case, finish your breakfast before you're late for your bus. I'm going to get dressed so I can get to the hospital early."

Chris left the room and Erin sat down, pouring so much maple syrup onto her one remaining pancake that it looked like an oil spill. David studied her small, thin body; the bulky knit top covering her nearly flat chest, the tight fitting jeans. She looked up.

"You have a problem?" she asked.

He shrugged. "No. No problem."

"Then I suggest you concentrate on eating. Maybe you can do something to fill out that anorexic body of yours."

"You ever hear that people in glass houses shouldn't throw stones?"

"Did you coin that yourself, David? Or is it something you read in one of your dirty magazines?"

His ears felt warm. She must have spotted the magazine on his dresser last night. He hadn't meant to even take it out of the box; now, he was sorry he had. He looked at her long, thin neck and imagined how it would feel to wrap his two hands around it and squeeze—hard.

Erin turned toward the wall clock, then stood up and grabbed her jacket off the countertop, stuffing her arms through the sleeves. "Tell my mother I'm leaving." She scooped up her books and a ratty brown shoulder bag, started for the door, then stopped.

"In case you were wondering, David, we *were* talking about you when you walked in. Now wouldn't you just love to know what we were saying?"

With that, she opened the screen door and slammed it behind her.

CHAPTER TWO

rin and David were gone by the time Chris got downstairs. The dishes were cleared, rinsed, and stacked in the dishwasher: David had apparently done them before leaving. Chris glanced at the clock—only 8:30, and her appointment with the doctor wasn't until ten. She poured herself a second cup of coffee and sat at the table, looking around the tidy kitchen.

Despite Erin's negative reaction, she wasn't sorry she'd taken David in. No. In fact, just his presence seemed to brighten the house. Certainly twelve rooms were too much for just the three of them. She and Neil had planned a large family, that was before Kevin . . . and Erin. Her second pregnancy had none of the wonder and magic of her first: she was excited one moment, panicky the next—riding an emotional roller coaster and gripping the steel bar for dear life. Finally Erin was born, and Neil convinced her to use birth control. He also did his best to convince her to move—away from the house, away from the park—but there she was adamant. "What's the point?" he'd ask when he'd find her in Kevin's room staring out the double windows.

They had done their homework before Kevin's birth and were fully prepared for late-night feedings, teething, colic. But almost as if he were determined to put one over on them, Kevin slept through the night from the very first week. "Should he sleep so much?" Neil asked her, more than once. "Maybe he's bored with us."

"He's only storing up his energy," she said. "You just wait." And they didn't have a long wait at all—by seven months, Kevin took his first steps; by nine months, he said his first words; and by ten months, he had learned to

climb out of the crib. She could still remember the first
morning she opened her eyes to see a small figure in
droopy-bottomed pajamas peeking in through their bedroom doorway. She sat up and rubbed her eyes, then
nudged Neil. "Get up, it looks like we have a visitor."

Neil yawned and raised himself up onto his elbow—
"Get over here, little wise guy"—and Kevin came
bounding to their bed, jumping up on the mattress like
a monkey set free. That was the first of many such
mornings: Kevin became their alarm clock. At 6:30
sharp he'd be there, usually toting a few of his books.
"Story, mommy," he'd say, placing a book carefully
under her nose on the pillow. She was the reader of
stories, and Neil was the reader of the Sunday comics.
And both Neil and Kevin were the cooks for all those
Sunday breakfasts in bed. Neil carried a huge tray
laden with coffee, milk, juice, toast, and cereal; Kevin
carried the newspaper ... She pulled her thoughts back
to the present. Neil *hadn't* really understood. The point
was: memories were all she had left of her first-born,
and she wasn't about to give them up, too.

But if you asked her at what moment she decided to give
David *that* room instead of the one on the third floor, the
one with the private back entrance, she couldn't say. It was
almost as if she never really made a conscious choice at all.
The same thing was true of the rent. She couldn't have said
when—or how—she came up with the figure she quoted
David. Twenty dollars a week and a few chores? Hardly
enough to cover the expense of a boarder's meals. In this
area, she could have demanded at least three times that
amount. What would Neil think? She smiled. David did like
the room though—that was evident from the moment he
walked inside, just by the way his eyes seemed to inspect
every bit of decor. And though it *was* a bit peculiar that he
didn't want it changed any, so what?

She gathered her keys, purse, and jacket, and headed
out of the house, resolved not to worry about any of it.

Erin would get used to sharing space and attention, maybe eventually look up to David. And David would be a big help. Most important, Neil would be coming home.

Rush-hour traffic had begun to thin by the time Chris reached Storrow Drive. She opened the glove compartment, slid Beethoven's Moonlight Sonata into the cassette deck and sat back. Her eyes followed the road as it arched deeply, rising and falling with the piano triplets, outlining the contours of the Charles River on her left.

She had traveled this road almost every day since July 12—the day Craig Phillips, Neil's assistant, telephoned her with the news. "Neil was in his office, preparing a case, then just slumped over in his chair." He'd said it quickly, succinctly; his time and his words always at a premium.

Chris waited, wanting and dreading more details. Finally she asked, "Will he live?" Any other feelings she had were pushed aside momentarily as she clung to Craig's reassurance that he *would* live. When she first saw Neil she had doubted even that. His face was as colorless and stiff as a sheet of ice. Only the eyes were his—heavy-lidded, deep-set blue eyes suddenly trapped in a body that no longer seemed to be his. Only the eyes could speak, and she had to listen so carefully.

S-t-r-o-k-e. The letters lined up in her head like an entry in an encycopedia. In the Middle Ages, strokes had been regarded as God's punishment for sinners. She remembered reading that somewhere, a scrap of useless information stored away and retrieved at an inappropriate moment.

"A stroke occurs when the brain's function is disturbed by interference with its blood supply," the doctor explained, drawing out each word as if that would insure her understanding. "In your husband's case, as indicated by the CAT scan, a rupture of a blood vessel."

"Why?"

"Arteriosclerosis. Just like bones, arteries become brittle with age. Sometimes overexertion or stress can trigger a hemorrhage—it's hard to say." He'd misinterpreted her question, but then she had asked a question impossible to answer. She meant: Of all people, why Neil?

Neil had been elected Middlesex County District Attorney less than a year ago. Though his law practice had brought in double his present salary, Neil welcomed the opportunity to shift the emphasis from the civil rights of the criminal to the civil right of the victim. "Somewhere along the way," he'd said, "the guy minding his own business got the shaft. Maybe I'm turning idealistic in my old age, but better late than never."

Unlike most elected officials, Neil had no higher political aspirations. He had one goal only: to prosecute crime no matter how expensively it was packaged. And if anyone knew how to do that, it was Neil. He had been one of the best criminal attorneys in the Commonwealth. And in the few short months he'd been District Attorney, he had shaken a beehive of corruption, some of it involving a Superior Court judge who'd been on the bench more than twenty years.

Chris drove the silver Volvo into the hospital parking lot designated for visitors, parked, and headed for the front entrance. When she walked into Dr. Frank's office, he removed his thick-rimmed glasses and waved them to a chair.

"Good morning, Mrs. Mathews."

She removed her jacket, folded it onto her lap and sat down while he opened Neil's thick file.

"How does this coming Monday sound for Neil's discharge?" he asked.

"Absolutely wonderful! Neil will be thrilled."

"Then I'll let you give him the good news." He sat back in his chair. "As we've discussed, he'll need a home therapist."

"One hour, three times a week. It's already been arranged."

"Fine," he said, sliding his glasses back on his face. "Normally my instructions are to keep the patient busy, stimulate his mind, don't allow him to become apathetic. But I doubt you'll have those problems with Neil, he seems driven all on his own. Your job will be convincing him to take things easy."

"Easier said than done. When Neil's determined, there's no stopping him."

He smiled. "So it seems, and by no means am I faulting him for that. His determination is what has allowed him to get this far—his progress since the stroke has been phenomenal. I'm just concerned about his working himself into a fit of rage when he runs into an obstacle he can't yet overcome. If he works at it, I feel certain that most—if not all—of his faculties will return, but it's not going to happen overnight."

Neil, fully dressed, was sitting by the window, staring out when Chris walked in. Although most of his memory had returned, there were still missing connections. Sometimes simple words escaped him; sometimes conversations or events would not come together in a coherent pattern. Chris had grown accustomed to the intense, almost anguished expression now on his face. Neil had always put great stock in his powers of concentration—a cure for any ailment, any problem. Concentration now was a grueling effort, a demand he imposed on a mind that wasn't yet capable of sustaining it.

He didn't know she was there until she leaned over and kissed the nape of his neck.

"Again, nurse," he said.

She swiveled his chair around to face her. "And just what is that supposed to mean?"

First his eyes smiled, then his lips; one side of his mouth curved up higher than the other. "You're getting those smiles down pat," she said. "Bet if you practice more often, you'll become an expert."

"Reasons. Give me some."

Chris pulled up a chair and sat down, facing him. "Well, if you behave yourself, stop driving the staff crazy, I just might be able to come up with something."

He made no effort to speak.

"What's today, Neil?"

". . . Wednesday."

"Right. Five days till Monday. And that's when you get your discharge papers." She could see he hadn't quite got it. "You're going home, Neil. Monday I'm taking you home."

He lifted his left arm, the stiff one, and slowly placed it on her knee. "It's about time," he said.

Tears filled her eyes, but she kept them back. Tears, happy or sad, only upset Neil.

"Back to work," he said.

"Not yet." She lowered her voice. "Give it more time, Neil. You're not ready to handle that kind of pressure, and you know it. Dr. Frank doesn't want you to rush yourself. Everything will come back, but you've got to give it time."

"Frank knows nothing."

"Maybe not. Let's just say Erin and I want to have you around a while, all to ourselves. Indulge us. Oh, and that reminds me—I have another piece of news."

He waited.

"We have a boarder, Neil. David Crane. Seventeen years old, a college freshman. He's really special—a little shy, rough around the edges, but he has a certain charm about him. I know you'll like him. He's a photography buff, I'm letting him use the old laundry room as a darkroom."

Puzzled eyes searched hers.

"He'll be helping out around the house. I could certainly use—"

He put his hand on hers. "I don't know, Chris . . ."

"What's not to know? Really Neil, he's a very special young man."

"Too young. The same age ..."

She took a deep breath. "I don't want you to worry, Neil. I mean, about me. I wouldn't have taken him in if I couldn't handle it."

A few moments of silence. "Where?" he said finally.

"I don't understand."

"Where is he staying? The attic space?"

Chris took another deep breath before she answered. "No. Not the attic room. I gave him Kevin's room, Neil."

Now his mouth and jaw stiffened, and she braced herself for more. But to her surprise, there was no more. Instead, his features relaxed, and he leaned over and kissed her.

CHAPTER THREE

David recognized Erin's game of "cat and mouse" right away. And why not—Fletcher had played it often enough with him. Of course, with Fletcher David was always the mouse, always wincing when the cat lifted his sharp claw. Sometimes it was up only to scratch his face, sometimes not. The idea of the game was—the mouse never knew. All he knew was, he had better wince. David could see the same pattern emerging in his relationship with Erin. Had she already told her mother about the magazine she'd spotted on his dresser? He tried to keep things in perspective: wouldn't Chris have said something to him at breakfast if she knew—instead of giving him the key to the darkroom?

Worried or not, he had things to do, so he went ahead and did them. For starters, he bought a *Boston Globe,* turned to the classified pages, and circled some job ads. One hour and two interviews later, he faced Tony Stelano in his ratty second-hand appliance shop in Boston's Back Bay area.

The man held out a thick, square paw, wholly out of proportion to his small frame. "They call me Steel," he said. Once David took his hand, he knew why. He didn't know if Steel did it intentionally, but a dull pain snaked up his arm, and he had all he could do not to pull his hand away.

"David Crane," he said. "I'm here about the job."

Finally Steel let go and David hid his hand behind his back and flexed his fingers.

"You got experience?" he asked.

"Some. I worked after school for two years in a laundromat. Mostly fixing the washers and dryers when they broke down."

"Ever do a television?"

David shook his head. "But I built a stereo from scratch once." He'd saved his money—the three dollars a week Fletcher let him keep from his paycheck—bought all the components and built one hell of a stereo system. It was so good, in fact, that Fletcher went ahead and sold it for five hundred dollars. Some of the profit went toward a new photo enlarger. "A present for both of us," Fletcher said. Just thinking about that now made him feel spacy, like the world was about to pull away again. He concentrated on Steel's face, trying to stay with it.

His face was now so close to it, he could count the pockmarks etched into Steel's skin. "What's-the-matter? You with me, kid?"

"Sorry. Just thinking."

"I got a rule around here. No drugs during working hours. What you do on your own time is your business."

"I don't do drugs."

The man's eyes traveled over David's body as if he were taking his measurements. Then he dug his fingers into his greasy black hair and scratched. "It's only part-time, mind you. Ten till three, Monday through Friday."

David nodded.

"I only pay minimum."

"That's okay."

"Show up tomorrow at ten. We'll see what you can do."

As soon as David left the shop, he headed across the street to a phone booth and flipped through the directory till he came to "photographic equipment." He wrote down an address on a slip of paper and turned to leave, then stopped short. A cop was walking his way, swinging his nightstick at his hip. David folded the door, lifted the receiver, and mimicked a conversation. When he looked up, the cop was gone. He threw open the door, ran to his car, and hopped behind the wheel. No more than twenty minutes later, he had a trunkful of supplies— enlarging paper, developer, stop bath, and fixer—and was heading home.

It wasn't until he pulled into the empty driveway that he realized he didn't have a house key. There was nothing to do but sit and wait for Chris. Or Erin. And that's when he started to think about Erin's threats. His fingers began to tap against the dashboard. The more he thought, the less he could understand why she was even playing the game to begin with. Not that it mattered much—all that did matter was, she'd picked him for her opponent.

He pulled his hands away from the dash and turned on some music, a soft instrumental. He sat back with his eyes closed, letting the sun warm his face through the windshield. Seconds later, he felt as though he was in a pitch dark chamber . . . floating. He felt safe.

David heard the giggling long before he knew what it was. Once he did, his body jerked forward so fast, he bumped his forehead against the steering wheel. He sat there, now fully awake, rubbing his head.

Erin opened the door. "Did I scare you, David?"

He didn't answer, just kept on rubbing his head.

She shrugged her shoulders. "You locked out?"

He turned off the radio, got out and opened up the trunk. She followed around after him.

"Whatcha got?"

He lifted the bottles and paper and set them down on the gravel driveway.

"The developing supplies!" she shouted. "Excellent. I thought maybe you'd forget all about them, but you didn't. Now we can get your darkroom all fixed up, and you can teach me—"

"I'd like to teach you to turn off your motor."

"What's that supposed to mean?"

"You know, Erin, it wouldn't hurt if you learned to slow down your mouth and talk like a human. Maybe you can take lessons. Or maybe I can remove your batteries for you."

She stared at him, then bent over. "I'll help you carry this in," she said as she lifted the two quart containers and juggled her armload of school books. He picked up the rest.

"Come on," she said. "I've got a key."

"I figured that much out for myself."

Once inside, she followed David to his room. He stopped her outside his door. "You can leave that right here," he said.

"Afraid I'm going to uncover more of your disgusting secrets?"

"I just don't like snoops. And I've got a suspicion you're an expert."

She set the bottles down. "I'm going to put my books in my room, then I'll help you set up."

"Who says I'm going to let you?"

She sighed. "Maybe we'd better stop playing games, David. The way I see it, you don't have much of a choice. My mom and dad are pretty open-minded, but not about dirty pictures. Personally, I couldn't care less but its not me you have to worry about.

He decided to chance it: "What *were* you and your mother talking about this morning?"

She smiled coyly, fluttering her long, dark lashes for emphasis. He lifted his hand and placed it on the back of her head. Then, with one quick movement, he balled up a chunk of her hair in his fist ... and squeezed. She didn't try to pull away, though he knew his grip was pretty strong.

"Tell me," he said.

"Let go of me."

"Tell me first."

"My mother told me to try to get along with you, that's all."

"And what did you say?"

"Let go, and I'll tell you."

He loosened his hold on her hair and dropped his hand.

"I said I'd try."

"What *else*, Erin?"

"Nothing else. Yet."

They stood there, eyeballing one another, testing to see who'd back off first. It turned out to be David. He looked down at his sneakers. "If you want to help, get moving. I'm going to start right away."

Erin ran down the hall to get rid of her books. David watched as she disappeared into her room, wondering what was to stop her from shooting her mouth off to her mother and ruining everything.

He supposed it sounded crazy—after all, he had only known Chris for a brief twenty-four hours—but already he knew he couldn't let that happen.

Erin handed David a plank of wood she'd found in the cellar, and he placed it across the brackets. Perfect. One long counter ran the length of the room to the washtub on the far right. He looked at the shelves overhead. They had cleaned everything from top to bottom, and the room was beginning to shape up.

"Can we bring in the equipment now?" Erin was already heading for the box in the hallway.

"Take it slow. That stuff is expensive."

"Trust me," she said, carrying in the most expensive thing of all.

David took the enlarger out of her hands and placed it on the left side of the counter. "Go get the trays."

Within seconds she was back with three plastic trays. "Where do you want these?"

"Line them up next to the sink." He carried in the chemicals and placed them on the shelf. "We're going to need some half-gallon jugs."

"What for?"

"To hold the stock solutions."

"What about plastic milk jugs?"

He shrugged. "As long as they're clean."

Erin ran downstairs to find the containers, and David went about setting up the rest of the supplies. By the time she got back, everything was in place. Chris followed behind her.

"Can I take a peek?" Chris asked.

David stood aside to let her in. "Sure. Come on in."

She walked in with her arms folded across her chest. But the minute she looked around, her arms dropped down to her sides and she smiled at him. "I'm impressed. It looks so professional."

"David's a regular Mr. Clean," Erin said. "Would you believe he even washed the ceiling?

David felt himself flush.

Chris's smile disappeared. "Well, perhaps you could take a few lessons from him," she said. "You know, not everyone views conscientiousness and cleanliness as negative traits."

"I didn't mean it that way," Erin said.

"Well, that's the way it came out."

Dead silence.

Finally, Chris said, "Dinner will be ready in twenty minutes. So if you two can pull yourselves away, I'll see you in the dining room at six." She walked out, then turned back. Maybe it was the way the light was reflecting on her—David wasn't sure—but at that moment her face looked almost like it was still somewhere in his dream. He wanted to reach out and touch it, to make sure it was still real, but of course he didn't. Instead he just stood there, waiting for her to speak.

"David, I told Erin earlier, the doctors are discharging Neil this coming Monday."

"That's good news," David said, not sure whether he meant it.

Her smile came back. "Maybe after dinner we can all sit down and talk about it. I'd like both you and Erin to know what to expect."

He nodded. Out of the corner of his eye, he could see Erin look back and forth from her mother's face to his as if she were an intruder listening in on a private conversation. Chris turned away and disappeared down the hall, but his eyes stayed right where she had stood in the doorway.

"You really like my mother, don't you." A statement, not a question. He didn't respond to it.

"Why?" she asked finally.

David shrugged. "She reminds me of someone I used to know."

Erin's dark eyes squinted as she looked at him. Tiny creases formed along her forehead, and she folded her arms across her chest. It was an expression and pose David had seen on Chris, but it didn't look nearly as good on Erin. He turned away and busied himself measuring out the powdered developer. Erin watched over his shoulder. "You know, I really didn't mean anything bad when I called you a Mr. Clean. I was only teasing."

He placed a funnel in the milk bottle and poured in the powder. "Forget it."

"Did you do this when you were little, David?"

"Do what?"

"Take pictures. And develop them."

He thought about it a moment. "Yeah. Real little. As a matter of fact, as far back as I can remember."

"How far is that?"

He looked at her, puzzled.

"You know what I mean—how far back *can* you remember? My dad and I made up a game once. The idea is to remember things you really thought you forgot."

"It sounds dumb."

"Maybe it is, but it's fun. My dad says we have all
kinds of memories stored up inside. And if you develop
your mind and concentrate hard enough, you can recall
all kinds of things."

"What's the point of it?"

Erin shrugged. "Maybe it's just a good way to get to
know things about the other person. For instance, my
dad told me a lot of stories about when he was little.
Once I remembered something that happened when I
was only four years old."

"What was it?"

"Well ... it wasn't too clear. I had fallen down the
front steps and needed my lip stitched. Actually I didn't
remember that part at all. What I did remember was my
dad in the hospital emergency room, making weird faces
at me, trying to make me laugh."

"Did you laugh?"

"No, not then. But I bet I did later." She smiled.
"How far back can you remember, David? Let's play."

He shook his head.

"Why not?"

"I just don't think I'd like it." Then, after a minute of
silence, "What did your dad remember?"

"Tons of things. His parents were terribly strict with
him. So he used to sneak out of the house through his
bedroom window to play with his friends."

"Did his folks ever find out?"

"Not then they didn't. Now, they're dead." She leaned
against the counter, looking up at the ceiling. "You know
... for a while I almost thought my dad was dead."

"You mean, when he got sick?"

"Yeah."

"But you found out he wasn't."

"Well ... my mother said he wasn't. But no one would
let me go see him. So then I thought maybe she was
lying to me and that he really *was* dead."

"I guess he was too sick to see you."

"He wasn't too sick to see my mother. She went every day. And Craig went too. Craig's his assistant—and *I'm* his daughter!"

"A lot of hospitals don't allow kids to visit. Maybe that was why."

"You only have to be twelve, and I'm almost thirteen."

As usual, Erin had a comeback. The only difference, David thought, was that this time she didn't gloat; this time, she looked up at him waiting, like—for once—she wanted *him* to win *his* point. "Strokes can leave people talking funny or forgetting things," he said finally. "Sometimes there is paralysis. Maybe he was in pretty bad shape."

"It wouldn't have made any difference to me what he looked or sounded like. I could have handled it."

David turned around and started to shake the solution. "Yeah, well maybe he couldn't."

She was quiet for a long while, then: "Can I help mix the chemicals?"

"What you can do is stop talking so much and go get some caps for these bottles."

After Erin and David helped Chris clear the dinner table, Chris sent both of them into the living room while she stacked the dishes in the dishwasher. Erin headed straight for the piano, lifted the bench top and took out some music; then, placing the sheets on the rack, she sat down and began to play. David stood near the piano and watched, fascinated by the way her fingers danced lightly and quickly across the shiny black and white keyes, pressing one note with her pinky, her tiny hand stretched like rubber up the keyboard, then another note with her thumb.

When she was through, she dropped her hands in her lap and looked over at him. "Did you like that?"

David nodded. "What was it?"

"The Syncopated Clock."

"Where'd you learn to play like that?"

"My mother. She studied at the Boston Conservatory of Music. Years ago, even before I was born, she even performed in some concerts."

"Why'd she stop?"

"I'm not really sure. I think it had to do with my brother. Probably when he died ..." Erin's eyes drifted away from him. He turned around to see Chris standing in the archway, listening.

"I was just telling David ..." Erin began.

"Let's talk about Daddy now."

Chris walked to the chair and sat down. Erin followed, sinking onto the carpet at Chris' feet. David sat on the sofa. Chris leaned over and with her fingers pushed strands of Erin's dark hair away from her face. "Daddy was overjoyed to find out he's coming home. Mostly, I know, because he can't wait to see you, young lady."

"He didn't really *have* to wait."

Chris sighed. "What's important now is, he's on the road back. He still has some difficulty expressing himself, but his speech has vastly improved. Now and then, if a sentence is too complex, you'll need to simplify it for him. And reading is still something of a chore."

"I could read to him."

"I'm sure he'd like that." Chris looked over at David as if she wanted to include him in the conversation. "David, you of course didn't know Neil before the stroke ... He was always very proud, very strong, and prided himself on always being strong. His condition now, his weakness infuriates him. He's not beyond having a temper tantrum."

A glass shattered in David's head. No, it wasn't in his head, it was on the floor. And Fletcher had thrown it—at him. *He started to run, but Fletcher grabbed him by the collar of his shirt. "Clean up the mess, Davie." He crouched down onto the floor and started to lift the pieces. "Not like that!" Fletcher shouted, then grabbing hold of his hands, he crushed them down on the glass, rubbing them back and forth ...*

His attention shot back to Chris; his eyes hadn't left her face, but he hadn't heard another word she'd said. Now she was looking at him, waiting.

"You can count on me," he said, hoping with all his might that those were the right words. He breathed normally when he saw her smile.

But of course Erin was there, and as usual she didn't miss her chance.

"Don't be scared, David," she said. "My dad wouldn't hurt a fly. He just sometimes sounds like he would."

"Who said I was scared?"

"No one. You just looked like you were expecting to meet Frankenstein."

"Enough," Chris said, looking at Erin. "I'm sure David can handle it. In fact, daddy is looking forward to meeting him. I expect they'll be friends in no time."

Erin looked away from both her mother and David, but not before David could see Chris' words registering on Erin's face: only a slight furrow of her brow, a pinch to her mouth. But he could tell right off—the idea didn't exactly appeal to her.

CHAPTER FOUR

Chris tapped first, but hearing no answer, turned the doorknob quietly and peeked in. Though the bedside lamp was still lit, Erin was fast asleep. She tiptoed to her bed, reached out and lifted the heavily bound book off her chest: then, marking her place, closed the book and set it on the bedside stand. That's when Chris noticed the title: *Beginning Photography and the Home Darkroom.*

She shook her head, feeling more than a little relieved. Here Erin was trying to impress—of all people—David. Just when Chris thought she understood how that active little mind operated, Erin would throw her off balance and remind her all over again how very much she was like her father. No one could ever be sure what was concealed beneath Neil's surface—unlike herself, who had never quite developed the knack of hiding her feelings.

She leaned over, pulled the covers up to Erin's chin, and touched her lips to her daughter's soft cheek.

"Night, mom," Erin's sleepy voice hummed in her ear.

"Night, angel." Chris turned off the lamp and went out into the hallway. Instead of going directly to her room, which she had every intention of doing, she found herself heading further down the hall. She heard a faint cough from David's room: the next thing she knew, she was standing at his door, wondering what she was doing there. She tried to walk away, but her legs just weren't cooperating at the moment. She leaned against the door, closing her eyes and resting the side of her face against the dark, smooth wood. The house was quiet, so quiet she could almost hear David's breathing.

40

She looked down to see her hand cupped around the doorknob. She yanked it back as if it were scorched and fled as quickly and quietly as she could to her bedroom.

Chris didn't sleep well that night; she couldn't easily ignore her trip to David's bedroom. How could she have done that? She'd wanted nothing more than to slip quietly inside for just a few moments, just to look at him. But still, what business did she have infringing on the young man's privacy? He was simply David, a boarder. Not Kevin. She didn't need a visit to her psychoanalyst to remind her of that.

When Erin showed up in the kitchen the next morning, Chris had been up for hours; the freshly perked pot of coffee was nearly empty. But, tired or not, she found her energy level slowly rising to match Erin's high spirits.

"I'm starved," Erin announced.

"No fancy breakfast this morning," Chris said, setting the box of raisin bran on the table and slipping two slices of wheat bread in the toaster.

"Can I fire you?"

"Not a chance. You're stuck with me." She decided not to mention the book; it would only embarrass Erin. "You know," she said, "I think I owe you an apology."

"You do?"

"Yes. I've probably been a little too hard on you when it comes to your dealings with David."

Erin just looked at her.

"The thing is, Erin, David's a very sensitive young man. I don't think he quite understands that your sometimes flip statements are not intended to ridicule him."

"What makes you think they're not?"

"Well, are they?"

Erin shrugged. "I guess not."

Chris sighed. "In any event I didn't mean to imply yesterday that you aren't conscientious."

"It doesn't really matter."

"I think it does."

"Dad always says the only important thing is what you know about yourself, not what others think they know about you. And since I know I'm conscientious, it really doesn't make too much of a difference."

Chris sat there studying her daughter, wondering how she could so admire that philosophy, yet know she'd just been told in so many words that her opinion was unimportant.

"Oh, I don't mean your opinion doesn't count, mom."

"Erin, how in the world did you read my mind?"

"I didn't. I just know how you think, that's all."

Chris sat there, not knowing what to say and feeling foolish. She supposed if Neil were there, he'd be leading the band in laughter. But Neil wasn't there, and she didn't feel much like laughing, particularly at her own expense.

Finally Erin broke the silence. "You really like David, don't you, mom?"

"Why? Don't you?"

"I asked first."

"All right. As a matter of fact, I do. Very much. Most boys his age are pretty much caught up in their own lives. Parties and good times are high priorities. David's different. I get the feeling there's so much more to him than he lets on—almost like he's afraid to show what's inside."

"Why should he be afraid?"

"Well, I don't really know. I do know that he's had a rough time of it. Apparently he was brought up solely by his father, whom he lost not too long ago. That couldn't have been easy. Losing someone you love can be devastating."

The toast popped up; Erin lifted out the slices and dropped them onto her plate, then used a knife to dig out a huge chunk of butter from the tub.

"Mom, did you ever think of investigating his past?"

"What do you mean?"

"You know, hire detectives."

Chris gulped down a mouthful of coffee and lowered her cup. "Erin, how could you suggest such a thing? And for that matter, *why* would you suggest such a thing?"

"You can sometimes find out interesting things about people. Things maybe you should know about. Dad does it all the time."

"That's for the purpose of investigating a case, Erin. David is hardly a file in your father's office. People don't go around snooping into other people's lives just for the fun of it. Apart from its impracticality, I find the idea very distasteful."

Having smeared every inch of her toast with butter, Erin raised it to her mouth and bit into it. The only response to Chris' comment was in her eyes—disturbed, thoughtful.

"Are you saying you don't like David, Erin?"

"No. I'm not."

"Then what *are* you saying?"

"Nothing. It was just a dumb thought."

"Erin, I'd like you to give David a chance. Surely that's not asking too much, is it?"

She rolled her eyes upward, sighing. "No," she said, "it's not. And I *am* giving him a chance, mom. Honest I am."

Chris slipped the newly made house key in an envelope labeled "David" and placed it on the kitchen table where he'd be sure to spot it, then went off to visit Neil.

Craig Phillips was at the hospital, waiting for Neil when she arrived. Craig had been out of law school only one year when Neil appointed him Assistant DA. According to Neil, he was one of the brightest young attorneys around, a real find. What he lacked in litigation experience, he more than made up for with his shrewd, analytical mind. "Besides," Neil pointed out, "if you want ideals, you've got to get your talent while it's young and fresh—before money has a chance to parade its importance."

"Neil's in therapy, Mrs. Mathews," Craig said, popping up from his chair. Though she'd told him countless times to call her Chris, he never did. Now he stood facing her, not a wrinkle in his navy three-piece suit. His blond hair curled softly over his earlobes; his complexion was unblemished, completely smooth except for a hint of peach-fuzz beard. Craig looked more like a choirboy than an attorney. But since Neil's stroke, it had become apparent to her that looks, in this case, were deceiving.

He handled the press with the aplomb of a diplomat and the cunning of a used car dealer. As an elected official, Neil's disability was news. Craig, determined to protect Neil's position, initiated two press conferences and posted up-to-date DA reports, never once failing to slip in Neil's views on current matters. So far as the media and public were concerned, Neil had suffered a mild stroke but was currently running the office from his hospital bed. Of course, during the first six weeks, this was completely untrue. Now, just mostly untrue. A judicious stretch of the truth, as he himself might have put it.

"Has Neil told you the good news?" Chris asked. "He phoned the office yesterday." Craig sat back down, shaking his head. "For a while there it seemed as if we weren't going to get him back. I'm not afraid to admit it—I was scared."

"You've been doing a marvelous job, Craig. I've been following the papers."

"Adequate. Only adequate. I'm not in Neil's league, not yet. We've got cases sitting on ice, waiting for him. Cases I wouldn't dare move on without his help."

"You must understand, Craig, he's coming home, but he won't be going right back to—"

"Don't listen to her, Craig." Chris looked up to see Neil standing in the doorway. Though powerfully built, he looked almost fragile as all six feet of him leaned against the aluminum bars of the walker. He lifted his right hand and pointed at Chris. "Earth Mother."

Craig looked first for Chris's reaction. When she smiled, he joined in.

"It's all right, Craig, I'm used to this man's abuse. You know the saying, in one ear and out the other."

Neil, now towering over her, bent over and planted a kiss on one ear, then the other. He sat down and pushed the walker aside, still looking at her. "A deal," he said finally.

"What do you mean?"

"A deal," he repeated. "I'll work at home."

"Not yet you won't."

His square jaw tightened.

"Neil, please. The doctor says it's important for you not to push yourself."

"Screw the doctor."

"Neil—"

He reached out and smashed his good hand against the walker, sending it sprawling across the room. Chris got up, fetched the walker and stood it up beside him. Then, kneeling in front of him, she reached up and ran her fingers through his thick, gray-peppered hair.

"God, you're impossible."

"A deal?" This time a question.

"Three hours a day. Max."

Out of the corner of her eye, she could see Craig staring out the window as if he hadn't heard a thing. But she would have had to be blind not to recognize the relief in his face at Neil's victory.

CHAPTER FIVE

s soon as David walked into the kitchen, he spotted the envelope Chris had left for him. While he poured himself a bowl of cereal, he rubbed the gold key between his fingers, feeling the craggy ridges one by one. When he was ten years old, he had seen a television special called, "Latch-key Kids." From that day on, he wished he could become one of those kids, running home with a key dangling from a string around his neck and opening the door to an empty house. But that never happened. Fletcher worked at home; he was always there, waiting ... David never did get a house key, either—that is, until now. He set the key down on the table and ate his cereal, not taking his eyes off it.

He'd wanted to come down earlier, to have breakfast with Chris, but the moment he heard Erin slam the back door in her normal uncivilized fashion, he heard Chris' light footsteps on the stairs. He lay in bed, his eyes closed, listening to the spray of the shower, then later the buzz of the hairdryer. He could see every single motion in his head. Nothing erotic, nothing like that, just the way women make a big deal of those things as opposed to men.

He remembered reading an article in a girls' magazine: "Twenty-five Steps to Proper Bathing." Pictures and all. After the author explained how to reach and wash those hard-to-get-at places, she moved on to teach the head-wrap: a towel is manipulated around the head in such a way that when the ends are tucked in, it makes a bonafide Arabian turban. Next she told her readers how to use a big thick towel to pat the skin so dry that it actually blushed. The article went on to shaving, clipping toenails, plucking

46

unwanted hairs, rubbing away rough spots with a little con-
cretelike bar, and lots of other gory details. Finally, the pow-
ders, the sprays, the lotions, topped by an "astringent
splash" to make the body tingle . . . Judging from the length
of time it took Chris to dress, David decided that she must
have taken every one of those steps.

By then he was too embarrassed to face her, so he
waited until she left to get himself out of bed. Once she
did, he got up and walked down the hallway to the big
bathroom, intending to tidy it. He should have realized
that Chris wasn't the type to leave a mess after herself;
except for the still damp tiles and the conglomeration of
scents, he never would have known she was there. He
pulled open the vanity drawer: tweezers, clippers, razors,
lotions—a virtual drugstore of supplies. Then he checked
in the hamper, and sure enough: resting inside were two
wet towels and a nightgown. Feeling a bit guilty, he shut
the hamper lid and climbed into the shower.

Now David spooned up the last of his cereal, rinsed his
bowl, set it in the dishwasher, and grabbed his jacket off
the back of the chair. He glanced at the clock, then took
the house key, leaving himself just enough time to stop
off and pick up a key ring before getting to work.

Maybe he'd get the kind with a rabbit's foot—he had
always wanted one of those.

Steel's first act of the day was to teach David how to
disassemble and repair a television set.

"Get it, kid?" he kept asking as he pointed out the
parts. David watched him manuever his king-size hands
around the tiny spaces, expecting one of his hands to
become wedged in so tight, he'd have to pry it free. But
that didn't happen. In fact, he was amazed at how nim-
ble those long, thick fingers were.

"I got it," David told him finally.

He stood up, sweating, ran a greasy cloth over his forehead and gestured toward the shelf.

"Okay, then go take apart that one. We're going to recondition it."

David took the twenty-four-incher and set it on the table. "How much does something like this go for, Steel?"

"Now, peanuts. Once we get through with it, it ought to bring in two hundred."

"Where do you get these?"

"You writing a book, kid?"

"Just curious."

"Curious people get into lots of trouble, kid, so I suggest you cure yourself of the habit. The only thing that ought to concern you is picking up your paycheck at the end of the week."

After that bit of conversation, David got to work on the TV. Customers came and went; one of them a shapely girl about fifteen whom Steel did his best to hit on. Only three people bought—the rest of the transactions were the other way around—Steel buying from the customers. One guy, who had a tattoo running down the length of his arm, brought in three TV sets and a stereo. Steel and he haggled over a price, then Steel reluctantly counted out some bills. It didn't take a genius to figure out what was going on.

By the time three o'clock rolled around, David decided the job wouldn't be half bad after all. For one thing, he liked to tinker. For another, Steel, despite his gruffness, tended to stay off his case. Most important, the job gave him time to think. And now, with his life all turned upside down, he had plenty to think about. It wasn't all perfect. There were Erin's threats and Neil's temper tantrums . . . there was even the fear that Kevin's memories might take hold of his thoughts the way they had when David was a kid. But today he managed to push all the bad things out of his mind. Today he pretty much thought about Chris.

Erin was waiting for David on the front steps when he drove up. He hadn't yet reached the bottom step when

she started hurling questions in his direction. "Where
have *you* been?"

"I go to school. Remember?"

"I thought classes didn't begin until next week."

"Orientation." He could have kicked himself; he certainly didn't owe her any explanations. "What's it to you,
anyhow?"

"We need to move some furniture into my dad's bedroom."

She followed David into the house, trailing upstairs
after him. Once he reached the landing, he followed the
smell of disinfectant to the room adjacent to the master
bedroom. Chris, kneeling at the bottom dresser drawer,
stood up and faced him. She wore jeans, a faded sweat-
shirt and sneakers; a wide blue headband framed her
face, puffing her short, dark curls to the back and empha-
sizing high cheekbones he hadn't noticed before. A
smudge of dirt was stamped on one flushed cheek like a
badge. She looked different. Not bad, just different.

"Am I glad to see *you,*" she said.

"I'm sorry—"

"No need," she said cutting his apology short. "Erin
and I were just anxious to get Neil's room settled. We've
done about all we can alone." She gestured toward a
broom, mop, rags, and cleansers. A bucket of gray water
with a layer of scum stood on the floor. "What we need
now are a few more muscles to help us get Neil's desk
moved in."

"Lead me to it," he said.

She smiled. "Follow me." Then, hanging lightly onto
his arm, she led him down the hall, Erin trailing at their
heels. Finally she stopped and turned: an alcove. Several
wide steps led to a double door. She slid her hand from
his arm, threw the doors open, then walked in. And
David followed.

He swallowed hard. The room was as big as a small
dance hall—a dark wood-paneled dance hall. But that

wasn't what bowled him over; it was the books. Shelves lined three of the walls, floor to ceiling, and hundreds— no, thousands—of books were lined up across the shelves.

"Neil is pretty much of a collector," Chris said.

"One whole wall is filled with law books," Erin chimed in.

"Has he read them all?"

"I don't suppose all," Chris said, "at least, not all of the law books. They're mostly for research."

When David didn't say anything, Chris walked over to Neil's large wooden desk and began to clear off the top of it.

"Get some boxes, Erin. We want to move these supplies into your father's room."

Erin ran off. "Is he—Neil—going to work at home?" David asked Chris.

"Yes, he is. Much against my better judgment, I might add. But since he is, I thought it would be easier having his desk in his bedroom."

"Doesn't Neil sleep in the master bedroom, with you?"

She stopped fidgeting with the pens, pencils, long yellow pads and looked up at him.

"Well, normally yes. But for awhile, under the circumstances ..." She stopped and licked her lips as if they were too dry to continue talking.

David wished he could have taken back the question. It was dumb and nosy. Most of all, it was making her uncomfortable, and that was the last thing he wanted to do. Then Erin stomped in and, for the first time, he was glad to see her. She threw down the boxes and they all began to clear out the drawers.

With very little help from either Chris or Erin, David managed to lug the desk down the five steps, down the long hallway, into Neil's room. He could tell by the way both of them watched that they were more than a little surprised at his strength. Of course, by that time he had pulled off his jacket and rolled up his shirt sleeves so they couldn't help but see his biceps. Sixteen inches: he had measured it once. Not so anorexic at that—right, Erin?

They had just gotten the last of the files and papers back in the drawers when the delivery truck pulled up outside. Erin ran down to open the door. Five minutes later, two Incredible Hulk look-alikes dragged in what was to be Neil's bed, piece by piece.

David watched as they ripped away the brown paper, as one piece connected onto the next, as they flipped the mattress into place, as ... He hung his head down and shut his eyes, resting them. Then, forcing them open, he looked again at the bed. And there he was: Fletcher, lying in a pool of blood. Huge flat feet dangled over the end rails, thick arms stretched toward the floor. David backed away, unable to shake the image. He felt himself trembling but couldn't will his body to stop.

David always operated on the assumption that a mind is programmed to accept what is real; so when that program short-circuits and scares the hell out of you, the trick is to loosen up as fast as you can. He quickly excused himself, went off to his room and, dropping onto the floor, wrapped his arms and legs into a basic yoga position. Then, with all the force he could work up, he suctioned every single thought right out of his head. "Freedom from the self," it was called, and he guessed he really escaped, because he didn't know or feel another thing until he heard a light tapping at his door. He opened his eyes and checked the bedside clock: 5:30—he had lost forty-five minutes.

He got up, feeling good—so good that when he opened the door to find Erin standing there, he actually smiled. And the funny part was, that smile of welcome really threw her off-balance. She stood there, speechless for maybe the second or third time in her life.

"What do you want?" he asked finally.

"Why did you run off like that, David?"

"I had to take a leak. Didn't know I had to ask your permission."

"It looked more to me like you'd seen a ghost." She looked genuinely concerned. "What happened?"

"Nothing," he said. "I just felt a little dizzy, that's all. Do you want to come in?"

She strolled in casually, her eyes taking in every little detail of the room. He wasn't worried; he had put all his private things back into the closet.

"Sit," he said, pulling the desk chair out into the center of the room. She sat down, but David didn't. He could tell right off that his towering over her made her feel uneasy. It reminded him of an article he'd once read on the power of strategic positioning.

"Nothing is changed," she said.

"What do you mean?"

"The room. You haven't changed a thing, not even the Disney characters."

"You got something against Donald Duck?"

She smiled. "No, I'm just surprised. Most people would have changed it."

"Well, I guess that makes me different."

"David, could we work in the darkroom tonight?"

He shook his head.

"Why not?"

He leaned against the wall, staring at her. Her knees were pulled together real tight as if she were scared he'd want to peek up her skirt. "And here I thought you were so smart," he said.

"What do you mean?"

"What was it you wanted to do in the darkroom?"

She shrugged. "Learn how to develop pictures, of course. What else?"

"Well, you can't develop them before you take them. Unless you know something I don't."

Her cheeks turned so red, they looked like they hurt. Finally, she stood up and headed for the door.

"I was thinking, Erin—"

She turned back.

"Maybe tomorrow I'll pick up some film," he said. "We can spend the afternoon in the park, taking pictures. How's that?"

"Can we, David?" she cried. And then she ran to him as if she wanted to throw her arms all over him, but she didn't. At the last moment she stopped short, embarrassed, and backed out of the room.

Once she left, David looked around. Maybe he ought to shove some of the baby stuff in the closet. But the truth was, he really didn't want to. He went over and picked up a Porky piggy bank from the shelf, slid his hand in his pocket, and taking out a couple of dimes, slid them in the slot. To his surprise, the pig oinked. He sat down on his bed with the bank, staring at it, thinking.

David had never known how or why Kevin had merged his mind with his. And still he didn't know how. But maybe now he knew why ... A kid who had all this would never give in to death easily. He'd do anything he could to stay alive.

CHAPTER SIX

Chris wasn't quite sure what had happened—all she knew was that ever since they had all worked together on Neil's room, David and Erin were thick as theives. That night, after they'd put away the dinner dishes, David brought out his 35-mm. camera.

"Sit over here," he told Erin, patting the sofa cushion next to him. "I want to explain the mechanics—how this thing works." Once she had settled herself beside him, he identified each part. "First of all, a camera has to perform three basic functions—"

"Wait a second, don't tell me." Erin closed her eyes and counted on her fingers: "It must create an accurate light image on the film, it must let you see the image as it's projected on the film, and it must regulate the amount of light on the film."

Chris suppressed a grin; David looked dumbfounded.

"How'd you know all that?"

"I'm not exactly stupid, you know."

David went on with his lesson. Chris sat and watched, wishing only that Neil were there to complete the picture and enjoying the fact that such wishes would soon be realized.

She lingered downstairs long after both of them had gone to bed. Finally, as if she had been waiting for something she'd known all along she would do, Chris went over to the piano, caressed the cool, velvety wood, then sat down and played. Not exercises, not scales to teach Erin. No hesitancy or stiffness either—her hands moved effortlessly along the keyboard.

Memories in her fingertips . . .

"I heard you playing last night, mom. You haven't for so long."

"No, I guess I haven't"

"Then why last night?"

"I don't know, Erin. I was feeling particularly happy. The piano sort of drew me."

"What were you playing?"

"Nothing special."

"I heard one piece over and over. What was it?"

"Oh, just bits and pieces of melodies I remembered. An ensemble, of sorts."

"Whatever it was, it was great," David said, walking into the kitchen. "It put me to sleep."

Chris laughed. "Well, now, I'm not so sure I should consider that a rave review." She passed him a platter of scrambled eggs and a blueberry muffin, still warm from the oven.

"Maybe it didn't sound like a rave, but I meant it as one. In the shower this morning I found myself humming that tune you kept playing."

"See, mom, I told you. It *was* one tune."

Chris looked from Erin to David then back again to Erin, trying to remember what it was she'd been playing. "I wasn't aware I was doing that . . ." she said finally.

"What difference does it make how many times you played it?" David said. "Or for that matter, what it was?"

"None. I guess none, David." She smiled. "In any event, I'm glad you enjoyed it." He was still looking at her. "What are your plans today?" she asked him.

"Signing up for courses, that sort of thing. I ought to be home around three-thirty."

"Don't forget the film," Erin said.

He nodded.

"What's this?" Chris asked.

"David and I are going to the park to take pictures."

Chris paused but only briefly, then picked up her purse from the counter. "Well, since this is a joint venture, why don't I make a small contribution toward film?" She took a ten-dollar bill from her wallet and handed it to David.

"You don't have to do that," he said.

"I know. But I want to."

"I have enough. No kidding."

"Please, David, take it." She placed the bill in his hand. "Besides," she said, "I might just confiscate a couple of those pictures for the family album. Be sure to take some of Erin and yourself."

Finally he conceded, stuffing the money into his pocket.

Chris found Neil sitting at the table by the window, diligently marking off "Friday" on the calendar. His unsteady hand drew an uneven line through the block.

"Aren't you rushing things? Friday still has a good thirteen hours to run yet."

"I'm a step ahead of them."

"Me being one of *them,* give us a chance to catch up."

"I want to get home. Now."

Chris leaned over, kissed his cheek and sat down next to him. "Patience, Neil. You're almost there."

"Erin knows?"

She took hold of his hand. "Of course she knows, she's counting the minutes." And then, hesitantly: "I was thinking . . . maybe I could bring her with me tomorrow."

"Why?"

"Because she still can't understand why you put your foot down on letting her see you."

"But *you* understand. Don't you?"

She sighed. "Understanding is not agreeing, Neil. I still think it was a mistake."

"Remember how I was? I didn't need a mirror to know."

"Do you really think anything could have knocked you off that pedestal she has you on?"

"I don't need pedestals—they support statues, not people. Still, there was no reason to put her through—"

"You've underestimated her, Neil. Erin doesn't flinch easily, she's tough. Not unlike her father."

"I saved her the nightmares."

"No, Neil. The nightmares come from fearing you'd *never* come home."

"We've been through this, Chris."

"I know. And I respected your wishes. But Neil, now it's different. You're speech has come along wonderfully. You're walking again. Your smile's a little rusty, but even that is coming back."

"I'll be home Monday. What's the point?"

"Just that if she could see where you've been—"

"I don't want her memories here, Chris. I want them home."

She sighed again. "All right."

A few moments of silence, then, "Has she been angry?"

"Not angry. Hurt."

Neil lowered his head onto his hands. If he were one to cry, it would be now. But tears were rare for Neil. Chris could only remember two occasions when he had cried: that day in the park, and Kevin's funeral. He stood up and, using his walker, went to the nightstand. He fished to the bottom of the tissue box and pulled out a roll of bills, then tossed them on the table.

"What's this?"

"Go shopping."

"Why, Neil?"

"Get a present for Erin. For yourself."

"But we don't need—"

"Go! Please!"

She stood up, taking the bills from the table and counting them out. "My God, Neil, there's over three hundred dollars here. Where in the world did you get this much cash?"

"Craig withdrew it for me."

"Were you plotting a getaway?"

A crooked smile, then: "You buy perfume. Get Erin something."

"Perfume, hmmm . . . any special fragrance?"

"Subtle, sexy."

"I'll do my best. And now that I think of it, I just might know the perfect gift for that daughter of yours. We'll make it a party. I'll have everything gift-wrapped, we won't open a thing until you get home." Chris threw her arms around him, hugging his body to hers, then drew back. "Oh, Neil, I have the most peculiar feeling. As if suddenly all the things in our lives are about to change."

"What things?"

"For one, you getting well."

"And another?"

"That's just it, Neil, I don't know what else. I just know there's more. Much more."

Chris hadn't been shopping in months, but within twenty minutes she was elbowing her way through busy aisles like a pro. Her first stop was the camera shop in Jordan Marsh were she bought Erin a 35 mm. camera like David's. Next she picked out a black leather photo album for David, suitably elegant for the new collection of photographs he was starting. She took the escalator to the third floor small appliance department, where she bought a mini-size tape recorder and a dozen blank tapes; it would be far easier for Neil to record than to write. Her last stop was the perfume counter, where she sniffed and sprayed and sniffed again. Finally—a muddle of bouquets—she left with a six-ounce bottle of Caleche.

She made a quick stop at Quincy Market for Neil's favorite bread sticks, then headed home, right in the middle of rush-hour traffic. It was nearly 5:30 when she pulled up in the driveway beside David's car. The front door was locked. She rang the bell—no answer. She shifted the packages to her left arm, then fumbled around in her purse for the key. After several unsuccessful attempts, she found the key, let herself in and dropped the shopping bags on the foyer credenza. She stood at the foot of the stairs and called out: "Erin . . . David." No response. And then she remembered—of course, the pictures. They must still be in the park.

She carried the packages up to her room, and came down to prepare a quick dinner. Less than an hour later, a casserole was bubbling in the oven and a string quartet was playing on the stereo. She went into the living room and pushed apart the floor-length drapes, looking across at the park: the sky was overcast, dreary. She hadn't noticed that earlier. Could they take photographs without sun? She supposed they could. A dull throbbing began in her temple. She was being silly—overreacting, Neil would say. After all, Erin wasn't alone, she was with David.

Yet somehow, she still felt that the park could be dangerous. For both of them.

CHAPTER SEVEN

The park was even bigger than David had imagined. They followed a dirt trail for at least a quarter of a mile, stopping to take photographs along the way. When they came to a waterfall on the top of a hill overlooking the playground, he told Erin to stop. "Let's get this."

He showed her once again how to adjust the light, then let her take the picture. They had used up most of the roll of film. David took the camera from her.

"Now let me take one of you," he said.

She shook her head. "Uh-uh."

"I promised your mother."

She rolled her eyes and backed up against a tree. "Okay. Go ahead." As soon as the shutter blinked, she ran up and took the camera back. "Your turn. Remember—she wants yours, too."

He took off his jacket, leaned his free hand against a tree and, with his other hand, held the jacket over his shoulder. A real macho pose. She pressed the button, then he sat down on the ground.

"Why don't you like to have your picture taken?" he asked.

Erin followed suit and sat down. She leaned her back against a tree; her small pale hands crunched the dry leaves.

"I don't know, I just don't like it."

"I'm surprised."

"Why?"

He shrugged his shoulders. "I would have thought someone like you wouldn't be camera shy."

"What do you mean, someone like me?"

What he wanted to say was flat-chested and skinny, but of course he didn't. Instead he said, "Someone with a body like yours."

She didn't answer.

"I don't mean anything bad by that. Just that you're built like a model."

"Well that's the last thing I'd want to be. I'm not the type."

"What type is that?"

"You know, empty-headed and scatterbrained."

"Where did you get that idea?"

She thought for a moment. "My dad, I guess. He thinks modeling, beauty contests, that sort of thing sets women's lib back about fifty years. He thinks it's a real put-down."

"Some girls have put themselves through college with money from modeling and beauty contests. Not all of them are scatterbrained. Besides, that's your father's opinion, not yours. Don't you have a mind of your own?"

Her chin tilted up. "Of course I do."

"Well, you could have fooled me."

They sat there a few minutes, not saying anything, mostly looking out at the white water foaming like seltzer over the dam. Finally Erin turned to face him.

"Do you really think I look like a model?"

"You'll never know till you pose for a few pictures. Some girls take lousy pictures. They're just not photogenic."

"But models do have to be pretty. I'm not that pretty."

Now David knew she was fishing. He reached out and put his hand to her face, cupping her chin and examining her even features from a few different angles.

"Maybe you're right," he said.

She pulled away. "I hate you, David." Then, "Did you really mean that?"

"Nah. A little make-up and I bet you'd be a knockout. Provided, of course, that you kept your mouth shut so you couldn't see those silver wires."

She was quiet for a few minutes, then she stood up. "We'd better get back. It's getting late, and I know my mother. She'll worry."

"She doesn't like the park, does she?"

"Why do you say that?"

"Just something I sensed this morning when you told her we were coming here."

"My mother never took me here when I was little. Once in a while my dad did. Mostly I just had to wait till I was old enough to come on my own."

"She must really hate it."

"That's the funny part, David. I don't think she does. Oh, she worries some when I'm here. But sometimes, when it's warm out, she sits out in the yard and stares across to the park like she really wants to go over."

"Then why doesn't she?"

"She never said so, of course, but I think she's afraid."

"Of what?"

"I don't know. And the weird thing is, my father seems even more afraid of her coming here than she does."

Chris *was* worried. When David and Erin walked in the house, she looked like a loud noise would have collapsed her right at their feet. She gave off a musty smell—a mixture of sweat and perfume?

"Where have you two been?"

"I told you, mom. We went to take pictures."

"Look at the time—it's nearly seven. Erin, you know better!"

"Don't blame her," David said, plunging right in. "It's my fault."

"It's not that late, and . . ." Erin stopped.

"She was a great student, and we were enjoying ourselves. I guess I didn't notice the time. Please don't be mad. Or if you are, be mad at me and not her."

"I'm not really angry, David. I was worried—about both of you."

"You shouldn't be. I can take care of myself. And Erin too."

All of a sudden she smiled. "I'm sure you can, David. I guess I tend to be a little too nervous."

"Next time I'll pay more attention to the time. I promise. I . . . well, I don't want you to worry."

She did something then that threw David completely off balance: she leaned toward him, tilted her head up, and kissed him on the cheek. Suddenly, he felt a rush of warm feelings, wanted to reach out and hug her, but instead he kept his hands at his sides.

She turned quickly to Erin. "Well, when am I going to see these pictures?"

"David and I are going to develop them after dinner."

"In that case, let me get dinner on the table. I'm anxious to see the work of that 'great student' David is bragging about."

Erin was strangely quiet during dinner, but the moment they got to the darkroom, her usual enthusiasm returned.

"What do we do first?" She had slammed the door behind her, leaving them both in the dark.

"First, we turn on the lights."

"But I thought—"

"Second, save your energy. Don't think."

He prepared three beakers of chemicals, then disassembled the developing tank and gathered the equipment.

"Hit the light," he said.

Erin again threw the room into darkness. "I can't see what you're doing."

"Keep quiet and I'll tell you. I've just pried off the end of the film cassette with a bottle opener. Now I'm snipping the end of the film to square it off." He dropped the scissors on the countertop and lifted the paper puncher. "I'm making a hole to catch onto the metal hook of the reel." Finally David wound the film around the reel, dropped it into the canister and closed the canister.

"Now what?" Erin said.

"You turn on the light and we pour in the developer."

After putting the film through a series of chemical baths, they hung it to dry. Less than ninety minutes later, now assisted only by the red beam of a special five-watt bulb, David exposed the photographic paper and developed film to light. Then he submerged the paper in a tray of developer. As the pictures took form, Erin, who had managed to stifle herself through most of the process, actually squealed.

"David, look! They're coming out right before our very eyes!"

David handed her the tongs and pointed to the next two trays. "Thirty seconds in each," he said. Once they were through, he flipped on the overhead light, held the pictures under running water and lined them up on the counter. Erin moved along the counter, examining each picture, and making noises that sounded like she had just invented photography.

"Let's show them to my mother," she said.

"They'll have to dry first."

"No problem—she'll come up here." With that, she took off, leaving David with the mess.

He was still drying trays when they walked in. Chris sized up the situation immediately.

"Looks to me like you sneaked out of clean-up duty, Erin."

Erin looked at David. "Why didn't you wait? I would have helped."

"I don't mind doing it," he said.

Chris turned toward the counter. "Well, let me see those pictures."

Erin handed them to her one by one, telling a story about each as she did. Erin had no story for the shot of David, but Chris didn't need one.

"I love it, David," Chris said. She studied it carefully. "You take a wonderful picture." Finally she looked up.

"Could you make a copy for me ... maybe blow it up larger?"

"Sure."

"That would be marvelous." She placed the picture carefully on the counter, then took the last one from Erin. She put her arm around Erin's shoulder. "Not bad, honey, but you look so stiff, so formal. It looks like someone is holding you at gunpoint."

"Actually," he said, "I think Erin's real photogenic."

"I agree with you, David. If only she'd smile. Maybe next time you can get her to relax."

That night David wasn't at all surprised when he heard the tap on the door; in fact, he was expecting it. For one brief moment he thought he'd pretend he was sleeping, but then Erin's cat and mouse game flashed through his mind, and he got up and opened the door. She stood there, looking like a painted Barbie Doll: she wore a thick, fluffy red robe that dwarfed her body and enough eye shadow and liner to make her eyes look like they took up her whole face.

"What do you want?"

"First of all, David, I want to know why you cleaned up the darkroom without me?"

"It was no big deal."

"I don't believe you."

"Why should I lie about it?"

"I don't know ... Maybe you wanted me to look bad in front of my mother."

David thought about it for a moment. Had he done that? He didn't think so. "That's dumb," he told her. "What's the second-of-all?"

She stared at him.

"I asked what you wanted, and you gave me a first-of-all. What's the second?"

She pushed her hair back, then licked her lips the way Chris did.

"I'm tired, Erin. It's late." he started to close the door. And if she hadn't put out her hand to stop him, that would have been that. But she did, and then finally asked the question he had been expecting.

"Do you really think I could photograph like a model?"

He nodded.

"Could I try? I mean, pose for some pictures?"

He gestured for her to come in; once she did, he quietly closed the door. She stood in the corner of the room as he gave her the once-over. Then he frowned.

"What's the matter?"

He turned around the desk chair and sat down with his elbows resting against the back. This time she stood, and he sat. It was still strategic positioning.

"What you're asking is, could you be a model—right?"

"Well, not really be one."

"Take pictures like one, then?"

She nodded.

"It's obvious you've got the face. The make-up looks good."

She smiled. "I didn't think you—"

He put up his hand to stop her. "The only question is, do you have the body."

Her face turned almost as red as her robe.

He sighed. "I mean, do you have the right lines, the right body structure to be a model."

"Well, do I?"

"The only way I'm going to know is if you take off your robe and let me see. You do have something on under that thing, don't you?"

Her hands went directly to the collar of her robe, pulling it tightly around her neck. "Sure. But why do I need to take it off?"

"Because in that robe you look like a sunburnt polar bear. For all I know, you could be a pile of sticks under there."

"David, you've seen me before without the robe. You know what I look like."

"But I never really looked at you from the viewpoint of model material. Do you think I walk around sizing up people for photographs?"

No response.

"You came in here for me to size you up, give you my semi-professional opinion, right?"

She nodded.

"Then I don't understand. What's the problem?"

She sighed. "All right—I'll do it."

Her fingers slowly rolled the buttons out of the button-holes. She manuevered her arms from the sleeves, then dropped the robe. It fell like a pile of scarlet fur on the carpet. She was wearing pink baby doll pajamas.

"Stand up straight," he said.

She stood like a soldier at attention while he studied her with the objective eye of a photographer: starting with her long, thin legs and working upward past the dark triangular shadow in her bloomers.

"Lift up that top a little so I can see your waistline."

Her hands trembled as they lifted the blousy top about six inches. Her waist seemed tiny enough to wrap his hands around. "Good," was all he said, and she pulled the material back down quickly.

Then he looked at her chest: small firm mounds lifted the thin low-cut top only slightly. But looking closely, he could see her nipples were dark, erect, perfect circles. He hated the kind that stuck in.

By this time, Erin's eyes were squeezed shut. "That's it," he said finally.

She opened her eyes.

"Now that wasn't so awful—was it, Erin?"

"No, I guess not . . . So what do you think?"

He stood up, went to the desk, and lifted his camera.

"I think I was right. Now we prove it by taking some pictures."

CHAPTER EIGHT

I t was nearly 1 A.M. when Chris heard the upstairs bathroom door close. She thought Erin had fallen asleep hours ago. But then it wasn't a school night; it was Friday, the beginning of the weekend.

She went back to her gift-wrapping, thoughts focused on an appropriate menu for Neil's homecoming. Shrimp. One of their favorites. She wondered, did David like seafood? She set the thought aside—as far as she could tell, David was hardly a fussy eater.

She recognized her daughter's bouncy steps overhead as she made her way down the hallway and back to her room. Chris removed the camera from the box and held it up—she couldn't have chosen a more appropriate gift. Erin was definitely captivated by photography. And, for that matter, by David.

Most of Erin's friends from grade school had contracted "boy fever" the moment they entered junior high. Although Erin was far ahead of the rest of her friends academically, when it came to boys, she lagged behind. Fortunately. The truth was, neither Neil nor Chris approved of girls her age jumping headlong into dating. But Erin's noninvolvement with boys did set her apart, and Chris knew her friendship with David meant far more to her than she would ever let on.

Chris finished the wrapping, topping each box with a lush satin bow to match the paper, then went around turning off lights. Finally she stacked the gifts in her arms and carried them back upstairs to hide, wondering which of the four of them would most enjoy the surprise. She suspected it might be her.

It seemed as though she had just hit the pillow when she heard the vacuum running downstairs. Chris sat up and looked at the clock: 10 A.M. She couldn't get out of bed fast enough—nor could she remember the last time she'd slept so late. Neil was always saying she woke the birds.

She washed and headed downstairs, tying the sash of her robe as she went. David was in the foyer, bent over the vacuum, humming a tune along to the noise of the motor. As soon as he saw her, he turned off the motor and stood up.

"Good morning."

"Are you always this ambitious on Saturdays?"

"I thought it was time I started earning my keep."

"Not to worry, David. You've done that already, in more ways than one."

"I hope I didn't wake you."

"Actually, you did, but I'm grateful. I had no intention of sleeping the day away. In fact I have to get Erin to her dental appointment at noon. Is she up yet?"

"Haven't seen her."

"Well, in that case, I'd better wake her up."

David came over and touched her shoulder lightly. "Wait, don't do that. Not yet. What I mean is, I'll wake Erin in a few minutes if you'd like." He looked down at his feet, twisting the toe of one sneaker into the carpet. "I made breakfast for you. Nothing that great, but—"

"How thoughtful of you, David."

"Well, it's not really a big deal. I mean, I used to do that for Fletcher—my father—a lot. So I guess I'm sort of used to doing it." Then he smiled; the tight set of his jaw relaxed and his jagged irregular features grew rounder, softer.

"Well," she said, "are you going to show me or are you just going to let me stand here and starve?"

David led her to the kitchen. He pulled out a chair and, with an elegant sweep of his arm, gestured for her to sit. The place setting had already been arranged; a glass of orange juice stood in the center of the plate. He took her cup and saucer and came back a few seconds later with a steaming cup of coffee. He added one Sweet 'N Low, no cream. Exactly the way she took it. Finally he opened a Dunkin' Donuts bag, took out a giant cinnamon roll and put it on her plate, then looked at the bag and shrugged.

"I didn't really make it all myself," he said.

She laughed. "I'm not accustomed to this kind of royal treatment, David. In fact, it's been years ..." She stopped.

"Did I do something wrong?" he said finally.

"No, David. You just brought back a memory."

"A bad one?"

"Not at all. A particularly nice one." She took his hand and pulled him down into the chair next to hers. "Come on—sit. Join me for breakfast."

"Maybe I should finish the carpets."

"They'll wait."

A mischieveous grin. "Wash the floors?"

She smiled up at him and shook her head.

"Well ... if you insist."

"Absolutely."

The next time Chris even thought of Erin's appointment was when her daughter came bursting into the kitchen, already dressed.

"Mom—my orthodontist! Why didn't you wake me?"

"Oh Erin, I'm sorry." Chris looked up at the clock; they had less than half an hour. "I'll go shower. You eat, and I'll be down in fifteen minutes." She headed out the door, then turned back. "Thank you, David."

He was already busy arranging a place setting for Erin. But all traces of the smile were gone ...

Erin hated to run errands with her mother, but today Chris left her no choice; to drive home and drop her off would have taken more time than she was willing to spare.

By the time they had made stops at the cleaners, the bank, the drug store, and the supermarket, Erin looked thoroughly morose and Chris felt more than a little guilty for putting her through the ordeal. It was nearly four o'clock.

"Want to stop for a soda?" Chris asked.

"No."

Chris slid the key in the ignition, turned on the motor and backed out of the parking space. "I know you hate wasting time on your weekend, honey, but tomorrow is another day."

Erin nodded.

Chris glanced at her. "What's wrong?"

"Nothing. I just want to get home."

"Of course this impatience wouldn't have anything to do with last night, would it?"

"What do you mean?"

"I mean the photo developing lesson—your pictures, your obvious eagerness to get back out there and take more."

"Well . . . I do like photography."

"And I think that's wonderful—it does seem like fun. I also think it's wonderful that you and David get along so well."

"Yeah. I guess."

She shook her head. "Erin, just once couldn't you admit it when I'm right?"

"About what?"

"David, of course. I had trouble getting you to agree to give him a chance. And now that you have, you found out you like him."

Silence.

"Come on—out with it."

"All right. I admit it."

"You make it sound like a tragedy. You've made a friend, Erin, and good friends aren't easy to come by, especially those that keep an eye out for your welfare. Like yesterday in the park, Erin—you heard him. He's very protective toward you."

"You talk like he's my brother or something. And he's not!"

"I was talking about your friendship," she said softly.

They were quiet for a minute or two, then Erin said, "I don't want to talk about David. I want to talk about my real brother. But *you* never do."

Chris took a deep breath. "It's hard for me, Erin. It still hurts."

"But he was *my* brother."

Chris nodded, though it wasn't a question.

"Then I have a right to know."

"What is it you want to know?"

"Anything. I'm just so tired of you keeping Kevin all to yourself."

"What do you mean?"

"I mean you never share your memories of him. Lots of times I just look at you and know you're thinking about Kevin. But still when I ask about him you don't want to talk, you always change the subject. It's weird. Except for the picture and his room being exactly the same as it was when he left it, it's as though Kevin never even existed."

"I never meant . . . All right, Erin, ask me anything you want, and I promise I'll answer."

"Okay. For starters, I knew he died in an accident. But you never really told me what kind of accident."

Chris's fingers squeezed the steering wheel so tightly, she thought her daughter would notice and say something. Instead, Erin just sat there, expecting an answer.

"A car accident," she said finally. "A . . . hit and run."

Erin moved forward; Chris could hear the squeak of the leather upholstery.

"You sound like you aren't even sure."

"That's not how I meant it to sound."

Erin sat, waiting for more. But what else could she tell her? *I lost your brother, Erin. And when he was found, no one could determine the cause of death. I never even saw his body. I never even said good-bye.*

The conversation continued to play:
Why was that, mommy?
Because I couldn't bear to look . . .
At your own son?
Daddy wouldn't let me look.
How did he stop you?
I would have broken again. And then there was you—I was carrying you.
Well, which reason was it? Why didn't you say good-bye?
God forgive her. She couldn't even remember.

CHAPTER NINE

David had been examining the pictures when he heard Erin and Chris come into the house. Funny how easy it was to distinguish people by their footsteps. In this case, of course, it wasn't a tough distinction: Chris's steps were soft; Erin's were like elephant clumps. Chris went right up to her room, and Erin went back and forth from the car to the kitchen, probably lugging bags inside. David leaned against the wall with his arms folded across his chest, waiting. Sooner or later, Erin would come up.

Sure enough, not more than five minutes later, he heard her across the hall, tapping at his bedroom door. Still he waited. Finally the darkroom door opened.

"I've been wondering when you'd get home," he said.

Why—you want to develop the pictures?"

"Nope. I have a surprise for you." David gestured behind himself to the clothesline he'd just hung. "Take a look, they're drying."

"You did them yourself?"

He nodded.

"They're so big."

"I blew them up. You can't really judge how photogenic someone is without a decent-size print. Come on, take a close look."

She looked at him, not at the pictures. "I'm scared."

"Why?"

She shrugged. He took her by the arm and pulled her next to him. "Don't be like that, they came out fine. And, I was right. You could be a model."

Erin looked down from his face to the first photograph, hanging at just her eye level. She stared at it like she

were examining a stranger. An older stranger. Which, of
course, was mainly David's doing. Rather than leave her
hair tucked back behind her ears, he'd pulled it forward.
The part was still in the middle, but in the photo her
hair fell over her forehead and lightly down the sides of
her face, giving her an older look.

Erin moved from one picture to the next, not saying a word. Finally she stopped, right at the photograph he had expected would stop her. Her pink
pajama bloomers were rolled down to bikini size. She
was hunched down on all fours, her head tilted up
and her mouth parted slightly. Best of all was the
angle of the shot—zeroing right down on her. The
camera caught perfectly the way her scoop-necked top
fell forward, revealing just a hint of small pale breasts
contrasting with the dark nipples. Everything about
the photograph seemed to say, "puppy in heat."

He could hear her catch her breath, then she looked at
him. "Did you know, David?"

"Know what?"

"That you could see . . . so much?"

"It was the camera that saw, not me. Besides, I don't
know why you're making such a big deal of it. You can
hardly see a thing."

"It's terrible, David. They're all terrible, but this one is
the worst."

He lowered his voice and dug his hands into his pockets. "I tried my best," he said.

"I don't mean to blame you, David. It's my fault."

He didn't say anything.

"I want to ask you something. It's important."

He knew the question already, but he let her go on.

"Can I have them—I mean, the pictures? I don't want
anyone to see them. Ever."

"I would think you'd want to show them at least to
your mother. Remember, she told you herself that you
ought to loosen up."

Erin looked again at the picture. "She didn't mean this."

"You'll never know unless you show her."

"Please, David. Please let me have them."

Even though he knew from the very start what he was going to do, he hesitated. He couldn't help getting a certain pleasure out of watching her squirm, and he wasn't even quite sure why. Finally he put an end to her suspense. He unclipped the clothespins from the tops of the pictures, stacked them, and handed the pile to Erin.

"I hope you appreciate what I'm doing for you," David said. "I started these at eight o-clock this morning. Just to surprise you."

Erin took the stack of pictures from his hands and held them to her chest. "I'm sorry, David. I really am. I'll make this up to you—I promise."

He watched her scoot out of the room and heard her run down the hallway. She would tear them up. Or maybe burn them. That's what he had done once ... He sat down on the stool and stared at the slats in the wooden floor, rubbing the sole of one sneaker along the cracks. Actually, he *was* surprised that she hadn't thought to ask him for the negatives.

But then again, why should he have been surprised? Had he thought to ask Fletcher?

A fellow throws two limes in the air; when they come down, they're suddenly lemons—the same texture, even the same size. But nevertheless, not what they started out to be. Well, that's how David decided it was with Chris and Erin that evening: he was seeing a side of them he never knew existed.

After a nearly dead-silent dinner, Chris headed straight for the piano. Erin, who until now had kept any questions to herself, asked, "Are you going to play again, mom?"

Chris lowered herself down onto the bench. "For a while," she said.

David followed her to the piano; creases pinched the sides of her mouth, and her hand trembled as she put her fingers onto the keys. Erin had probably given her one question too many today which, David knew, was enough to make a wreck out of anyone. He leaned his elbows on the wood, cupping his chin in his hands, waiting for the music to begin.

As if someone had pressed a button, Chris' fingers began to move. And though she'd been vague about the tune she played a few nights earlier, she played the same one again now. He didn't take his eyes off her for a minute: occasionally, her clouded eyes would look up and meet his. The music was eerie, almost as if it were coming from two different sources. One set of notes coming from the piano, the other, from his head.

Partway through the concert, Erin must have gotten up and left, but David honestly couldn't say when. He was aware only of the music. Two hours must have passed before Chris stood up. She swayed slightly, and he put out his arm to steady her.

"Heavens," she said, "I must have bored you silly."

He shook his head. "No . . . I liked it, it made me think of things."

"What kind of things, David?"

He shrugged. "I'm not sure. Maybe not really things at all. It just made me happy, I guess."

She stared at him for a moment. "I'd better be going to bed," she said finally. "I'm afraid I'm not quite myself this evening."

He turned off the lights, then walked with her up the stairs. They said goodnight at her door, and he headed in the opposite direction toward his room. He fell onto his bed, fully dressed, putting his arms behind his head and staring at the roughly grained ceiling. He was David, David Crane, his father was Fletcher . . . And Kevin was dead . . .

No matter what, he musn't forget that. Still he could hear the music

He must have heard it right up to the moment he nodded off, because when he woke the next morning, he was still fully dressed. And he could feel the smile on his lips.

David was relieved to see that Chris was back to normal at breakfast. Erin was still quiet, but as far as he was concerned, her change was an improvement. Not that he really expected it to last long.

After breakfast, Chris joined David and Erin in the living room. He was leafing through one of Erin's teen magazines; Erin had set up a chess computer and was busily matching wits against the machine.

"Are you two going out to take photographs?" Chris asked.

David and Erin looked at each other. He was the one who finally answered. "Sure . . . if Erin wants to."

Erin turned off the computer and stood up. "All right."

He looked at Chris, remembering his conversation with Erin. "Sure you don't mind being alone?" he asked her.

She smiled. "Not at all. I have a few chores to catch up on. Then this afternoon I'll be going to visit Neil."

"If you want, I'll help with the chores," Erin said.

"No, honey, you go on ahead. I've already spoiled part of your weekend. I'm not about to feel guilty for spoiling the rest."

Twenty minutes later, David and Erin stood near the waterfall high on the hill, overlooking the playground. Neither of them seemed that interested in taking pictures. He sat down on the ground and so did she.

"I know I really upset you yesterday," she said.

"Forget it."

"I don't want to forget it, I want to try to explain."

David leaned back on his arms and closed his eyes, wishing she wouldn't. "You don't have to, Erin."

"But I want to. You put in all that time and trouble, and I was the one who asked you to do it in the first place."

"No big deal."

"Those pictures made me feel awful, David. You're not a girl, so I don't really expect you to understand. But seeing myself that way ... those poses ... well, it made me feel almost dirty."

He nodded his head, opening his eyes.

"You *do* understand?"

He nodded again.

She looked at him, puzzled. "Then why did you take them to begin with?"

He sprang forward, grabbed her by the shoulders and shook her.

"Why did you *let* me take them?" he said.

It was a while before she could answer, and when she did, her voice was choked: "I trusted you, David."

"That was your mistake, Erin. Don't trust anyone. Ever!" He jumped up and ran to the edge of the hill, looking out at the playground—and at the house across the street. It was like looking at a very old postcard and not being able to remember the trip. His eyes were watering up; he took a deep breath, then felt a brush at his sleeve. Erin.

"Why are you saying these awful things? And acting this way?" He shrugged. "I tore them up," she said finally. Still he didn't answer, and she went on. "Because all I could think about was my dad. You know, what he'd think of me if he saw them."

David kept his eyes on the house in the distance.

"And just the thought of that made me feel sick. I could never face him, David.

"So relax," he said. "You tore them up."

She nodded. Her brown eyes stared into his, and her little pink tongue raked over her lips. For a moment, he thought she was going to ask about the negatives. But she didn't.

CHAPTER TEN

For the first time since Neil's hospitalization, Chris had to force herself to make the visit. She hadn't gone last evening as planned, and if she didn't show up today, Neil would worry. She put off leaving the house, tidying her bedroom, stacking the puzzle books neatly on her nightstand, then headed for the car.

Why now, when everything was going so well, had she reacted that way to Erin's questions yesterday about Kevin? Erin had even accused Chris of behaving as though David were her brother. Had she unconsciously been doing that? The minute they got home, she'd made a dash for her bedroom and holed up there for the rest of the afternoon, unscrambling anagrams, working crosswords. Fill the blanks and everying else would fall into place . . .

But even at dinner, she hadn't been able to rid herself of the ache inside. She had played the piano—for David.

Later, he walked with her upstairs, obviously concerned. Had she looked as unstrung as she'd felt? She felt embarrassed that she had allowed him to see her like that.

Chris pulled into the hospital parking lot and stayed in the car a few moments, trying to put yesterday afternoon and evening out of her mind. Finally she got out of the car and went inside, taking the stairs to the second floor. The moment she saw Neil's tall form in the doorway of his room she broke into a run. His arms went around her, but his grip was feeble—no longer the powerful haven she'd grown accustomed to. She pulled away and looked up. "Missed you," she said.

"What's wrong, Chris?"

"Nothing. Can't a wife miss a husband?"

"Sounds suspicious to me."

Chris laughed and tapped the bar of his walker. "Come on, walk with me, and I'll tell you all the elaborate plans for the homecoming."

"Oh? Someone coming home?"

"Not if that someone doesn't quit teasing . . ."

"Okay—I'm ready. Tell me."

"Shrimp scampi's the entrée. To be introduced by fruit cup with lemon sherbet."

"Vegetable?"

"Broccoli."

"Dessert?"

"Angel food cake."

"Fatten me up, huh?"

"That's the plan. And I bought us all gifts."

"Me too?"

She shortened her footsteps to keep pace with his. "Of course, you too. How would it look having no gift for the guest of honor?"

"Bad. Very bad."

"I even picked up something for David."

She could tell immediately, he didn't recognize the name. "You remember, Neil. David's our boarder, the college student."

Silence.

"I bought him a photo album. I told you about the darkroom he set up. He's starting a new collection of pictures. I thought an album would be perfect." He nodded, and she went on. "It's bound in black chamois, with textured fabric sheets—one of those things that lasts forever. I just know he'll love it."

They reached the end of the corridor, and Neil went to the window. "And Erin?"

"What about Erin?"

"What did you buy her?"

"A Nikon 35 mm. camera."

He turned to face Chris, his eyebrows arching. "That's the boy's hobby," he said finally.

"Oh, but you don't know the latest news, Neil. Now, it's Erin's hobby too. David's taken her under his wing, teaching her everything. They're becoming great friends."

"I see."

"Wait till you meet him, Neil. You'll like him."

"I'm sure," he said, then turned away, looking out of the window.

Except for the dim ray of light thrown from the foyer chandelier, the house was pitch dark when Chris walked in. She slipped out of her raincoat, hung it in the closet and headed upstairs. As soon as she reached the landing, she saw the bright light coming from Neil's bedroom. She walked quietly to the doorway and stood there, watching Erin. She was leafing through one of Neil's law books.

"What are you up to?" Chris asked.

Erin jumped; her hand flew to her chest. "God, you scared me."

"Sorry, I didn't mean to. It's so dreary and quiet around here—where's David?"

"I don't know. In his room, I guess."

"You two didn't have a falling out, did you?"

"No, nothing like that." She turned back to the books. "I just decided to move some of dad's law books to his room. I brought in the Massachusetts Rules of Criminal Procedure. He uses them a lot."

"He'll like that, Erin." Chris went over, picked a few of the black books from the stack on his desk, and helped Erin arrange them alphabetically on the shelf.

"About yesterday," Erin said.

"Yes?"

"I'm sorry. I didn't mean to force you to talk about Kevin." She shrugged her shoulders. "That's not really true. I guess I did mean to force you, I just didn't mean to get you that upset."

"I shouldn't have reacted the way I did."

"It's not your fault. People can't much help how they feel."

"No, I guess they can't."

"I just wish . . ."

"Go on, Erin."

"I just wish you didn't miss him so much. I mean— you do have me."

Chris reached out and ran her fingers through Erin's silky hair. "Of course I have you. Don't think I don't know how lucky I am . . ."

"But?"

"But Kevin was my first born. A mother feels a special bond with her first. It's all so new, so miraculous . . . so, as you would say, awesome."

Erin swallowed hard.

"A mother feels a strong bond with a daughter too, Erin. It's a very special relationship. Like no other." Erin looked at her. "Do you understand?" Chris asked.

"I guess."

"Well, then, let's get these shelves arranged for your father. And let's remember how lucky we are that he's coming home to us."

"That's L to N—it goes here." Erin took the volume from Chris' hand and slipped it in place.

Between Neil's homecoming and David's first day of classes, everyone was up earlier than usual the next morning. But breakfast turned out to be a wasted effort. Chris couldn't touch a bite, David seemed on edge, and Erin was far too excited to think about food. Instead she played with the french toast on her plate and said for the third time, "Please, mom. Let me stay home today."

"For the last time," Chris said, "No."

"It's only one day. I can make up whatever I miss."

"I don't like your missing even a day. Besides, your father will be tired when he gets here. This way, he'll have the opportunity to nap before everyone gets home." Chris turned to David. "As for you, young man—try to relax."

She stopped his protest before it began. "Since yesterday, you've been as nervous as a cat." Chris reached over and took his hand in hers. "I know you'll do just fine in school. So whatever it is worrying you, please stop."

She could see that she wasn't getting through to him. His hand was cold, and if she wasn't mistaken, even trembling . . .

Chris wanted everything to run smoothly, which it did—until she got Neil safely in the house. The drive home had tired him more than she anticipated. And there they were in the foyer, facing a flight of stairs which, to Neil, must have looked like Mount Everest. She found herself wishing that David was there. But he wasn't, so she put one arm around Neil's waist and shoved his walker aside with the other.

"Lean on me," she said.

Neil's eyes looked doubtful. Chris was a small-framed 5'4", but not quite as fragile as Neil liked to believe. "Trust me, honey," she said.

Neil, for lack of an alternative, grasped the railing and threw his other arm around her shoulder. Slowly, step by step, they made their way up. Halfway there, he stopped.

"What's wrong, Neil?"

"I'll let you catch your breath."

"Don't worry about me. I'm fine."

"Up to carrying me the rest of the way?"

"Just like a man—give a foot and they want the whole leg."

"A nice leg," he said, grabbing hers.

She wriggled free of his hand. "Behave yourself, Neil. Or we'll both end up at the bottom of these stairs."

As soon as they reached the landing, she ran down again to bring up the walker. By the time she returned, she was out of breath.

"I don't want you doing this," Neil said.

"I won't have to. Before you know it, you'll be taking those stairs two at a time. Meanwhile, of course, David will be able to help you down for meals."

He nodded.

"Would you like me to have a stair elevator installed, Neil? That could easily be arranged if you—"

"No, I'll walk." He took her hand and squeezed it. Then, using the walker, he headed down the hallway. She stopped him just as he reached their bedroom.

"Remember, Neil—we decided, temporarily, since you need the hospital bed . . ."

"Right," he said. "The guest room."

"Look," she said, leading him across the hall. "The children and I moved in your desk, your books." But he didn't look in. Instead he turned back toward the bedroom they'd shared for twenty-two years. "Neil, I *could* move the bed."

"No," he said. "I'd rather this. For now."

By the time she'd settled him in and left the room, he was dozing off. He was out like a light when Erin's bus pulled up at the street corner at three. And it was only minutes before she heard Erin's footsteps and shout: "Is dad home?"

Chris went to her, hugged her and whispered, "Yes, but I want you to be very quiet."

"What's wrong?"

"Nothing, honey—absolutely nothing. But daddy's sound asleep and I'd like him not to be woken up."

"Can I just go look at him?"

"Not until he's up."

"Darn it, I just want to—"

"No, Erin."

A flicker of anger in her eyes, then she sighed ...
"Okay," she said and headed upstairs.

"Now, Erin, you won't go—"

"I said I wouldn't, didn't I?"

Not much later, Chris looked up to see David standing in the kitchen doorway. Before she could ask him how school had gone, he said, "Is Neil home?"

"Yes, he's resting until dinner. He's anxious to meet you, David."

"Can I do anything?"

Chris looked down at the shrimp she was deveining. "Not at the moment. But Neil will need your help coming downstairs this evening."

"Sure. Anything at all."

She looked up again, surprised to find him already gone ...

CHAPTER ELEVEN

The moment David reached the landing he headed for Neil's room, unable to wait any longer. Even before he cracked open the door, he heard the soft snoring. He took a deep breath and tiptoed in, moving close to his bed, studying the suddenly familiar face propped on the pillows: thin lips slightly parted; a fine line of saliva running from the corner of his mouth and collecting on his square chin. Tiny lines around the mouth wrinkling his complexion like a hastily ironed shirt. Thick, dark graying hair and brows.

He was spread out on top of the covers. His broad shoulders seemed a mismatch for the rest of the skin and bones that followed. His feet touched the bottom bar of the bed, but in spite of his size—he was almost as tall as Fletcher—he looked wilted. Like the power had been bled right out of him.

David couldn't decide if he was disappointed or relieved. Another memory had been given substance, but with Chris it had felt as comfortable as stepping into an old pair of sneakers. It wasn't as comfortable with Neil. Goosebumps popped up along his arms as he backed away from the sleeping figure. He shut the door to Neil's room and came face to face with Erin.

"What were you doing in there, David?"

"Just looking."

"At what?"

"Him. Your father."

She put her hands on her hips and squinched up her mouth like she had been sucking a lemon.

"You had no right to sneak in and spy on him. Why

didn't you wait until he was up, until he invited you in?"
David started to walk away, but Erin grabbed his arm.
"Answer me—why'd you go in there?"

He yanked his arm back. "What's it to you?"

"Plenty—he's my father! If anyone should have been
first to see him, it should have been me. Not you!"

Just then they heard the deep voice call out, "Erin."
They both froze, listened—and heard it again. And the
next thing David knew, Erin was gone. He hadn't even
seen her move from the spot, but he could hear the
springs dance as she jumped onto Neil's bed.

David leaned against the wall outside the door and listened, until he heard them laughing. Then he went down
the hall to his own room.

At about five o'clock there was a knock on David's
door. By then he had washed, brushed his teeth, shaved,
changed his shirt, and even put on his one necktie; he
ran to the door, still combing his hair. He slipped the
comb into his back pants pocket and opened the door to
Chris. For a second he wondered if Erin had told her
about him sneaking into Neil's room, but he stopped
wondering when he saw her big smile.

"Don't you look nice," she said.

"Tonight's a special night. I thought . . ."

She grabbed his arm. "Come on, young man, I want to
introduce you."

He held back. "Maybe you'd all rather be alone first."

"Not at all, David. You come along."

He trailed after her, feeling foolish, almost like a little
kid being dragged off to the dentist. When they got to
Neil's room, Chris gently pushed him ahead. Neil was sitting on the edge of the bed, fully dressed, Erin standing
at his side like a guard.

"Neil, I want you to meet David."

For the first time, David could see his eyes: big,
blue question marks with x-ray vision. Lawyer's eyes.
And the way they examined David, he felt like he

was being sucked into a vacuum. Neil stuck out a hand, and David took it in his. A glove filled with water. He pulled away.

"Heard a lot about you," Neil said. "The family's pretty taken with you. What's your secret?"

David could feel the heat traveling up his neck. Simple conversation, but as usual, just when he needed some simple words, they rolled right out of his brain.

"Hear you're a photographer," he said.

He nodded, then Chris came to his rescue: "David and Erin took some lovely pictures at the park."

Neil put his arm around Erin, pulling her down beside him, and she nuzzled her face into his shoulder. "Take any of her?" he asked.

Erin perked up at his question—and David found his tongue. "Yes," he said. "She takes a good picture. Maybe you'd like to see them later."

"You mean you took more than one?" Chris asked.

By that time, Erin had pulled away from her father and was sitting straight up, staring at David the way people do when they want to get your attention without attracting anybody else's. David went out of his way not to look at her.

"Actually, no," he said. "Erin's a little camera-shy. It surprised me—I would have thought she'd love center stage."

Everyone smiled, even Erin, though David knew her smile was one of relief. Then Neil stood up. "Time to eat," he announced.

Erin and Chris snapped to attention. Chris set his walker in front of him and they all followed behind as he made his way to the stairway. Once there, Chris gently pulled the walker aside.

"David will help you," she said.

David took over, sliding his arm around Neil's body, supporting his weight as Neil slowly took the first step down. Sometimes things have a way of feeling just right—like a perfect photograph. And that's how this felt to David. Chris and Erin looked at him with respect. Of course, he couldn't see Neil's face, but by the way he leaned against him, he for those moments had given him his trust.

And David had the feeling that trust was something Neil rarely gave.

The good feelings David had didn't last long. In fact, they ended as soon as they sat down to dinner. Neil watched his every move, like he expected him at any moment to begin shoveling food into his mouth with the heel of his shoe. David spent more time using his napkin than his knife and fork. As soon as that ordeal was over, Chris hustled them all into the living room, and another ordeal began: "Hear you're from Laconia," Neil said. "What made you choose B.U.?"

"It has a good reputation."

"Where else did you apply?"

"Nowhere else. I wanted to come here."

"Didn't want to be in a dorm?"

"No."

"Not easy to find a decent room."

"I guess. But I had all summer to look."

"Oh? When did you get here . . . to Boston?"

"June. Late June."

"Where'd you stay?"

David wondered what he'd say if he knew he'd slept most nights in his car . . . "The YMCA," he said, a half lie.

"Why did you leave home so early?"

"I wanted to make sure I found a place to live. Besides, there was nothing holding me there. My father died in June—I left right after."

"That's too bad." Neil studied David's face for a few moments, then, "How did he die?" Chris gave Neil a warning look, but he ignored it.

"A stroke," David said, hoping his answer would shut him up.

It didn't. "Your mother?" he asked.

"She deserted me—us. Fletcher and me."

This time Chris spoke up: "Why don't we talk about something else, Neil?"

But he wasn't about to lay off. "Fletcher?" he asked.

"My father." And then David answered Neil's look as if it were his voice. "He wanted me to call him Fletcher. That's what he wanted."

"And your mother?"

"I told you—she left us!"

"What was *her* name?"

Now David's mind drew a total blank; his hands started to shake so badly, they wouldn't stay still. He wrapped his arms together at his chest and tucked his hands inside to steady them.

Again: "Her name?"

"I don't remember!" The moment the words were out, David was on his feet. Somewhere in the distance he could see Chris' face; her lips were moving, but he couldn't hear a word. He turned and ran out of the living room and up the stairs, not stopping until he reached his room. Then he collapsed on the bed, squeezing the palms of his hands over his ears.

What's your name?

Kevin.

The snake curled overhead like a thick cord of fire, moving closer.

Softly. *What's your name?*

Kevin.

The snake rattled its body—sparks spitting through the darkness.

I want my mommy!

Mommy left Fletcher ... Mommy left Davie.

The snake circled, and circled ...

Whose little boy are you now, Davie?

The snake came down and bit. Not Davie ... Kevin!

The next thing he knew, his nostrils were filled with a wonderful frangrance. A cool, gentle hand stroked his hair, his forehead. He could feel every single knot inside him loosening ... untying.

David didn't open his eyes, he didn't move ... He didn't even want to breathe. If he did—he'd wake up, and no one would be there ...

CHAPTER TWELVE

Chris closed the door to David's room and made her way down the stairs, holding onto the railing for support. When she entered the dining room the conversation between Neil and Erin came to a stop. Erin was first to ask; "What's wrong with David?"

"He's upset, Erin, surely you could see that."

"But why? All dad did was ask him some questions."

Chris looked at Neil, then back at Erin. "Please go to your room, Erin. I'd like to speak to your father alone."

She began to protest, then sighed deeply and stood up. She leaned over Neil and planted a kiss on his cheek. "Night, dad."

"Night, princess."

When Erin reached the archway, she turned. "This whole house has changed since you've gone, dad."

It took Neil a moment to answer. "How, Erin?"

"I don't know, really. I just know everything is different. And I'm not so sure I like it."

"Well ... I'm home now."

"I'm glad." She opened her mouth to say something else, but stopped, then she ran up the stairs and Chris sat on the sofa across from Neil. There were so many feelings, so many words brimming inside her, she didn't know where to begin. Finally she just said, "Why?"

"How is he?"

"Sleeping. Why did you do that to him?"

"Just questions. I'm interested in him."

"You badgered him, Neil. As if he were a hostile witness on your damned stand. What did you hope to accomplish? Even Erin is reacting to your obvious mistrust of the boy. As for me, I just don't understand it. What did he ever do to you?"

"No. To you."

"What does *that* mean?"

"He's not Kevin."

Chris sat forward, staring at him. "So that's what it is. You think I've magically transformed him into Kevin."

"I see the way you look at him, the way you talk to him."

Neil's face seemed to go out of focus. Chris reached up her hand to wipe her eyes. "I see. Chris will fall to pieces. Chris will embarrass you again in front of the whole world . . ." She lowered her head onto her hands.

Neil had stood up and made his way to the sofa. Now he sat beside her. "Chris . . . don't. I'm just afraid for you."

She jerked her head up, catching him off guard. "Tell me, Neil—assuming I had gone off the deep end, assuming I had fantasized this young man into Kevin, did that give you license to grill him, to call up painful memories he obviously couldn't handle?"

"No."

"And is it so very peculiar for me to care about him? Does that make me crazy?"

Neil's speech was noticeably slower, less clear. "Boy's re . . . action was odd. Can't you see?"

"He's been hurt. Maybe it's something you just can't relate to, but I can. Not everyone operates like you and your daughter. Not everyone who stumbles can simply pick themselves up, wipe the dust from the seat of their pants and go on again like nothing ever happened."

Silence.

Chris buried her face against the sofa.

"Don't cry. Please."

It took her a few moments to stop. When she did, she sat up and faced Neil.

"He's not leaving," she said. "Do you understand me? He's not leaving!"

"I never said he should."

"But you're behaving as if that's what you want."

"I want you to be happy ... and well. That's all."

Chris helped Neil upstairs; he seemed even more tired than before, but somehow they managed. Once she settled him in, she went to her room, and sank down onto the bed. Was Neil right, was she still trying to find Kevin? Was she looking at David and seeing her dead son? No, it wasn't true, she was sure it wasn't true. Chris opened the nightstand compartment and pulled out a book— "Jawbreakers," puzzlers for the experts. She lifted a razor-sharp pencil from the top of the stand, turned to the first unused sheet she could find, then set to work, determined to break the code. She didn't, but somewhere around 2 A.M. she did fall asleep, fully clothed.

Plick ... Plick ... The hands had no face, no body. They crept toward the crib like two flaming spiders burning their way through the darkness. The smell of singed flesh made her want to vomit. Instead, holding her breath, she ran to the baby, lifted him and hugged him to her breast. Plick. Slowly, she backed away, watching as the hands turned toward her. Then she ran ...

But not fast enough. Now the angry snaps fizzled in her eardrums, and long fingers reached out and curled around the baby. He screamed. She threw herself onto the ground, hiding him beneath her. She could feel the hot fingers crawl over her back and sides, probing, but she didn't dare move. She didn't dare make a sound ...

When she finally lifted her head again, the hands had disappeared, along with the darkness. Her bedroom light was on, and Neil was there. "What are you doing, mommy?" he said.

Only the baby called her that. Not Neil.

"Answer me," he said.

"The hands, Neil. I had to protect the baby."

"Where is he?"

"Safe, Neil. Under me."

"Why can't I hear him?"

Slowly she rolled away, uncovering the baby. He was lying so still.

"He's dead," Neil said.

She shook the little body—it didn't move.

"You killed him, mommy."

She snatched the baby up off the bed and cradled him in her arms; she touched his neck—he squeaked. Couldn't Neil see he was still alive? "Hush little baby, don't you cry ..."

"Throw him away. He's dead!"

"Mommy's gonna sing you a lullabye ..." Then the baby's little fingers stretched apart, wrapping themselves tightly around her finger. "Look, Neil. See?"

Neil leaned forward and took the baby out of her arms. First she felt the heat of his hands, then she screamed...

Chris awoke, shuddered, sat up. Her forehead was damp with perspiration, but still her body felt chilled. She leaned back against the pillows and pulled the blankets up around herself.

It had been so long since she'd had a nightmare about Kevin. Or, if she had any, she hadn't remembered them. This one stayed with her—every part. Neil's face loomed out at her from the dream, and she suddenly wished he were with her. If she could see his face now, the Neil in the dream would disappear.

She thought back to earlier that evening. She meant what she'd said to Neil: she would not allow him to drive David away. So she cared about David—did it really matter why? Was it necessary to dissect every emotion in search of a motive? Only in a courtroom, or a psychiatrist's office. She heard a bump along the carpet and sat up, looking toward the doorway. Neil was standing there, his walker in front of him.

"A dream?" he said.

"I woke you. I'm sorry."

He made his way closer to the bed. As he did, his features became clearer: the strong, square chin, the high-bridged straight nose. He stopped in front of her, leaning over to lift the puzzle book from the bed and tossing it onto the nightstand. Then he lowered himself onto the edge of the bed.

"About Kevin?" he said.

She nodded. "And you, too."

"Was I bad?"

"Yes," she said, knowing they were no longer talking about her dream. "Very bad."

"A second chance?"

"Do you think you deserve one?"

"First offense, your honor."

"I shall, of course, have to check over your record."

"It speaks for itself."

"Will you give David a chance, Neil? Get to know him? That's all I ask. I want you to open your eyes and see what I see."

"What do you see?"

"Someone sweet and vulnerable and loving. Someone who's been hurt very badly. Who needs us." He closed his eyes as if it would help him to see. "Please, Neil. For me."

Finally: "For you. Whatever makes you happy."

She tilted her head up and kissed him, then moved back. "There is one more thing . . ."

He sighed.

"I think it was a bad idea, your sleeping in the spare bedroom. I just thought it would be more comfortable for you."

"And now?"

"Now I'm only concerned about my comfort. And this bed is obviously too large to afford one person a decent night's sleep. They say rattling around in bed alone causes nightmares."

His fingers found her cheek and stroked it. "No," he said. "You were right. It's better this way. Just for a while."

She could feel her face grow warm; she swallowed hard. "Whatever you think, Neil."

He kissed her lightly, then stood up. "Get undressed, Chris. Go to sleep."

Chris watched him hobble away, out of the room. All she had wanted was his closeness, his warmth. Had he been afraid she wanted more? Go after him, explain, make him understand ... She did none of those things. Instead she sat still and let the sense of urgency dissipate. She listened to the thump of the rubber tips on his walker as he entered his room, then moved along the carpet to his bed.

Chris turned off the lamp and lay back down on the pillow, still not bothering to undress. The sheets seemed cool. She tried to concentrate on pleasant thoughts: Neil was going to give David a chance. Tomorrow she would give them all their gifts. Neil was, after all, getting well ...

Just before she fell back to sleep, one dark thought slipped through: David was all alone with his nightmares. And for that matter, so was she.

CHAPTER THIRTEEN

As soon as David opened his eyes, he remembered last night, then buried his head again in the pillow. How would he ever face Chris after running out like that and making such a total fool of himself? For a few seconds he considered packing his bags, slipping out of his bedroom, out of the house. But the thought only lasted a few seconds. Even as it went through his head, he knew he wouldn't—couldn't—leave Chris. Besides where would he go?

The first time he had asked himself that question was in June, the day he graduated high school. Fletcher hadn't gone to the ceremony; he was in his bedroom packing when David got home.

"I'm gonna be moving on, Davie," he said, opening his dresser drawer.

"Where're we going?"

"Open them ears, boy. You didn't hear me straight. What I'm saying is, things are getting out of hand—the law is about to clamp down on the business. The best thing I can do is take off. Alone."

Fletcher always referred to his work as "the business." Though David knew it had to do with selling photographs, he never once asked him what it really was. And now that it was closing, he still didn't. All he said was, "What about me?"

"You're a big boy now. Too big."

"Where will I go?"

Fletcher shrugged like he hadn't bothered to think about it. "Wherever you've got a mind to, I suppose. What about the west coast, L.A. Seems to me you used to talk about being one of those surf boys."

David took a deep breath, then "When you going?"

"Tomorrow. That's when the rent's paid till, and that's when the new folks will be moving in."

"What about the furniture?" A dumb question—like he really cared.

"It stays with the house."

The muscles in the back of David's neck pulled, like someone had yanked a cord. "No," he shouted. "You won't go, not without me—I won't let you!"

Laughter. Fletcher's face reddening with each crow. Finally out of breath, "So that's how it is, Davie? Can't bear to see your old man go." He went out into the parlor, came back with the black photo album, and sat on his bed. His voice went syrupy, and he patted the mattress. "Come on, son. Sit next to Fletcher."

The cord pulled tighter; a pain shot through David's head.

"Come on," he said again. "No tricks—I promise."

David sank down onto the bed, facing him. Fletcher put the book on David's lap. "For you, boy, a going-away present. Any time you miss Fletcher, you just open up this here book and take a look."

David said nothing. A noise—way off in the distance—rumbled toward him . . .

Fletcher slid his hand to David's knee and rubbed it. "And now, Davie, *you're* going to give your daddy a going-away present. It's been a long time since you showed daddy how much you love him. This one will be for old times—"

Water—gigantic waves—crashed through David's skull, roaring in his eardrums. He jumped up—the book falling to the floor—pressing his hands against his ears, yelling words at Fletcher he couldn't even hear himself. Fletcher jumped up and grabbed for him; David swung out, but Fletcher caught his punches in mid-air, then he brought up his knee to David's groin, and a searing pain sliced through him, sinking him to the bed. Time must have passed because the next thing David knew, his jeans were open, the waistline wound down around his knees and Fletcher was coming down to him . . .

Fletcher didn't see David pick up the hunting knife from the night table, he didn't know, not till the point of the blade slammed into his stomach . . . Fletcher's mouth opened, his eyes bulged and his body lurched back, throwing him across the bed, the back of his skull smashing the footboard. Then nothing. Except blood—lots of blood. And as suddenly as the roaring in David's ears had started, it stopped . . .

Right now, David didn't want to think about going anywhere else. He rose from the bed and lowered himself to the floor. Then folding his arms and legs in yoga position, he tried to wipe every single thought from his brain. He concentrated so hard, he could feel sweat drip off his nose. But when he stood up an hour later, his mind felt clearer. Oh, he still remembered last night, what Neil had done to him, but the hurt was pushed further back in his brain. Along with Fletcher.

He had just stepped out of the shower when he heard the knock at his door. He quickly wrapped a bath towel around his waist, then went to the door, cracked it open and peeked out: he saw the aluminum walker before he saw Neil.

"Can I come in?" Neil said.

David opened the door, pulling the towel more tightly around him. "I'm not dressed."

He came in anyway. First he examined the room as if he'd never seen it before, then he examined David. "About last night," he began, "a lawyer's foible—too many questions."

David didn't know what "foible" meant, and he really didn't care. He just wanted him to leave. But he didn't. "Sorry I pushed like that," Neil said.

"It's okay."

"Are you all right?"

"Why shouldn't I be?"

Neil had the sense to drop it. "I'll shower after breakfast. Maybe you could help?"

David nodded; Neil turned and thumped out. David went to the doorway and watched him heading for his room. When he reached it, David looked away, and that's when he saw Erin standing on the landing.

As soon as she caught his attention, she ran over to him; he backed into his room and she stood outside the door. "What was my father doing here?" she said.

"He came to invite me to a tea party."

"You're trying to win him over, aren't you?"

"Not at all. I don't like tea, I refused his invitation."

"You may think it's all one big joke, David, but let me warn you ahead of time, my father's not so easy to fool. You saw how he was last night—he already suspects you."

"Of what?"

"Not being who you say you are."

"You're right, Erin. I'm not really David Crane."

"Then who are you?"

"I'm an impostor." He raised his arms to his head, flapping his hands like ears. "Hey ... what's up, Doc?" he said, then pointed behind him to the Bugs Bunny character in his room. "Look, Erin. See the resemblance?"

"I'm just wasting my time talking to you. Maybe the best thing would be to talk to my father—then I can tell him what I really think of you." She turned and marched away.

"Wait, Erin. Where are you going?"

She stopped. "Read my lips, David. I'm going to tell my dad what you're really like. And maybe, just maybe, he'll throw you out on your butt where you belong!"

"I wouldn't do that if I were you."

"And why not?"

"Because I'd hate for him to get all upset."

"I don't think getting rid of you will upset him at all. In fact, I think he might enjoy it."

"Do you think he would enjoy finding out about your plans to become a model?"

"That's a lie, David." Then, "Would you tell a lie like that?"

"I didn't say I would."

"Even if you did, he'd never believe you."

"You're right, he probably wouldn't." David grabbed the doorknob and started to close the door, then stopped. "Of course, he might very well believe the pictures themselves. Not that anyone would ever show them to him."

"You forget—the pictures are gone."

That's when David smiled. Not on purpose; he just couldn't help but compare this game to all the other cat and mouse games he had played before with Fletcher. Of course now *he* was the cat, and it sure was a hell of a lot better place to be. "Your next lesson in photography, Erin," he said. "One you should never, ever forget. Photographers always keep their negatives. Just in case a customer changes his mind and decides to order more copies."

This time, he did close the door.

Erin had gone off to school, and Neil had decided to eat in his room. Once David delivered Neil's breakfast tray, he came back downstairs and sat at the kitchen table. It was cozy—just Chris and himself. She had already eaten, but she poured herself another cup of coffee.

"Are you feeling all right, David?"

"I'm fine."

"You were so upset last night, I was worried. I hated to leave you alone, but when you finally fell asleep—" She must have seen his surprise because she stopped right there. "You don't remember, do you?"

It was strange: he hadn't before then, but her words set off some kind of chain reaction in his brain. He remembered the feelings clearly, but until this very moment, he hadn't realized that it had been Chris who was responsible for them. He stared down at the table, too embarrassed to even look at her.

"I hope you don't mind my coming in like that," she said.

"No, I don't mind." Then finally he worked up the courage to look at her. "Thanks," he said.

"For what, David?"

"I don't know. Being there, I guess."

They sat in awkward silence for a moment, then Chris took his plate, piled it with sausages and eggs, and put it in front of him. "I want you to understand, David, Neil didn't mean any harm last night. He sometimes jumps in without noticing he's treading on sensitive ground."

"I understand," he said, lying. What else could he say? *Neil did know; he meant to shake me up. There's a side to your husband even you don't know.*

"I want you to get to know him, David. He's really a wonderful man. I'd like you two to become friends."

It felt like a piece of sausage had lodged in David's throat. He quickly lifted his glass of milk and gulped some down, pushing the sausage along with it. Chris waited for him to say something; when he didn't she put her hand on his. "Please try, David."

Just her saying those three words was enough to put a dent in his defenses. There was nothing less he wanted now than to be Neil's friend—not after what he had done. But he knew that for Chris' sake, he would try. He got the opportunity about five seconds later: Neil's intercom buzzed. Chris jumped up, went to the counter and pressed the button.

"Yes, Neil?"

"Send David," the tinny voice commanded.

"I'll come, Neil. David's eat—"

He stood up. "It's okay, I'll go."

Chris smiled, then turned back toward the voice box. "He's on his way."

By the time he got upstairs, Neil was already preparing for his shower. He had taken clothes from his dresser drawer and laid them across the top bar of his walker. A pair of black socks, rolled in a tight ball, dropped to the floor and bounced under the bed. David crouched down and picked them up. "I'll carry them," he offered.

"No need," Neil said, taking them from his hand. "When's your first class, David?"

"Not till ten, I've got lots of time."

Neil headed out into the hallway, his clothes still hung over the walker's bar. He followed after him like a puppy, twice retrieving the sock ball. As soon as they got inside the bathroom, Neil began to undress.

"Need help?"

"I can manage."

David backed against the wall, trying not to watch, but in such a small space it was almost impossible not to. Neil's flesh drooped on his body like a sagging hemline; his penis, though limp, was long and thick. He had once read that guys with big noses were hung big; Neil's nose was big, but unlike David's beak, it was straight as a arrow. Neil looked up, and David quickly looked down, counting the tiny blue ceramic tiles on the floor.

When he was ready, David adjusted the water temperature, helped him step over the side of the tub, and closed the sliding doors. Then David leaned against the wall, directing his eyes away from the frosted glass as he showered. Finally Neil turned the water off, and David helped him step out onto the bath mat.

"A towel," he said. David handed it to him, then, "Thanks. You can go."

"If you want—"

"Go. I'm fine."

David made a hasty retreat, feeling as if, by assisting Neil in his morning hygiene, some dirt had rubbed off on him. For the first time, he was almost anxious to get to work. Not that Steel was anyone you'd ever choose to be with, but David could usually count on him to ask no questions. He never had to try to read between the lines. Or worry that he might say the wrong thing.

CHAPTER FOURTEEN

The physical therapist had just left when Craig pulled his car into the driveway. Craig came up the walk with his arms full of files; Chris held the door open for him.

"You didn't waste any time, did you?"

"I'm sorry, Mrs. Mathews. Neil called this morning and asked me to run these by." As he spoke he was already headed upstairs.

"I'm giving you one hour, Craig," she called after him. "See that Neil doesn't renege on his bargain."

"I'll try my best, Mrs. Mathews."

His best was not good enough. Ninety minutes later, Chris took matters into her own hands; she made up a tray, carried it upstairs, and announced, "Time's up," the moment she entered the room.

Craig immediately stood up. "I'm sorry—"

"Sit down, join us." She passed him a cup of tea, swung the over-the-bed hospital stand in front of Neil's chair, dipped a bread stick into low-fat cottage cheese and held it out. "It's your favorite, Neil. Straight from Quincy Market."

"Thanks."

Chris sat down, gesturing toward the thick file open on Craig's lap. "What's the case?"

Craig looked at Neil.

"Just old business," Neil said.

"Oh? What kind?"

Neil normally discussed his work with Chris, but this time he dodged her question. "Great bread sticks. Try one, Craig."

Craig leaned over, took one and bit into it, nodding his approval.

"What do you think of the therapist, Neil?" she said finally.

"Personally or professionally?"

She smiled. "Let's start with professionally."

"He knows the right muscles to pull."

"I'm sure he'd be pleased with such a glowing report. And personally?"

Neil shrugged. "A cheerleader."

"Give him a break—I assume he's only trying to encourage you. Most people enjoy a pat on the back."

A brief scowl, then onto the next thought: "Get a bar in the bathroom."

"Why, Neil?"

"I want to shower alone."

"Was there a problem with David this morning?"

"No. He was helpful."

"Well, I'd feel better having someone in there with you."

"Get the bar! Please."

Craig chose that moment to bow out. "Thanks for the tea, Mrs. Mathews." He turned to Neil. "I'll leave the files."

"The book too," Neil said. "And don't forget tonight."

Craig looked a little sheepish. "I'll be here by six."

Chris started to follow Craig out of the room, but he put his hand up. "No problem, I'll see myself out." And with that, he was off.

Chris looked at Neil. "What's this about tonight? You promised to limit the work to a few hours a day."

"No business. Dinner."

"You asked Craig to dinner?"

Neil nodded.

"Why?"

"Why not?"

"You've never asked him before."

He shrugged. "That's why. About time we had guests."

Chris piled the cups back onto the tray. "Are you going to nap before lunch? There's time."

"I will. And, Chris ..."

She sighed and lifted the tray. "Yes, Neil. I'll call someone about the bar right away."

Erin was so quiet and pale when she got home that afternoon that Chris felt her forehead to check for a fever. Erin pulled away from her. "I'm okay," she said.

"Well, you don't look it."

"I'm going up to see dad."

"If you aren't well, I don't want you going near him. He can't afford a setback."

"I told you, I feel fine."

"Did something happen in school?"

"Leave me alone. You're always nagging. If it's not at dad, it's at me." She lifted her books from the table and ran out of the kitchen before Chris could even respond to her outburst.

Ten minutes later, she came downstairs as if nothing had happened. "Mom, do you have another key to the darkroom? I want to blow up some of our pictures."

"Why don't you wait until David gets home? It won't be long."

"I want to get started now."

"Well, I'm afraid I can't help you. First, I don't know where the duplicate key is. And second, if I did know I wouldn't give it to you. The darkroom is David's, not yours. Going in there would be an invasion of his privacy."

Erin glared at her.

"Surely you can understand that, Erin."

"No, I can't. All I ever hear any more is David this and David that. What about dad and me? Don't we count at all?"

Chris stared at her daughter, wondering where all the anger was coming from. "That's unfair, Erin," she said finally. "Do you doubt—have you ever doubted for one minute—how much I love you and your father? How much you both mean to me?"

"I guess not."

"Only guess not?"

She sighed. "I know."

"All I want, Erin, is for us to be a family."

"That includes David, of course."

"Yes. That includes David."

"But David isn't family."

"Have you two had a falling out? Is that what this is about?"

"No."

"Then what *is* the problem? I can't believe you're turning on him like this. Not after all he's done to be your friend."

"And I can't figure out if you're dumb—or just crazy!"

Chris didn't even think about it; she took one step forward and slapped her daughter's face. She had never struck her before, and she couldn't believe she had done it now. "I didn't mean—"

"It doesn't matter!" she shouted through the tears in her voice.

Immediately, Chris pulled her into her arms. "Of course it matters. I don't know what came over me—I'm sorry, Erin."

She twisted away. "I'm sorry, too."

Her words were the same as Chris's, but Chris knew she wasn't referring to what had just happened.

Chris hadn't heard David come in, but she immediately recognized the humming; she called him into the kitchen. She must have looked as bad as she felt, because when he saw her, his expression turned to concern. "Is something wrong?"

"Sit down, David."

"Something *is* wrong."

"Nothing serious. I just thought maybe you could help."

"Sure. Anything."

"Actually, the problem is Erin."

"Is she hurt?"

"No, nothing like that. She's very upset, though. And I'm afraid I haven't handled the situation well at all."

"What happened?"

"That's just it—I don't really know. Has there been any difficulty between you and her?"

He shook his head. "Did she say there was?"

"No. But something is bothering her, and I can't figure out what it is. Perhaps seeing her father this way has been harder for her than I expected."

David's voice lowered. "Maybe it *is* my fault."

"Why do you say that?"

"I might have said something or done something to upset her without my even knowing it. I don't understand girls all that much. Sometimes you can get them mad at you without even trying."

Chris laughed. "They do tend to be emotional. And, sometimes, overdramatic. But from what I've seen, David, you're very sensitive—I doubt that you're at fault. It may be a combination of things getting her down. She's been through a lot these past months with her father away."

"If you want me to, I could talk to her."

"Would you, David? At her age, sometimes it's easier to open up to someone other than a parent. I'm sure you remember how it was for you."

He looked down at the floor for a moment, then back up at her. "I have a feeling that Erin and even Neil don't know how lucky they are to have you to talk to."

Chris stood up, leaned over and kissed his cheek. "You know, David, you should win some kind of award for tact. You always seem to say just the right thing, at the right time."

CHAPTER FIFTEEN

ven before David reached his bedroom, he heard the noise from inside. It didn't take a genius to figure out who was spying. He tiptoed the rest of the way to the door, then threw it open. Redhanded and guilty.

Erin squealed and jerked her hands upward, like she'd set off a mousetrap. It was funny, but neither of them laughed. Finally, she turned around to face David.

"I want the negatives, David."

He pointed to the dresser; all four drawers were open. "Well, you're wasting your time. They're not there."

"I found that out. But I still want them."

"Why didn't you just ask me?"

"If I had, would you have given them to me?"

He shrugged. "Probably not."

"They're my pictures. I have a right to them."

"I explained to you, Erin, negatives belong to the photographer."

"What good are they to you?"

"None, I suppose."

"Then why do you want them?"

"Because they're good. Maybe some day you'll change your mind and want them developed. I could even put together a portfolio for you that you could show to prospective employers."

"How can you look me straight in the face and say that? You as much as told me yourself how disgusting they were!"

"When did I say that?"

"You remember—in the park."

112

"You misinterpreted what I said. I never said I didn't like the pictures."

"What if I don't want a portfolio, David?"

He stuck his hands in his side pockets. "Then I won't make one."

"What about the negatives?"

"What about them?"

"Would you ever develop them?"

"Did I say I would?"

"No. But what you said this morning...It sounded like..."

"What?"

"Like you wanted to punish me. Or maybe even my father."

"I don't want to do anything bad to you, Erin. Or your father."

"You say that now, but how do I know it's true?"

"I don't know. I guess you'll just have to believe me."

"But I can't trust you, David. You said so yourself."

"Try thinking of trust like religion, Erin. You believe because you want to. Not because you have evidence to base it on. Do you want to trust me?"

She nodded.

"Then it's simple. Isn't it?"

She started out of the room, then stopped. "David, I know you don't know my father very well, and maybe last night he didn't make the greatest impression . . . but he's really a nice man."

"Then we'll both have to take good care of him, won't we?"

She stared at him for a few seconds, said, "I'll see you at dinner," and left. He closed the door after her, went to his bed and lay down on the spread. He started to drift off to sleep, happy he'd kept his promise to Chris. Erin felt better . . . and so did he.

At 5:30 Chris knocked at David's door and asked him to help Neil downstairs. Neil was leafing through a thick book when they entered his room. He slammed it shut and pushed it aside.

"I thought you might want to come down a little early," Chris said.

Neil stood up and reached for a file.

"Uh-uh, remember our agreement," Chris said. "You've done plenty for today. Now is the time to relax. You did say Craig isn't coming on business?"

"Strictly social."

David stiffened; Chris sensed it and turned to him. "Craig is an associate of Neil's. You'll like him, David." She turned back to Neil. "Leave your work up here where it belongs. So help me, Neil, if you start talking law at dinner, I'm going to jump up on the table and do a tap dance."

"Sounds like a real attention-getter."

"So long as I make my intentions clear . . ."

"Absolutely."

As soon as David helped Neil to the parlor, he ran back up to put on his necktie. The doorbell rang just as he was heading down again; he stopped and watched Chris let Craig in. David summed him up immediately as a pretty boy. He would have bet a week's pay that the soles of Craig's shoes were as spotless as the rest of him. He didn't much like the type, but he had to admit, it intrigued him. How did the Craigs of this world manage to never get dirty?

Bad timing: he reached the bottom of the stairs just as Chris turned to show Criag to the living room. She spotted David, and in that odd way they had of communicating, she contradicted his thought. "Perfect timing, David," she said.

David stood there, waiting for—and dreading—the formalities.

"This is Craig Phillips, he's Assistant DA on Neil's staff... This is David Crane, our—" She stopped herself, smiling. "Now, how can I say boarder? Somehow that sounds all wrong. What I really mean to say is, David is the newest member of our family."

That really threw him and probably Craig, too. Instead of a brief glance and quick handshake, Craig shook his hand firmly and looked him square in the eye. Like he was someone special.

Craig pulled his hand back. "I hear you're from Laconia," he said. Chris must have told him. Or maybe Neil. David nodded.

"Nice country up that way. When I was a kid, we had a summer cottage not too far from there. Halfmoon Lake—ever hear of it?"

"I don't think so."

"Well, it *was* pretty small. What's that big lake up there? The one where they have sailboat races?"

"You mean Winnipesaukee?"

"That's it. That must be fifteen miles long."

"Even bigger. Twenty-two miles."

"Did you ever watch any of the races?"

"Only once. I was usually too busy working."

They started walking to the living room. "I used to work summers myself," Craig said. "Nick's Restaurant, right across from the lake. It was actually more of a glorified hot dog stand than a restaurant."

David sat down next to Craig on the sofa, across from Neil's easy chair. Chris went to the bar, uncorked a bottle of wine and poured it into four long-stemmed glasses. She set them on a tray and carried it to the coffee table. Everyone reached for a glass.

"Would you like some, David? It's burgundy," Chris said.

He hesitated.

"If you'd rather, we have ginger ale."

"No. This will be fine." He lifted the glass and took a swallow. He had never tasted wine before; it seemed sour. He smiled at Chris, then took another sip.

"Look who's here," Craig said, looking toward the archway. Erin came prancing into the room. "The most beautiful future lawyer ever to hit the Commonwealth."

Erin ran over to Craig and hugged him. "Missed you, Craig."

"Don't worry, you'll be sick of me soon enough. I'm going to be coming around often now that your dad is home."

Chris stood up and put down her wine glass. "Erin, how about you and me making a salad and putting the finishing touches on dinner?" Erin sighed and followed Chris into the kitchen. David started to get up, but Chris called out: "Don't you dare, David. I'm leaving you in charge to make sure that the conversation doesn't turn to law."

Craig turned to David. "Where did you work, David?"

"A laundromat," he said. "I fixed machines."

"Mechanically inclined, huh?"

He shrugged.

"I always envied anyone who could take apart a machine."

"Taking it apart is easy," Neil said. "It's putting it back."

Craig laughed; so did David. David heard the ring of his laughter—off key, for sure. Neither of them seemed to notice.

"Kidding aside," Craig said, "It's a real art. Unfortunately I have zero aptitude for it."

"No choice but to go to law school?" Neil said.

Craig rested his arm on the back of the sofa.

"Something like that. You use whatever talents you're given. I had two choices: I made the greatest frankfurters and shakes on the East Coast. And I could push around paper faster than the wind. So here I am." He looked at David, but gestured slyly toward Neil. "He collects it and I push it."

David had never been part of a conversation like this before. It moved so fast, it was making him dizzy. Or maybe that was the wine. He said the next thing that came into his head. "I thought of becoming a psychiatrist myself."

"Is that right?" Craig said. "I have a friend in the field. I'll tell you, it's not a bad business. His cases are interesting, and he's making good money."

"A tough business," Neil said. "Bad enough to deal with your own nightmares."

"I don't know," Craig said. "Seems to me you could get a lot of satisfaction from helping people that way. And there's not a one of us who doesn't occasionally need help with a problem. What do you think, David? You must have given this some thought."

"Psychiatrists are fine for those people. But there's a lot of crazy people in this world. I don't think psychiatrists should tamper with them at all."

"I suppose that all depends on how you define 'crazy.' Give me a hypothetical, David."

"Well . . . how about a person who isn't who he thinks he is," he said.

Craig took a sip of his drink and so did David. "You mean, he perceives himself differently from what he is?"

"That's everyone," Neil said.

"I mean he's carrying around more than one person," David said. "And he's not sure which person is real."

"Like a split personality?"

"No—not split. Separate."

"Those cases are pretty rare," Craig said. "You're talking about two or more personalities sharing one body, each taking on a definite role."

"Not really that, either. One personality is buried—it doesn't play a role, it's just there. It doesn't even get to breathe."

"Then how would this person even know it exists?"

"He could feel the body he was carrying around inside him," David said. "It would weigh him down."

"Certainly not your everyday neurotic," Neil said.

Craig smiled. "I'm not a psychiatrist, David, but I'd certainly think this guy you're talking about would need one."

"Yeah, but he'd never go near one," David said.

"Why not?"

"He's afraid."

"Of what?"

"Letting the other personality out."

"Why would that be so frightening?"

"Because the other personality belongs to someone who's dead. If it comes out, there's a chance it might take over. And then this guy we're talking about—he dies."

Now both Neil and Craig looked at him. Finally Craig said, "Well, I know psychotherapy is a pretty painful process. But I haven't yet heard of any fatalities."

"Suicide," Neil said.

"I suppose. But, David, what's this guy's alternative?"

"Do nothing."

"I assume you wouldn't recommend that. After all, you're the budding psychiatrist."

"Well, he could ... I don't know." David stopped talking and looked down at the floor.

No one spoke for the next few minutes. Finally Craig said, "You taking pre-med, David?"

He shook his head. "Liberal Arts. I've got time to change."

"School's a good time. When I was there, I couldn't wait to get out. Now, sometimes, I wouldn't mind being back."

"A reflection on me?" Neil said.

Craig laughed, then looked at David. "He's not an easy man to work for—he doesn't know the meaning of the word 'stop.' I don't envy you, David. At least I get to part company with him at five, six, seven o'clock. God knows what it's like to *live* with him."

"Chris makes anything bearable." David hadn't even known he was going to say that until the words came out; the wine must have loosened his tongue. He looked at Neil to see how he'd take it.

Neil laughed. "Yes, she's quite a woman. That is, if you like them smart, and sensitive, and beautiful."

Just then Chris walked in with Erin behind her, carrying a half-dozen platters and bowls between them. "Who's smart, sensitive, *and* beautiful?" Chris asked.

"One of the nurses in the hospital," Neil said.

"Maybe on second thought you ought to talk about law, Neil." She put the platters on the table and turned, smiling. "Not to change the subject, of course, but dinner is served."

CHAPTER SIXTEEN

hris' introduction of David to Craig had been prophetic: that evening it was like they were a family. Although the idea hadn't been hers, having Craig to dinner worked out perfectly. Just his presence seemed to put both David and Neil at ease. Of course the burgundy hadn't hurt, either. Even Erin was almost back to normal. Not quite as talkative or energetic as usual, but the anger she'd felt earlier had definitely exhausted itself.

After Craig left at nine o'clock, they opened their presents. They took turns; Neil was first. "Great," he said, pulling the miniature recorder from the box. "I'll carry it everywhere."

"Oh no!" Erin groaned. "Now, we'll have to worry about every word we say to you. We'll never know when it's on."

"That's the idea. Just be sure that what you say is for the record."

"Well, for the record, Neil," Chris said, "don't you dare."

Erin picked up the gift in front of her. "I'm next," she said, already tearing at the paper. She looked at the picture on the box. "A camera!" Then pulled it out and examined it. "A Nikon—like David's. Thank you." She leaned over and kissed her father.

"You're sure you'll use it?" he asked.

"Of course, dad—I love it!" She pecked Chris' cheek, then turned to David. "Your turn," she said.

He was all thumbs trying to open his gift, but once he did, he ran his hands along the album cover, feeling every inch of the soft textured leather. Finally, he looked at Chris. "I never saw anything like this—it's really great." He hugged the album to him and Chris reached over and kissed his cheek. "Use it well, David."

Suddenly a look of dismay: "But what about you, Chris? Where's your present?"

Chris picked up the tiny box beside her. "Here's mine. It's not exactly a surprise, but I was given very precise instructions as to what to buy." She opened the box, unscrewed the bottle and generously dabbed the perfume along her neck and behind her ears. She leaned toward Neil.

"Take a sniff," she said. "Is this what you had in mind?" Neil buried his nose in her neck; she pulled back, laughing. "No fair, you're tickling."

"Get back here."

She put her head back and he sniffed again. "Well?" she asked.

"Yes. Definitely sexy."

Erin was enjoying their little performance, but David looked embarrassed. Then he stood up.

"I've got a surprise, too."

With that, he picked up the used wrapping paper and rushed out of the room, leaving Chris with an odd sense of having watched this same scene before.

She looked at Erin. "Do you know what this is all about?"

Erin shook her head. Two minutes later David was back, carrying something flat and rectangular, more or less wrapped in the torn paper. He held it out to Chris, and as she took the gift, she looked into his eyes: worried, uncertain. And at that moment, she remembered . . .

The beautiful lace nightgown, a birthday gift from Neil. Then Kevin jumping down from his chair lifting the torn paper from the box. "I got a surprise, too."

Two minutes later he was back. "Close your eyes, mommy." She closed them. "Put out your hands." He put the gift in her hands.

She opened her eyes and looked down; one long strip of scotch tape wrapped twice around the package, holding it together. She opened it: ten acorns strung together on a black shoelace. A thick knot holding the ends together. She held it up, then looked down at Kevin and smiled. "A necklace?"

He nodded, his eyes still worried.

Chris held it up again. "Look what Kevin made for me, Neil. Isn't it beautiful?" She remembered Neil's tirade the day before when he was late for court and found his left shoe minus its lace. Neil reached over and examined the necklace. "A really sensational job, son," he said.

She bent down and hugged Kevin. "I love it, honey— thank you." Then she pulled away. Still that look ... Finally she took the string of acorns and put it over her head, letting it settle around her neck. His dark eyes widened. "You will wear it, mommy?"

She laughed. "Of course I'll wear it. What else would I do with it?" Now came his big smile ...

"Is something wrong?" David was asking.

She was holding the wrapped gift in her hands, staring at it. "Nothing ... Nothing at all."

"Open it."

She carefully removed the paper and lifted out the photograph of David in the park, enlarged and gold-framed. She studied it carefully, then stood up and hugged him.

"Oh, David—it's beautiful. Thank you!" She held it up to show Erin and Neil. "From here on," she said, "it will sit on the mantel beside Erin ..." She looked at Neil. "And Kevin."

Chris carried it right then to the gray stone fireplace and stood it on the mantel, right in the center.

That night, Chris fell asleep almost instantly. She awoke at six and lay in bed for a few minutes, enjoying a marvelous feeling of anticipation. Then she got up, threw on her robe and headed across the hall. Neil was sitting in bed, leafing again through the thick black book Craig had left the day before. He rubbed his fingers slowly back and forth along his chin, scowling. She stood in the doorway, watching him.

"What's so intriguing?" she said finally.

He continued to stare into the book.

"Neil—are you all right?"

He looked up, rubbed his eyes, then closed the book. "Sleep well?" he asked.

"I sure did." Chris went to the window and pulled open the draperies, letting the sun pour in the room, then pointed to the book. "It looks to me like a stack of magazines in there." He didn't comment. "Confidential?" she said.

"Yes."

"You realize, of course, this is the first time you haven't confided in me. Now, you've really got me curious. What kind of case is it?"

Neil shook his head.

"All right, I won't ask." She went over and sat on the edge of his bed. "Besides, I'd rather talk about last night."

"Oh?"

"It was special, wasn't it?"

He lifted his hand and cupped Chris' chin. "Yes. Very special."

"Then it wasn't just me?"

"I don't understand."

"David's being here. You're beginning to see how right it is."

"I told you Chris—I want what makes you happy."

"Not just me, Neil. You and Erin, too. He really cares about Erin. Why just yesterday, Erin was very angry, and David—"

"Angry about what?"

"I'm still not quite sure. I do know what set her off—I refused to let her into David's darkroom without his permission. But I actually think it had more to do with everything she's been feeling for these past few months."

"My stroke?"

"Well, it hasn't been easy on any of us. And like you, Erin tends to hold everything in. It's a wonder her frustration and anger haven't come out sooner."

"And David?"

"David talked to her. I don't know what he said, but apparently it was what she needed to hear. By last night, she was fine. Growing up isn't always as easy as we remember, looking back, and I'm glad she has David to turn to." She put her hand over his. "And you, Neil—you can't tell me that you didn't enjoy David's company last evening. Even before dinner, the three of you seemed to hit it off just fine."

"You listened?"

"Well, I couldn't hear what you were saying, but I could hear you talking. I could tell David was joining right in with you and Craig. Admit it, it's nice having him here. It feels natural. Almost as if he was meant to find this house and come to live with us."

"How *did* he find it?"

"A sign. I put a sign in the window."

Neil gave her an odd look. "Not an agency?"

"No. I was going to list it with an agency, but I never got the chance. In fact, I hadn't even had the sign up for more than a few hours ... Now, doesn't that convince you that fate played some small part?"

"My God—anybody ... It could have been anybody."

"But it wasn't, Neil. It was David."

He didn't say a thing for what seemed like minutes. Then: "Why Kevin's room?"

"I didn't want him living in the attic. It somehow didn't seem right. Tell me honestly, Neil—would it have seemed right to you?"

She hadn't noticed until then, but Neil's hands were clasped together, the palms rubbed back and forth rhythmically.

"Are you all right, Neil? I shouldn't have gone on and

on like this." She started to get up from the bed, but he took hold of her wrist.

"I'm glad you did."

"Then you understand about David?"

"Not all of it. Not yet. I need more time."

She wrapped her arms around him. "Of course, honey. Take all the time you need."

Neil again had breakfast in his room. Erin ran a little late, had a bowl of Grape Nuts, and scooted out just in time to catch her school bus. David came downstairs right after Erin left. Chris watched him pause at the fireplace and look at the pictures on the mantel before he came into the kitchen.

"It looks good up there, doesn't it?" she said.

He nodded, smiling; he was smiling so much more often these days.

"Sit down, young man. Have breakfast." As he sat, he reached out and laid two ten dollar bills beside Chris' plate. "What's this, David?" she said.

"Rent. I'm sorry I'm late, it was due yesterday."

She looked from the money to him; it seemed inconceivable that it had only been one week since he'd come. She didn't want to take the money from him, but finally she did. She slipped it into her pocket.

"Is something wrong?"

"No, David, not at all. You know, I wasn't joking when I introduced you to Craig last night. I meant what I said: as far as I'm concerned, you're just like one of the family."

He looked down at the table. "But I'm not, really. Then there's Neil ... what does he think?"

"Actually, he's beginning to take to the idea. You've got to understand something, David. The only reason Neil has seemed wary of having you here is because of me. He was worried about me."

She could see by his expression, he didn't understand,

and why should he? "You see, David, Neil and I once
had a son—"

"I know."

"Then you must know his name—it was Kevin."

"His picture's on the mantel. Next to mine."

"Yes." Chris could feel her hands trembling; she tightened them around the coffee cup. "He was special.
Bright, beautiful ... It took me a very long time to get
over his death." She could feel the tears coming; she
didn't want that, not now.

David put his hand on hers. "I once knew a little boy
who died," he said.

"Was he someone close, David?"

"Very close."

She waited, but he didn't add anything. Finally she
went on. "You see, Neil was afraid I'd forget who you
really are."

"What do you mean forget?"

"I don't know if I can make you understand ..."

David sat patiently and waited. He knew Chris needed
to talk.

"Pretending can be fun, David. Certainly we all do
it. But sometimes it gets out of hand ... A person
can move deeper and deeper into his dreams until
one day he imagines something to be so real, he
can't tell any longer that it's not. He sees only what
he wants to see. Like looking at one person and seeing someone else."

"And you've done that?"

"Yes. I'm afraid I have."

"And what happened?"

"I realized I was wrong. It took me a long time to face
it. But I finally did."

"It must have been hard."

"Harder than anything I've ever done—before or since.
And Neil was afraid I might try to do that with you."

"Change me into Kevin?"

"Yes, in my mind. But that's not going to happen, of course. I won't ever let that happen to me again." She dropped her eyes for a moment, then looked up. "In any event, having you here, means a lot to me. To us."

David sat down and picked at his breakfast, without saying another word. She could almost see him thinking. Finally he looked up from his plate. "I wouldn't mind, you know."

"Wouldn't mind what?" Chris asked.

"If you wanted to think of me as Kevin ... if it made you feel better. I wouldn't mind so much."

CHAPTER SEVENTEEN

"Step on a crack and break your back." When David was ten years old, he spent one entire year trying to avoid stepping on a crack. Once he lasted for three months straight. He kept a little plastic card calendar under his mattress and every night before he went to sleep he'd pull it out and cross off another day of success.

His plan was more complicated than most—exactly two steps to a sidewalk square and never a foot on a crack. He had it all worked out in his mind. If he could last one whole year, then he would get the two things he wanted most: his head would stop hurting and he would no longer be David. Sometimes he thought the two things were really one thing, but he couldn't be sure.

It made no difference, either way: just like always, Fletcher found him out. Fletcher never said a word to him about it. Instead he followed him to school, and all of a sudden, his long leg swept right under David, threw him off balance and, in that one instant, wrecked the whole three-month ritual. Then he stood over him and said the same thing he'd said for as long as David could remember: "You're crazy, Davie. And someday everybody's gonna know it."

In school that day, David looked up the definition of "crazy." Webster defined it as unsound of mind, mentally unbalanced. But he knew better: crazy was a pounding in the head that hurt so much it was all you could do to not put a gun to your head and pull the trigger. Instead you walked around, gritting your teeth, doing all the things you could think of to do to pretend everything was all right. And you did all that because the truth was—you wanted to live. Way back somewhere, you thought if you played by the rules for a long enough time, without tripping even once, the hurt would go away. But it never did.

That morning Chris had confided her deepest secrets to him, told him of her pain. She had tried her best to make it sound like that was then and this was now, but he knew better. What she'd been doing all along was just trying her best not to step on the cracks in the sidewalk ...

David was having trouble concentrating on his work. Everything Steel had taught him seemed to have drained from his consciousness. All he could think about was the lunatic thing he had suggested to Chris that morning—why had he said it? But even while he asked himself why, he knew that, if given the chance, he would say it again. Now he stood in the back room of the fix-it shop, staring at an empty television frame and a hundred odd components lying on the table beside it. Every piece looked like every other piece. He lifted a circuit and stared at it.

Steel pulled the doorway curtain aside and stepped in. "What's taking so long, kid? You should of been done an hour ago."

David didn't answer.

"Cat got your tongue?"

"I don't feel so good, Steel."

"You're not going to puke, are you?"

"I don't think so." David felt lightheaded and sweaty; he tore open the top button of his shirt. "Maybe I should leave."

Steel lifted his big hand to his face, and with a black fingernail dug at a pockmark on his cheek, drawing blood. "Go on," he said finally. "You're doing shit anyhow. I'm gonna dock you for the time though."

David nodded, grabbed his jacket off the hook and left. Driving home, he rolled down the car windows and let the cold air whip against his face. Craig was just getting into his car when David pulled in the driveway; he raised his hand, waving, and David waved back. Chris must have heard him coming, because she was standing in the foyer when he walked in. "David, you're early," was what she said, but her eyes said, what's wrong?

"I cut class, I don't feel so good."

Chris touched his forehead. "No fever. I hope it's not flu season coming early this year. Maybe you'd better go upstairs and lie down. I'll bring you some tea."

"I'm sure it's nothing."

"You're probably right, but it won't hurt to get some rest."

Within ten minutes, Chris was upstairs, carrying a cup in one hand and a portable TV in another. She set the tea down beside him, then the television. "I thought you might like some entertainment." She plugged the set in, then came over to the bed. "What bothering you, David? You look tied up in knots."

"My stomach feels funny, that's all."

"It's this morning, isn't it? You didn't understand."

"Yes, I did. Honest."

"David, you look very uncomfortable, as if you're unsure of me, of what I might say or do."

"Oh, no. It's not you at all. Never. It's just that, well, I just get like this sometimes. For no reason."

"I would never do anything to hurt you. You believe that, don't you?"

He nodded.

"I care about you, David."

Then he asked—he had to. "Like you cared about Kevin?"

She stared at him.

"You wish I were Kevin, don't you?" He pushed himself up on the pillows, trying hard to smile. "You know, I could be if that's what you want."

"No, David. You just be yourself." She pushed her dark hair away from her face and licked her lips. "Besides," she said, her lip trembling. "You can't just magically transform people into someone else."

"You did. And so did I once."

"What do you mean?"

"There was once a little boy I wanted to be. I used to pretend I was him."

"Children often fantasize, David. Particularly when they're lonely."

"He seemed real to me."

"What was the little boy like? How was he different from David?"

"He was happy . . ."

She reached out, tentatively, and began to stroke his forehead. "And David wasn't?"

He shook his head. "The other boy could always think of fun things—things that I wouldn't have thought of in a million years. And he could really laugh—you know, like he really meant it . . . Finally, though, I stopped pretending."

"Why?"

He wanted to tell her, but what would he say? *It wasn't a child's fantasy at all, it was real. The little boy I made myself into wasn't just any little boy—he was your Kevin. And if it were up to me, I would have stayed Kevin forever, but I couldn't. Because he died . . . And if it hadn't seemed all so real, I wouldn't have been so scared that I would die too.* Oh, he could say all of that—and then she'd know for sure he was crazy. Instead he just repeated what he'd said that morning: "I wouldn't mind if you wanted to pretend I was Kevin."

Chris looked around the room at the red lantern, the wooden Disney characters, the books, then in such a soft voice he could barely hear her, "I used to read to him," she said. "Every night before he went to sleep."

He didn't say anything, he couldn't. Her words were like big beautiful bubbles floating just within his reach; if he reached out to touch them, they would pop.

She faced him again. "Why, David? Why would you want to go back to pretending?"

"We would both know the difference. It wouldn't be like it was real."

"Then what would be the point?"

"I don't know, maybe it would take away some of the pain."

"Whose pain?"

"Yours. And mine."

She drew in her breath sharply, then hurried out of the room. David wanted to call out to her, to say something—anything—that would get her to come back. But the words stuck in his throat.

Even though David managed to sleep for a couple of hours, he woke with a dull ache in his head. At three o'clock he heard a knock on his door. "Come in," he called, hoping desperately that it was Chris. It wasn't. Erin carried a cup of tea and a dish of toast and set them on the nightstand.

"My mother thought you might be hungry."

He sat up. "Where is she?"

"Downstairs."

Erin was waiting for him to ask her more, but he didn't. Instead he took a slice of toast, bit into it and said, "Have you thought more about the portfolio?"

"I don't have to think about it. I told you, I'm not interested."

He shrugged. "Whatever you say. That's a nice camera your folks gave you last night. You ought to take it out and use it. This is the best time of year for colors."

"I will."

"Yeah ... when?"

"When I'm in the mood."

"Don't you like your present?"

"It's okay, I guess." She looked at the television on the desk. "My mother give you that?"

"Temporarily. Just while I'm sick."

"What's the matter with you?"

"My head hurts."

"Maybe you have a brain tumor."

"Naw. More likely I'm crazy."

She walked to the door, opened it and turned. "Congratulations, David. That's probably the first honest thing you've said since you walked in this house."

Chris sent word by Erin that the two of them would manage to get Neil downstairs for dinner; he was to stay in bed, and a tray would be sent up. But when Erin brought it at six o'clock, he couldn't touch a bite. All he could think about was Chris and her ignoring him that whole day since their talk.

He got out of bed, opened the door and listened: he could hear Erin and Neil's voices coming from the dining room. And then he heard Chris'—two octaves lower than theirs. It was so soft he couldn't even make out her words. He closed the door, turned on the television to "Family Ties" and got back in bed. At seven, Erin came back for the tray. She took a good look at it as she picked it up. "What's the matter—don't you like chicken?"

"Sure. I like you, don't I?"

"Actually you made a wise decision, David. If I were you, I wouldn't have touched it either. You never know who in this house might have decided to flavor it with arsenic. I hear that you can't even tell when you're eating it, at least not until it's too late."

Normally, her comments wouldn't have fazed him. But now, with Chris mad at him, Erin's backhanded threat hit home. His head hurt so bad he was afraid he might scream. He bit down on the edge of the blanket. "Get out," he said.

The moment she left, he put his hands on each side of his head and pressed hard as if somehow counteracting the pressure that welled up inside. He pinched his arm, trying to draw the pain away from his head, but that didn't help. The television audio blared forth in some language he no longer understood. Finally he started to count, first slowly, then faster. Maybe when he reached a thousand, the pain would stop.

CHAPTER EIGHTEEN

As soon as Chris left David, she had rushed down the hallway to her room, grabbed a puzzle book and tried to concentrate on the jumble of words. Finally she tossed the book aside and lay down on the bed with her eyes closed. And then, as if a movie film had begun to unroll in her head, she remembered . . .

One chubby leg onto the chair, then the other. Turning and facing the salesman, Kevin put in his order: "One pair of big-man shoes, please."

The stocky salesman crouched down, unlaced his shoes, took them off, and slid his foot into the steel measuring apparatus. "A heavy date?" he asked Kevin.

A puzzled look, then: "I need them for work."

The salesman nodded. "What kind of work is that?"

"I'm a turney—like my Daddy."

"An attorney," Chris said.

He tried again. "An at-turney."

Because of a slight toeing in, Kevin had until now worn high orthopedic shoes. Today he was to have his first pair of low shoes, and he'd been looking forward to the shopping trip for weeks. Last night, at bedtime, Neil had managed to up Kevin's excitement even more: "As soon as you get those shoes, have mommy bring you up to my office. We'll let her go shopping, and you can work with daddy."

He turned from Neil to her. "Can I, mommy?"

"Will you let me sleep a half-hour later in the morning—till seven?"

"Sure I would. Why wouldn't I?"

Neil and she laughed; Kevin always made them laugh. "All right," she said, "You've made yourself a deal."

He jumped up, bounced on the mattress as if it were a trampoline and clapped his hands. Now, he sat very businesslike waiting to be shown his new shoes. The salesman came back carrying several boxes; he opened each one and held the shoes up for Kevin's approval. Each time, Kevin shook his head.

"Kevin, there must be *one* pair you like?" Chris said finally.

He shook his head—adamant.

She held up a pair. "These look very nice to me, Kevin."

"They're nice. But I don't like them."

"Suppose you tell me what it is you don't like about them."

He placed his little finger on the detail on the front of the shoes. "Daddy's shoes don't have squigglies."

She looked at the salesman. "Do you have a plain pair?"

He disappeared again into the walls of boxes, and three minutes later was back. He opened a box and held up a plain brown pair of shoes. "Now how about these?"

Kevin didn't answer.

"Let's try them on and see how they fit," she said.

Kevin nodded. Using a shoehorn, the salesman put the shoes on Kevin, then laced and tied them. "Stand up," he said, and Kevin bounced down from the chair. He pressed his thumb on Kevin's big toes, then looked at Chris. "Seems a good fit to me."

"Walk around, honey," she said. "See how they feel."

Kevin ran to the mirror, looked down at his feet and frowned.

"Do they hurt, Kevin?"

"Nope."

"You don't like them?"

Suddenly he charged to the other end of the store, searched through a row of shoes on a shelf, grabbed a pair of men's shoes and brought them back to her.

"Here's the ones, mommy!"

"But these are too big for you, Kevin."

"I want these. Only littler."

Finally, she understood. She looked up at the salesman, laughing. "Do you have black shoes in this young man's size?"

As soon as the salesman opened the box and took out the shiny black shoes, Kevin's eyes lit up. He dug his hand in his back trouser pocket, pulled out a red plastic wallet, and, removing the dollar bill Neil had given him, held it out to the salesman.

"I'll take them," he said.

"Can we see if they fit first?" she said.

"Sure, mommy."

They fit. Kevin turned to her, the dollar bill clutched tightly in his fist. She shrugged and turned to the salesman. "It seems you've made a sale."

He was showing them off to a man in Neil's waiting room when she got back from shopping. The freckle-faced man in the dark three-piece suit turned from Kevin as she walked in. Maybe another attorney. "Quite a boy you've got here," he said.

She smiled. "He's very proud of those new shoes."

"And rightly so. Why, they make him look all growed up." No, not an attorney. A client.

Kevin beamed. "He wants *me* to repuzent him in his case."

"I see. Well, where's the chief attorney?"

Kevin pointed to Neil's office. "He's telling a letter to Louise."

"Isn't that where you should be, young man?" Chris asked.

"My fault, ma'am," the man said. "He was on his way back from the little boy's room." He gestured to the lavatory across from the secretary's cubby. "Seems I held him up. Never in all my life seen such a smart little lad. How old is he?"

"I'm one week more than three. Halloween is my birthday."

Actually Kevin had been born on November 2, but at Kevin's request, at that year's party she had used Jack-o-lanterns and orange and black streamers as decorations. But instead of correcting him, she nodded politely to the man, took Kevin's hand and walked him into Neil's office.

"Missing someone?" she asked.

Neil quickly finished his dictation, and Louise went back to her desk. "I'm afraid your son may have stolen a client." Neil looked up at me, puzzled. "The man in your waiting room."

"I'm not expecting anyone." He pushed the button on the intercom and Louise came on.

"Yes, Mr. Mathews?"

"Tell the gentlemen waiting I'll be right with him."

"There's no one out here, Mr. Mathews. Were you expecting someone?"

"No, I wasn't." He released the button and shrugged. "Must have changed his mind."

Kevin and she stopped at Friendly's for ice cream, then drove on home. As they got out of the car, he pointed across to the playground. "Can I go on the monkey bars, mommy?"

Chris looked over at the playground: the swings and see-saws had already been taken down for the winter. The park was empty. "I don't know, Kevin. It's chilly, and there's no one else there."

"Just one climb to the top, mommy."

She laughed, dropped the bundles back in the car slammed the door. "All right. *One* climb to the top." She took hold of his soft hand, crossed him over the street, then let him run on ahead ... toward the playground.

Suddenly the film went blank. By the time she reached the playground—Kevin had disappeared.

She sat up in bed, running her fingers through her

hair, wondering how it was possible—after so many years—for the memory to still hurt as much as it did. Wasn't time supposed to heal? Or was Neil right, after all ... did she want to replace Kevin with David? She had immediately rejected the idea when Neil suggested it, but David seemed to believe it too. Only their reactions were different. Neil was appalled; David seemed to welcome it. In any event, she couldn't even allow herself to think about what David had suggested ... It was preposterous—rational people didn't do things like that. It would be wrong ... for both of them. Wouldn't it?

She got up, slipped into sandals and ran a brush through her hair, then stopped off at Neil's room. He was at his desk, staring at the black book opened in front of him. The color had somehow seeped out of his face, leaving a sickly palor.

"What is it, Neil?"

She waited, but he didn't answer. She crept up slowly behind him and placed her hand lightly on his shoulder—he jumped, slamming the book shut.

"Get out," he said. "Please."

"I'm sorry. I didn't mean to startle you."

He put his hand to his forehead, shielding his eyes.

"Neil ... there *is* something wrong. Tell me."

"I want to be alone."

"Not until you tell me why you're so upset."

He lifted the book, this time smashing it down on the desk top, scattering dozens of papers to the floor. "Go!" he shouted.

She turned and ran ...

Although she was sure Neil's rage was related to the case he and Craig were working on, and not to her, it disturbed her. After two hours of procrastination, she dialed the DA's office and asked for Craig, hoping she could trust him enough not to tell Neil she'd called.

"Craig Phillips here."

"Craig, this is Chris."

"Hello, Mrs. Mathews. Listen ... I want to thank you again for last evening. I enjoyed it very much."

"Our pleasure, Craig. Actually, I called because I'm worried about Neil."

"What's happened?"

"Nothing. It's the way he's acting."

Silence.

"I'm sure it has to do with the case you're working on. He's so secretive, it's not like him at all."

"It's a complicated matter, Mrs. Mathews."

"It's got to be more than complicated. He spends all his time with his nose buried in the file—or in that folder full of magazines. And the more time he spends, the more upset he gets. Maybe he shouldn't be working on whatever it is."

A long pause. "I'm afraid there's not much I can do about it. This case is his baby. He began the investigation even before he had the stroke."

"Was he working on it that day?"

"I'm not sure. I suppose, it's possible."

"Then I must be told what it's all about."

"I'm sorry, Mrs. Mathews. You're going to have to ask Neil."

"Craig, if I have to get up in the middle of the night to search the files, I will. But I thought it might be easier to ask you. I'm sure I don't have to remind you how sick Neil's been. I will not allow him to endanger his health this way."

"Take it from me, he won't stop. Your knowing won't change that."

"Maybe not, but I can't help at all unless I know what's bothering him. And I intend to find out—one way or another."

It was several seconds before he answered. "Child porn," he said finally. "Neil stumbled on a publication put out from Middlesex County. And it's pretty grue-

some business, Mrs. Mathews. Not just nudity ... I suspect Neil didn't want to upset you."

"When will it be over? The case, I mean."

"We've already closed down the publication."

"Why haven't I read about it?"

"Neil has insisted we keep a tight lid on it."

"Why?"

"There are other considerations ... We're trying to
find the participants."

She swallowed hard. "You mean the children?"

"Yes. And the adults."

"I don't understand."

"Many of the children were abducted, taken from their
homes. We're talking about pederasts contributing photographs of themselves and their victims."

She sucked in her breath. "A man and a child?"

"More specifically, a man and a male child."

"And you're trying to find them."

"In all cases the adult's face has been blotted out of the
photograph, but when we confiscated the publication
records, we came up with dozens of names. We've got law
enforcement agencies throughout the northeast looking."

"Have you found any children?"

"Some. You can only keep this sort of thing so quiet.
The fact is that the perpetrators now know the publication has been shut down."

"And they're running?"

"With children in tow. But Neil has no intention of
giving up on them. He's even considered making a deal
with the publisher if he can help us locate more of the
participants."

She sighed. "You're right, Craig. I won't be able to
stop him. And now I'm not so sure I want to. But I *am*
worried, this whole business may very well have triggered
his stroke to begin with. He's obviously taking it very personally—not that I can't understand why. But even that's
unlike Neil."

A silence, then: "Mrs. Mathews, there is one more thing maybe you should know. It might explain why Neil's so determined to go after this."

"What's that?"

"The names we found ... Neil recognized one of them."

"What do you mean?"

"Years ago, when Neil was first doing criminal work..."

He paused and she nodded, though she knew he couldn't see her.

"He defended this guy. He got him off on a charge of child molestation. On a technicality."

Dinner had seemed incomplete without David sitting across the table. Chris had purposely stayed away from his room, not trusting herself to go near him. She knew that what David proposed was wrong, but still there was a part of her ... At this point, her head ached and she wasn't sure what worried her more: her conversation with David, or her conversation with Craig.

Neil had managed to completely hide his frustration at dinner. Chris watched him as he chatted with Erin and wondered how many times he'd managed to fool her before. Strange how some people wore their feelings right on their sleeves while others camouflaged them so easily. Of course, it didn't mean that the hurt was any less—it just didn't show.

She waited until dinner was over and Erin went up to get David's tray and do her homework before broaching the subject. "I spoke to Craig today," she said.

"He called?"

"No. I called him."

His eyes asked and she answered.

"I had to know what was upsetting you, Neil."

"You had no right—"

She leaned over, placing her hand on his. "I had every right. You're my husband. And I can't just sit back and be silent while I see something is ripping you to pieces."

"Don't interfere."

"I had no intention of interfering—not that it would do any good. I just want to talk about it. Maybe I can help."

He shook his head.

"Why, Neil? Can't I—for once—help you?"

"Nothing to help," he said finally.

"You're always the strong one. Always the one who keeps a level head, does whatever is necessary, never falls apart. Even with the stroke, Neil. If it hadn't been for your determination to come back, I never would have been able to deal with it. For once, lean on me. Just a little."

She saw his eyes soften, and she went on. "Craig told me."

"What did he tell?"

"Only the nature of the case. And that one of the men involved was once your client."

He lifted his stiff hand, raising it to his forehead.

"You couldn't have known, Neil."

"I put him on the street."

"Wasn't it you who always told me, everyone deserves a good defense?"

"Words. I was young then."

"And now?"

"I know better."

"Are you suggesting that attorneys make the judgment of guilt? I suppose it's tempting, but I would assume the whole legal system would fall flat on its face. It is, after all, based on the presumption of innocence."

He leaned back in his chair, hands gripping the arm-rests, eyes closed. "At the expense of those children. All those children."

"And it could have been our son." The thought was so

terrible, her voice shook. "That's what you're thinking, isn't it?"

He opened his mouth to speak, but instead of words, a tiny cry like the squeak of an unoiled spring came out. He just sat there, stiff and silent. She knelt on the floor beside him, put her arms around his waist, and looked up at him.

Not one tear, but she could see the pain in his eyes. Was it for all the children, or just for Kevin?

CHAPTER NINETEEN

D avid lay in bed looking upward, using the scarce light from the television to create ghostly figures on the wall with his fingers. It was almost nine o'clock when he heard the steps, then the knob turning. He tucked his hands under the covers, banishing the figures.

She tiptoed to his bed and looked down at him. When she saw he was awake, she asked, "How do you feel, David?"

"Better. A lot better."

Chris sat on the edge of his bed and ran her hand lightly over his forehead. "We missed you at dinner."

"Are you mad?"

"Why would I be?"

"I thought when you didn't come to see me this afternoon . . ."

"I just needed some time alone. To think."

"About Kevin?"

"Yes. And about you." She studied his face in the darkness, then so softly he almost couldn't hear her: "Would you like me to read to you?"

Drumsticks rolled in his chest: he nodded.

"What would you like to hear?"

He reached out, pulled a book from the shelf and handed it to her. Pinocchio. She didn't have to tell him; he could tell just by looking at her face, it had been *his* favorite too. She stood up, turned the volume of the television way down, then came back to his bed, sat down and read. At first her voice sounded tense—and David didn't dare to look at her—but then when she got involved in the story it relaxed. And so did he.

He remembered the parts of the story before Chris got to them. He knew just how the lonely, white-haired Gepetto was going to hammer out a puppet; he waited anxiously for the moment the puppet would come to life; he dreaded the dark lies and Pinnochio's nose growing longer and longer ... Before he knew it, the story was over and Chris had quietly shut the book.

"Do you want anything before I leave?"

David shook his head.

"Then I'll turn off the television so you can get some sleep." She paused for a moment, as if unsure what to do next, then leaned over and kissed his cheek. She stood up and stared at him, irresolution still showing on her face.

"Good night, David."

He was sure she had called him "David" on purpose, her way of telling him she knew who he really was. And that was okay—it hardly seemed to matter at all. She stood up. A click, silence, the television light shrank to one tiny dot, then disappeared. And the door closed.

It wasn't until that moment that the strangeness of it all hit him. Not the strangeness of Chris reading to him as if he was some kind of little kid. But him remembering that story so well. Fletcher had never once read him a story. In fact, aside from his Old Testament, there hadn't been a single real book in the house the whole time he was growing up.

David woke up the next morning feeling so relaxed that he wondered if he hadn't gone and slept the day away. He sat up and looked at the time, relieved to see it was only seven A.M.

Erin was just finishing breakfast when he came down; Chris was slicing a banana into two bowls of cornflakes.

"Well, mom," Erin said, "looks like you won't have to be taking breakfast to David." Her words said *hey, mom, good news*, but her expression said she thought it was anything but good.

"Are you sure you're all right?" Chris asked him.

"I feel fine."

"But are you up to going to class?"

"Now you don't want to push yourself, David," Erin said sweetly.

"Erin's right," Chris said.

"Really, I'm okay." He looked at Erin. "In fact, I've been thinking . . ."

"You *have?*"

David ignored her and went right on: "With all that's been going on here, we haven't had time to test out your camera. Why don't we go to the park this afternoon and take some pictures?"

Erin didn't answer, and Chris gave her a look.

"You do want to try out your new camera, don't you?" he asked.

"Of course."

"Then I'll pick up some film for both of us."

She was stuck and she knew it. She nodded.

Chris set one bowl in front of David, then picked up the other and set it on a tray with a mug of coffee and an English muffin. "You two excuse me—while you make plans, I'm going to take daddy his breakfast." She stooped over, kissed Erin's cheek and left the room.

Erin waited until her mother was out of hearing before she said, "I really don't want to go."

"Well, I want you to."

"What difference does it make to you anyhow?"

He shrugged. "None, really. But it does make a difference to your mother. You wouldn't want her thinking you didn't like her gift. Or that you didn't like me."

"What I want is to be able to tell her how I really feel."

"And how's that?"

"Like the best gift she could give me is to throw you out of this house."

"What's stopping you from saying it?"

"You know very well, David. The pictures."

"I don't see why. I never said I'd use them.

Her dark eyes studied his face; he was careful to keep it blank. "You know, David, sometimes when I look at you, I wonder what's inside your head. What you think is not the same as what you say. It's almost like you twist the truth around on purpose. Why are you afraid to tell it—is it that bad?"

"What makes you think I lie?"

"Tell me, David—do you really go to college?"

"That's a dumb question."

"Really? David, this is Erin you're talking to, not my mother. Tell me—where are your textbooks? I suggest you buy a few just to keep up appearances. My mother isn't *that* dense, she'll get suspicious eventually."

Even coming from Erin, the words surprised him. "That's a lousy thing to say about your own mother."

"I suppose it is, but it's true. At least, she's dense when it comes to you."

"If you must know, the textbooks are late coming into the bookstore. Those things happen in college."

"Do they really? Well, I just wanted to check things out for myself, so yesterday I got a brilliant idea—why not call Boston University and find out from them why David doesn't have any books?"

"You called the bookstore?"

"I couldn't very well do that, David. After all, I don't know the names of your courses. And besides, my dad always says, 'Start right at the top—don't fool around with underlings.'"

"You called the president of the college?"

"Of course not, David. My dad says you have to zero in on just the right person. You see, going to the top is really useless unless the top has the information you want. So I sat down and thought about it—who's important, yet not so important that he wouldn't even know you're alive. And of course there was still another consideration . . ."

She stopped there, waiting for him to ask. As much as he hated to give her the pleasure, he did: "What other consideration?"

She smiled. "You see, David, when you're doing this kind of investigative work, you have to come prepared with just the right question to get the answer you want. I mean, I couldn't very well call up some department and say: *Hello, how are you, by the way does David Crane go to your school* ... So after thinking all of this over, I finally put my finger on just the right person to call."

She stopped again. And again he bit: "Who was that?"

"The head of the business office. I said I wanted to know the balance of my brother's—David Crane's—bill. I almost choked on the word 'brother,' but he didn't notice. I explained that my mother wanted to send out a check ahead of time for the balance of the tuition. And as you might expect, he ran right away to get your file. But then the strangest thing happened ...

"You can probably guess what, but I'm going to tell you anyway—he couldn't locate a file on you. Would you believe, you weren't even in their computer? As far as the college was concerned, you didn't even exist." She stood up, leaned over and examined his hands. "Now if I didn't know better, David, I'd think those greasy fingernails of yours came from a class in shopwork." She put her finger to her mouth as if she were thinking. "But they don't teach shop at Boston University, do they?"

He couldn't think of one single thing to say, but it didn't matter. She wasn't through yet. "Now for once, David—tell the truth. You *would* use those pictures to hurt my father. And me. Wouldn't you?"

His voice crackled. "Only if I had to, Erin."

"I already figured *that* out." Her eyes narrowed. "But now you have about as much to lose as I do—don't you? After all, my mother would find it hard to forgive her perfect David for a lie like that." She clicked her tongue. "Goodness, what would she think? Maybe I should have

known better than to pose for those pictures to begin
with, but remember ... I'm only twelve years old.
"*You're* the one who tricked me into it, and *you're* the
one who took the pictures. What's your excuse?"

"You think you've got it all figured out. Don't you?"

She put on her jacket, collected her books and shoulder bag and went to the door. "No. Not all of it—not yet.
I still don't know what your purpose is. Why you want to
be here so darn much. And ..."

"And what?"

"And I still don't know what makes you lie, David.
What truth are you hiding?"

After thinking about it nearly all day, David decided
Erin's detective report wasn't quite as threatening as it
had seemed that morning. Her delivery was flawless, but
despite what she knew or suspected, as she said herself,
he still had those pictures. Report or no report, she
wasn't about to chance her father seeing them.

When he got home from work, he found a note tacked
to the kitchen bulletin board: "Dear David, went food
shopping—be home soon. Erin's in her room. You two
have fun in the park.—Chris." He reread the message,
then headed to Erin's room, his face lit up by a broad
smile.

She wasn't there. He stopped at Neil's door, put his ear
to it. Silence. He cracked it open and looked in: Neil had
fallen asleep at his desk. Without thinking much about it,
he tiptoed to the bed, pulled off one of the covers and
draped it over Neil. It wasn't until he'd closed the door that
he again thought of Erin. And as soon as he did, he knew
where she was. He ran, swung open his bedroom door, then
stopped suddenly: Erin was sitting on the closet floor with
Fletcher's photo album in her lap—just about to lift the
cover. This time, she didn't jump.

He stepped forward, holding his hand out. "Give it to
me."

"I thought there were no old pictures, David. I thought they weren't good enough to take along."

A swishing sound, like a water faucet turned on full blast in his ears. "I don't want to hurt you," he called out over the noise. "Give me the book!" He could see her mouth moving, but he couldn't hear the words. He flung his arm out and ripped the book off her lap. "Now get out!"

She stood up; then, so fast he didn't even see it coming, she grabbed for the book. It flew out of his hands, landing on the floor, one page tearing loose. Erin crouched down to look: her mouth opened, her hands shot up—one hand crossing the other—and covered her mouth. He shoved her aside, snatched the page up, and slid it back in the album, then fell across the bed, the sound of water now roaring in his eardrums . . .

Somewhere out there was Erin's voice, trying over and over again to cut through the noise. Finally, it did. "Was that you, David?" Then, louder, "Who was that awful man? What was he doing to you?"

The boy rolled into a ball on the bed, facing the wall.

"Lay down nice, Davie—like a big boy."

He wanted to climb into the wall.

"Do what I say, Davie."

There was a crack in the wall. If only he could make himself tiny enough, he could squeeze right through . . .

Then the hands grabbed Davie's arm, rolling him onto his belly, hooking circles of rope around one wrist, then the other. Around one ankle, then the other. Each rope pulled tightly as it stretched to fit over the tall bedpost. So tight that soon the boy would not feel his hands or feet.

The man pointed to the other end of the room. "See that?"

Davie looked to where his finger was pointing.

"A camera, Davie. When I pull this here cord"—he touched a string next to the bed—"we're going to take a

picture. *Together. Now, what's the rule in taking a picture?"*

He had taken his picture lots of times, he should be able to remember the rule. But he didn't have to remember; the man told him: "Look at the camera and smile." *Then he took off his clothes, too, breathing so hard Davie thought maybe he would die. He didn't die—he got in beside him.* "This will feel nice, Davie," *he said. But it wasn't nice at all . . .*

When it was over, the man untied him, then put him in a hot bathtub so the big dark red rings around his wrists and ankles would feel better. "Next time will be better, Davie."

He was still crying, but now the cries were real soft, like they were buried deep in his belly.

"Because next time, you'll lay nice and smile."

Fletcher was right. After that, he always laid nice. And he always smiled.

CHAPTER TWENTY

Jack caught Chris' eye, smiled, then left his booth and headed in her direction. She'd been shopping at the A&P ever since he became head cashier. Recently he had been promoted to store manager. She pushed her nearly full cart toward him, tossing a bunch of bananas in on the way.

"I like that new touch of gray, Jack. It gives you an air of dignity befitting the job."

He ran his hand along the side of his hair. "Don't tell anyone—it wasn't in the plan. Just old age catching up."

"Why, you're no older than I am."

"Not everyone ages as secretively as you, Chris."

"I knew there was a good reason you made it to the top. You know just what to say to keep the women coming back."

"Really, Chris, you're looking better than I've ever seen you look."

She smiled. "Thanks. I'm feeling better than ever."

"Does that mean the husband's finally come home?"

"It does indeed. But that's not all—we have a boy living with us now. A new member of the family. His name's David."

"Is that right? Sounds like you're stuck on the kid."

She laughed. "I guess you *could* say that."

"How old is he?"

"Seventeen."

"I have one of those at home, too. Better watch out—they'll eat you right out of the house." Then he looked down at her shopping cart. "Of course I'm not complaining . . ."

Chris counted ten bags at the check-out counter; she set two of them and the *Boston Globe* on the kitchen counter, then looked up and saw Erin. "You're home early, honey. Have fun?"

Erin poured herself a glass of milk. "We didn't go."

"Why not?"

She shrugged. "David wasn't feeling good."

Chris stopped unpacking the bags. "What's wrong?"

She licked her lips nervously. "I don't know."

"Erin, please bring in the rest of the bags, I'm going to look in on him. When you're through, why don't you take the newspaper up to daddy."

She hurried upstairs and knocked lightly on David's door. No answer. She went in and sat down on the edge of his bed. He was just lying there, stormy blue eyes staring up at the ceiling.

"I should never have let you go to school, David. We had better call a doctor."

He shook his head.

"It wouldn't hurt to have a check-up. It's the second day in a row you haven't been well." And then she saw the tear swell at the corner of his eye and slowly spill over. She put her hand to his forehead—not feverish—and ran her fingers through his dark hair. "Do you miss your father, David?"

His lips tightened and he shook his head again, barely moving it.

"I'm right here with you, David. I won't ask any questions. When you're ready, you'll tell me what's upsetting you."

Suddenly he sat up and threw his arms around her, his body trembling like a child waking from a nightmare. She held him close, rocking him, letting him bury his face in her shoulder. She could feel his warm tears sliding down her neck. *Please, David,*

whatever it is—let it come out. Let me help. Chris
didn't say a word; she just sat, holding him. Whatever it was—for now, it was better that he cry.

It was a long time before David finally pulled away. All
the muscles in Chris' arms were stiff, but it was worth
the discomfort to see the calm, clear blue eyes that now
looked into hers.

"Feeling better?" she asked him.

"I want to go out in the yard and rake up the leaves."

She laughed. "What in the world brought this on? I
admit, I all but had to swim through the leaves to get to
the car, but ..."

Now he laughed. She had heard him laugh before, but
it always seemed a little forced. This time it was easy,
natural.

"I don't know," he said. I just have this nutty urge."

"Well, now ... I once knew a woman who worked off
excess energy scrubbing floors. She said it calmed her,
made her feel good. Do you suppose you might have
something in common with her?"

He pointed to Chris. "You?"

"Never. My irresistible impulse is quite the opposite.
And, I'm afraid, quite a bit crazier."

"Tell me."

"Now, this is of course in complete confidence ..."

"I'd never tell anyone."

"All right. I love to kneel down in the dirt and get it all
over me, feel the earth on my bare skin. You understand,
I can't very well do this without attracting a lot of stares.
So to satisfy this insane impulse, I garden—who ever
heard of a clean gardener?"

He thought a moment. "I think I'd like that. Gardening, I mean."

"Then I'll teach you. In the spring."

"Will I still be here?"

"Of course, David. Why wouldn't you be?"

"I don't know."

"You're not throwing me aside that easily, young man. You're stuck, now—I've already signed you up for my gardening course. Tomatoes, cukes, radishes, pumpkins . . . and, of course, tons of dirt."

"Pumpkins?"

"Apparently you are not aware of the notorious Mathews Pumpkin."

David grinned.

Chris held up her right hand. "I do not lie—a seventy-five pounder. It made its debut on the Boston six o'clock news."

"Wow! Do you have any this year?"

"Yes, but none even close to that guy. Maybe next year we can break the record." She stood up. "Meanwhile, the rake's in the garage and I had better see about dinner."

He lifted a torn photo album from the floor, stood up, went to his closet and tossed it into a box. Then followed her downstairs.

While Chris prepared dinner, Erin knelt on the floor with her arms resting on the window sill, watching David outdoors. "Why don't you help him?" Chris said finally. "There's another rake in the garage."

She shook her head and leaned her chin across her arms. "I'd rather watch."

"What's daddy up to?"

"I read him the newspaper for a while."

"Good. The small print is still hard for him." Chris looked over at her. "And now?"

"Now he's busy again with that case he's always working on. He talked to Craig twice on the phone. And I got him an old file that was stored away in the library."

"Oh? What was the name of the file?"

"Louis Flannery. Do you remember the case?"

Chris thought for a moment. "No, I'm afraid I don't."

She wiped her hands on a paper towel, then went and knelt next to Erin, glancing out at David crouched down, stuffing leaves into a green bag. "Daddy has been so preoccupied with that case lately, I know he hasn't been giving you as much time as you'd like. But it's very important to him, Erin. And I'm afraid he won't stop until he ties up all the loose ends."

"What's it about?"

"It concerns children, Erin. Children who have been abducted from their homes."

She turned to Chris. "You mean kidnapping?"

Chris nodded.

"Why's that so important to him?"

"Because of Kevin."

Her forehead wrinkled. "But Kevin wasn't kidnapped."

No—they found Kevin's body ... but that was more than a year later. Where was he until then? Chris put her thoughts aside and swallowed hard. "No, of course he wasn't."

"Then why?"

"I suppose, when you lose a child, it really doesn't make a lot of difference how. The loss alone makes you understand what other parents go through, even under dissimiliar circumstances." She kissed Erin's cheek and stood up. "Come on, now—help me set the table before your father starts suffering from lack of nourishment."

Erin grinned. "You know what just happened?"

"No. But I have a feeling you're going to tell me."

"You mean you really didn't notice?"

"I can't say that I did."

"Well, I did. You just talked to me about Kevin. And for the first time, you did it without getting all angry and upset."

Chris hadn't even thought about it. But Erin was right.

Dinner was only fifteen minutes behind schedule, but Neil's impatience mounted with every minute.

He came to the kitchen twice to check Chris' progress. "Neil," she said finally, "someone would truly think you were starving."

"I am."

"Then who's cleaning all those plates of food I carry upstairs all day long?"

"What food is that?"

She lifted the telephone. "In that case, I'd better call in an exterminating service—we obviously have mice."

He put his hand over hers, taking the receiver away and hanging it up. "Let's not be hasty. No need—" Someone had begun fooling around on the piano. Neil stopped and turned toward the living room, listening to the tune.

"Maybe it's Erin," Chris said, walking to the living room with Neil behind her. But it wasn't—it was David. One hand lay in a fist on his lap, the other on the piano keys, two fingers picking out a melody.

"Do you recognize that, Chris?"

She listened for another few measures. It was the tune she had heard David humming occasionally. But how would Neil know that? "What do you mean?" she said.

Neil didn't answer; he just stood there staring, first at Chris, then at David. David must have sensed that he was being watched, because he looked up and jerked his fingers off the keys.

"That was very good, David," Chris said. "And you say you've never played before?"

He shook his head.

"Then you must be a natural."

He laughed, awkwardly, and stood up. "That tune ... funny, but it's been going through my head ever since you played it last week."

"I played it?"

"Over and over again. Remember? Erin wanted to know the name of it, but you had forgotten."

She stared at him, not knowing what to say. Even now,

she couldn't remember playing it. Or even hearing it played. Finally she said, "Why don't you go get Erin for dinner."

He left the room, and she turned to Neil. "What did you mean when you asked me if I recognized it?"

"It's not important, let's forget about it."

"I want to know, Neil. Tell me—please."

He reached out and took her hand. "*You* composed that piece, Chris," he said. "For Kevin."

Dinner began on an almost somber note. Now Chris couldn't get the song out of her mind or the knowledge that she'd hidden it away all those years. David was the one to finally lighten the mood. "When I was doing the leaves," he said, "I took a look at the pumpkins out back."

Chris looked at Neil and Erin. "I was telling David about our super pumpkin." Then, to David, "Well, do you think we can come up with a respectable specimen by Halloween?"

"There's one there that's pretty big. I'd say thirty, thirty-five pounds."

Erin perked up. "The best part of carving the pumpkin is getting to eat the seeds—all baked and salted. Yum."

David looked baffled.

"You mean, you've never eaten pumpkin seeds?" Erin asked.

"Fletcher." David glanced at Neil. "My father didn't like me going out at night alone. He thought I'd get hurt. Besides, Halloween is my birthday."

Chris stopped eating, and Erin said, "Oh, so you celebrated *that* instead?"

"No. We didn't really celebrate anything."

"Oh. My brother's birthday was Halloween, too."

Chris looked at her daughter. "Where did you get that idea, Erin?"

"I saw pictures of his birthday party in the box in the

attic."

Chris cleared her throat. "One year we used Halloween decorations for his party, but his birthday was not on Halloween. Actually it was November 2, two days after."

Then she looked at David ... And he nodded.

CHAPTER TWENTY-ONE

That night Chris played the piano for everyone—one of Brahms' Intermezzos, she told David. Every now and then David could sense Neil looking at him, but never returned the look. Erin wasn't so easy to ignore; she sat on the floor, not far from him, sometimes gawking as if she'd spotted a big black bug with striped horns lounging on her sofa. But David didn't let her get to him. Instead he let the music fill him right up to the top, sometimes spilling over, humming along softly with it.

Later that evening, David took Neil upstairs. Usually he thanked David, but this time he said, "You were in my room?"

He didn't answer, not sure what Neil was referring to.

"This afternoon. The blanket was on me."

He remembered and nodded.

"Don't," Neil said. "Not unless you're invited in."

David smiled, and the best part was that he knew Neil couldn't figure why, though he probably would have given anything to know. David was imagining what it would be like to stick those pictures of Erin right under his nose ... The image stayed with him—that is, until Chris came into his room a half hour later to read to him. She tucked him in and made every bad thought he had ever had disappear.

It was strange: the happier Chris made him—and she did make him happy—the more frightened David became when she wasn't with him. It was a different kind of fear than he'd felt with Fletcher. For one, he began to carry Erin's negatives around in his back pocket. David knew she couldn't get to them in the darkroom which was always locked, but there were other possibilities. A skelton key, a duplicate. Even Erin picking the lock. None of those things seemed likely, but now he was afraid to take chances. There was too much at stake.

For another, David began to have weird dreams. One, in particular, he had over and over. He could see, hear, talk. But it was as if his body had been formed from stone; it didn't move. The beautiful lady in the dream held out her arms. A soft, hypnotic voice called out, "David, Kevin."

He nodded his head, wondering how she knew his name. He wanted her to come to him, but a guard, about three feet tall with arms as thick as baseball bats and a long silver tongue blocked her way.

"You must come here," she told him. "I've been waiting for you."

"I would but I can't. Don't you know—stones don't move."

"Make yourself, you must make yourself. Then we'll put everything together again."

"All the king's horses and all the king's men couldn't—"

She cut in. "But *we* can, David Kevin. We can make it like before."

Before. The word swam around in his mind, making no sense. Finally he asked, "What is before?"

"First you must move yourself, then you'll know."

He gritted his teeth, every nerve, every muscle put to work separately. Suddenly—like a geyser broken loose, steam thrusting him forward—he moved. "I did it!" he cried.

"Now turn around and look who's behind you."

"Who?"

"Look. Don't be afraid."

He held his breath and turned, very slowly ... And that's when the dream ended, every time. Before he could make out who was behind him.

He must have cried out at those times, though he didn't remember doing it. But always, when he woke up, Chris was at his side, holding him until he'd fall back to sleep. Sometimes David wondered if she wasn't just a part of the dream, but then he'd know she had really been there by the look in her eyes the next morning. "I'm all right," he'd say, even though she hadn't asked the question out loud.

When Chris was out of sight, Erin and David pretty much ignored each other except for the subtle digs they'd toss back and forth like a ping-pong ball when they passed in the halls or got stuck alone in the same room.

"Off to classes?" Erin would say, and David would parry with, "No, I'm off to buy more film so we can do your portfolio."

One day Erin asked, in front of Chris, "Can I look at some of your textbooks?" She had a smirk on her face, but by that time he'd taken her one good suggestion. David had walked straight into the B.U. bookstore, scouted the aisles and picked out titles he might have bought had he really been going to college: *Abnormal Psychology, The Philosophy of Existentialism, The Guide to Good Writing.* It was funny when you thought about it: here he was having Chris read him children's stories a couple times a week, and on his own he was reading material that was so deep he sometimes had to read it three, four times before making sense of it.

David went upstairs, got the textbooks, then brought them down and set them on the table, totally enjoying the look on Erin's face. Chris picked up the book on existentialism and leafed through it.

"What do you think of this philosophy?" she asked. "I studied it myself in college. In fact, I wrote a paper on it."

"It's different. Sometimes it makes me feel hopeless. But other times, I really feel close to what it says."

"Give me an example."

"Well, like this 'choice' thing. They say it's not only possible to choose, it's impossible not to. Because to choose not to choose is a choice in itself."

Erin looked up. "That's a funny way of looking at it."

"Yeah, it is. But it seems to make sense."

Erin paused a moment, then nodded. "I guess when you really think about it, it does."

Chris studied David's face, frowning. "Do you know what existentialists say about courage, David?"

He shook his head.

"It requires more courage to suffer than to act, more courage to forget than to remember. I think that was Kierkegaard."

He just looked at her, wondering if she was thinking about herself and Kevin or about him and maybe what was causing his nightmares.

The week before Halloween, Erin knocked at David's door; it was the first time she'd done that in weeks. He called out, "Come in," thinking it was Chris, then looked up and closed his psychology textbook. "What do you want?"

"I'm going to go outside and pick a pumpkin to carve. My mom told me to ask you if you wanted to help."

"And what about you? Do you want my help?"

"I'd just as soon you kept your nose in your book and left the pumpkin to me." She turned toward the bookshelves. "Though I'd think the books my mother reads you are far more appropriate to your mentality."

David could feel the heat in his face; he hated it that she could see his face turn red. "What are you talking about?" he said.

"Oh, let me see. Tom Sawyer, Huck Finn and other such books befitting a college freshman." She drew on the last two words, then pointed to the shelf-full of fairy tales. "Probably those too."

"You must be hallucinating."

"I don't think so—I listened at your door."

"When?"

"A couple of nights. Of course, I never did stay for the happily-ever-afters. I was too bored. I outgrew children's stories a few years back." She put her finger to her chin and squinched up her nose. "I wonder, David, what happens after the stories."

"What does that mean?"

"Oh, I think you know. What do you and my mother do then—take dirty pictures of each other?"

He was up and off his bed before she had even closed her mouth. He grabbed her by the shoulders and shook her so hard he thought her neck was going to snap. "How would you like it if I wired up your jaw so tight you'd never talk again?" he shouted.

Two tears rolled down her face, and that's when he stopped, dropping his hands to his sides. "My mom never read to *me*," she said.

"Why not?"

"I don't know. She just never would."

"No one ever read you a story?"

"My dad did."

"Well, isn't that just as good?"

She didn't answer.

"Besides, maybe she had reasons. That doesn't give you any right to talk dirty about her."

Then she looked up at David with puffy, red eyes. "Who are you to talk, David? Maybe I say things, but you do them! What about those pictures of you and that man? How could you do those disgusting things?"

He sat down, resting his head in his hands. "I didn't want to do them, Erin."

"But you did do them, and that's what counts."

Erin left soon after, but he thought about what she'd said all the rest of the day. That night, when Chris came to his room, he asked her, "What about people who don't have choices?"

She looked at him, her warm eyes now troubled. "Everyone has choices, David. One way or another."

"But what about someone who is ..." He couldn't finish the sentence, but he didn't have to.

"Forced to do something?"

He nodded. That was exactly what he'd meant.

"Well ... existentialists would say everyone has freedom of mind, of spirit. You may be forced into an act or even be locked behind bars, but you do have a choice of attitude—what you feel inside."

"You mean if you hate what you were forced to do, it doesn't count?"

"That's an oversimplification, David, but that's the idea. People are ultimately responsible for their acts. However, if an act is forced upon someone against his will, and that person does all he can to reject the act, he can't be blamed for it. Remember—no one can take away your freedom of attitude. No one."

There was one more question he had to ask. "Do you really believe that, too, Chris?"

She put her hand to the side of his head, running her fingers through his hair. "Yes, David. I do."

It took him a long time to fall asleep that night. Finally he did, still thinking about what she'd said.

The next day Erin and David picked the pumpkin. When it came to carving, as usual they had different ideas. Finally Chris settled the dispute: "We have several pumpkins out there. Why not get another one, then each of you can carve away to your different drummers."

The other pumpkin was smaller, but David agreed to take it. They spread newspaper on the table and set to work, armed with carving knives and an apple corer. They picked out the seeds, setting them aside for baking. When they were done, they put candles inside, then set the tops back on. After that they went to the front porch and set the little and big pumpkins down next to each other—like parent and child. Erin backed down the front steps to see how they looked. "It figures," she said.

"What?" He came downstairs and looked. First at Erin's pumpkin—it was big and evil, with sharp menacing teeth—then at his. "I don't see anything wrong," he said.

She sighed. "You wouldn't. Pumpkins are either scary or smiley. Yours is neither, David."

He studied his again. The mouth was slashed straight across, with blunt, even teeth. It didn't have any expression at all.

CHAPTER TWENTY-TWO

Chris had noticed a definite change in her daughter. It was subtle—nothing she could really put her finger on. At odd times she'd catch Erin watching her. When Chris noticed, she'd quickly turn away, busying herself elsewhere. Erin was polite, agreeable—in fact, too agreeable. She kept up with her schoolwork and did everything that was expected of her. But she had lost that unrelenting self-confidence that seemed always to set her apart from the rest of the world. No matter how hard Chris tried to get her to open up to her, she was unsuccessful.

Erin spent a great deal of time with Neil, and for that Chris was thankful. Neil had always been able to get through to her more easily than she. But this time, with the case consuming so much of his energy, he took less notice of her during the times she was with him. He was continually on the telephone—pushing law enforcement agencies, gathering leads—or had his nose buried in the files. Or the book. Why he still tortured himself by even looking at that book was a mystery to her.

"Why don't you ease off—let the police do their work?" she said. "Erin could use more of your attention."

"I have to find him, Chris. I can't stop till I do."

"You said *him*, Neil. Can you hear yourself? You've turned this into some kind of one-man vendetta. We're talking here about a number of children, a number of criminals. Why is it that you're obsessed with only one?"

"That's not true."

"Don't lie to yourself." Then her voice softened. "I'm not suggesting you don't care about the others. But the obsession is with this one man you mistakenly defended years ago. You are not responsible for the actions of every man you helped set free. Is there nothing I can say to convince you how irrational your behavior is?"

He shook his head.

"What about your intention to make a deal with the publisher?"

"We did that."

She looked up, surprised. "And?"

"We've made three more arrests. Reunited two of the children with their families."

"The other child?"

"We're still looking for his family. We have some leads—hopefully we'll find them."

"Then you *have* made progress, Neil. Wonderful progress. To look at you, no one would guess."

Silence.

She sighed. "But you haven't found Louis Flannery yet, have you?" It was his turn to look surprised. "Erin told me his name," she said.

He seemed to shrink in his chair. "No. Not Louis Flannery. Only an old post office box number that seems to lead nowhere."

"Where was it—the box office number?"

"New Hampshire. Kingston." Then he picked up the file on his desk, opening it and shutting her out. He didn't look up again. The subject was closed.

Even more than Chris worried about Neil and Erin, she worried about David. For weeks, he'd been plagued by nightmares. Sometimes he'd cry out and she'd hear him; sometimes it was only an ominous feeling, a message sent to her in her dreams. But always she'd act on her instincts, and always they were right. She'd go into his room and find him shaking, curled up in a tight ball, his fingers scratching at the sheets as if looking for something to hang onto. She was the someone. Never fully awake, he came right to her, letting her hold him until his nightmares faded, until his body relaxed and was able to sleep peacefully.

At first she feared that their peculiar relationship might be causing the nightmares. Was it good for David, for them to pretend like this—that he was Kevin, a young boy? And that she was his mother? Even as she worried, she knew that it was those times—her reading or simply talking to him before he went to bed—that were her happiest moments of the day. And then two things dawned on her: First, the pretense was only partial; the bond between them was real. Second, the terror had always been there, buried inside him. The only difference was that now it was coming out.

Still, she knew so little about him. She'd made it a point not to question him, not to push herself into terrain that was private. All she knew with certainty was that David had suffered—more than his father dying, more than never knowing a mother. And she ached for him because without even knowing what was hurting him, she knew how the hurt felt.

Three days before Halloween, Chris told Neil, "I've decided to have a birthday party for David."

"But it's—"

She stopped him. "I know, Neil. So close to Kevin's birthday. But it's all right. I can do it."

"You're getting in too deep."

"That's not true."

"I've heard you going to him. At night."

Her lips felt dry; she licked them. "He has nightmares, Neil."

"And what do you do?"

"I just sit with him. Comfort him the best I can."

"He's almost eighteen, Chris. He's not a child. Yet that's how you treat him. That's how he allows you to treat him."

"Is that so wrong?"

"Yes, it is. It's not healthy. Not normal."

"In other circumstances I might agree with you, but not with David. With David, it's different."

"Different how?"

She took a deep breath. "I have this feeling about him, Neil . . . It's almost as if in some way he missed out on ever having a childhood. Like somehow he'd been gypped out of it."

Neil stared at her. "Even if that were so—and we don't know that it is—you can't give it back to him. No one can. You know that as well as I."

"I can try."

"Be rational, Chris. Besides, why would you even want to try? Until six weeks ago, the boy was a stranger. And still we know nothing about him."

"We know as much as we need to."

"No, Chris. We don't."

"What's got into you? I thought you had accepted David into our home. Were you just pretending, all along?"

Suddenly, he stood up from his desk and, without his walker, headed for the nightstand. Before he took two steps, his legs folded under him and fell to the floor with a thud. She ran to him and knelt down.

"My God, Neil. What are you trying to do? Are you hurt?"

He pointed to the nightstand, his lips drawn into a tight line of anger. "Go . . . open the drawer."

She pulled at his arm, trying to help him up.

"Leave me. Do what I say."

She stood up, went to the nightstand and opened the drawer, then looked at Neil, puzzled.

"Take the report."

"What report?"

"Take it out . . . read it."

Then she spotted the thin manilla folder. She lifted it out and opened it. The top line, all in capitals read: RE DAVID

CRAME, 177 RANEER DRIVE, LACONIA, NEW HAMP-
SHIRE. She looked down at Neil. "What is this?"

"You can read."

"It's about David," Then, she sucked in her breath.
"You've had him investigated?"

"I did what I had to. For your own good."

"*My* good? How dare you?" She closed the folder and
dropped it into the drawer as if the mere touch of it had
stung her fingers. "Tell me—who did you get to do your
dirty work?"

Silence.

"It was Craig, wasn't it? That was what the dinner was
all about. And here I was, stupid enough to think it was
a simple social visit. You wanted him to look David over,
confirm your suspicions."

A moment's pause, then, "Which he did."

"I'm not interested!"

"Please, Chris—read it."

"It's your report, you read it."

"The boy hasn't told us the truth. Don't you care?"

She turned, walking away, but Neil's voice stopped her.
"Dammit! You stay here—you listen!"

She turned back, waiting.

"He did graduate high school in Laconia as he said,
and he did work part-time at a laundromat, but his father
did not work for a newspaper."

She said nothing.

"He was self-employed. I don't know by what means. I
haven't been able to find out."

"Is that all, Neil?" Her words dropped out like chips of
ice.

"No. His father did not die. Their lease was up, and
his father moved." ·

"So his father moved, and David went off to college.
That hardly makes him a criminal."

"Only a liar."

"Sometimes there are reasons."

"Don't defend him."

Then, as calmly as she could manage: "The truth is, Neil, I don't give a damn what your report says. I *know* the boy that's here, the one who lives with us. He's sensitive and loving—and I care what happens to him. Whatever reason he has for lying. And when he's ready to tell me what it is, he will. Until then, I will not push him. So don't bother sending your spies out again."

His intense blue eyes looked into hers. "Why would a boy say his father was dead when he wasn't?"

She didn't answer.

Then, almost in a whisper: "His father never even left a forwarding address. Neither did David."

"What does that mean?"

He shrugged. "Nothing. I guess nothing."

She turned to see Erin standing in the doorway. Chris wasn't sure how long she had been there; judging by the look on her face, long enough to hear plenty. She swept past her, then turned back toward Neil.

"I'll send David in to help you up."

She knocked on David's door and asked him to help Neil, then headed right downstairs to the kitchen. She took a pad and pen from the drawer and sat at the table, making out a list. It would be a costume party, combining both Halloween and David's birthday. There would be a huge chocolate double-layer cake, decorated like a pumpkin. She had baked that cake before. For Kevin's third birthday party. And a gift for David ... What would he want more than anything? She wanted it to be something special. Very special. She would have to think about it ...

She looked up to see Erin staring at her from the doorway. "I'm sorry you had to hear all that," Chris said.

She shrugged. "What are you doing?"

"I'm planning a party for David. A combination Halloween-birthday."

"You mean with costumes?"

"Yes. And each of us is in charge of making his own. That way, no one will know what to expect. So get your creative juices flowing, I'm expecting something truly unique."

"Just us?"

"Yes, Erin. Just the family—your father, you, me and David."

"Will it be a surprise?"

"The birthday part will be. We will, of course, have to tell David about the costumes."

A moment's pause. "I'll get him a present," she said.

"That would be nice, Erin."

She turned, started to walk away, then stopped. "Mom?"

Chris looked up again.

"I love you," she said.

Chris stretched out her arms and Erin walked into them. "I love you too, Erin. So much. It's just that—"

She put her finger to Chris's lips. "I know. But I don't want to talk about it. Not now. I just wanted you to know that." She disentangled herself from Chris' arms and ran out of the room.

Chris went back to her list: A prize for the most creative costume; they could play charades, Trivial Pursuit ... maybe even bob for apples, though that might be a problem for Neil.

Suddenly she threw down the pen, folded her arms on the table and put her head down. Neil's words came thundering back at her: *Why would any boy say his father was dead, when he wasn't?* Chris hadn't answered Neil— but she knew the answer, as well as she knew her own name.

Because he wished he were. David wished Fletcher was dead. Which led right to the next question: Why?

CHAPTER TWENTY-THREE

The whole situation was strange—Chris coming to get him like that, then rushing off. David ran into Neil's room just as Erin came out, looking like she'd just seen a cobra. The moment he saw Neil on the floor, he hurried over and helped him to his feet.

"What happened?"

"What does it look like?"

"It looks like you fell."

"Trust your instincts."

"I guess what I mean was *how* it happened." Neil didn't respond, so he asked, "Anything else before I go?"

He grabbed hold of the walker. "Yes. There is."

David waited.

"I want to know why you've come to this house. And what it is you want here."

David looked toward the door, and Neil read his mind. "Chris isn't here—you can tell me the truth."

"There is no truth. I mean . . . I don't want anything."

"Everyone wants something. Everyone."

"I'm not everyone."

"No, you're not. Who *are* you? Tell me something about yourself."

"I'm David. David."

Neil studied his face, then, "I'm a lawyer . . . Did it ever occur to you that maybe I can help? Trust me."

"You can't trust Neil," he said, his words surprising even him. Was it because they were familiar—had he said them before? Suddenly a wheel cranked in his head, running slowly: they had been waiting, in the car. Such a long time. Sleepy, so sleepy. *Where's my daddy? Please,*

*find him. You said my daddy would come ... you said
that—remember?* Then came the words he'd just spoken:
You can't trust Neil. The voice was Fletcher's. The wheel
stopped turning, and he looked up at Neil. He had said
something. Now he was saying it again.

"Why not, David?"

He shook his head, not knowing. "Where's Chris?" he
asked.

"What are you afraid of?"

"Where's Chris?" Now an edge of panic in his voice.

Neil sighed and sank down into his chair. "Downstairs.
She's downstairs."

David rushed out of the room. Again he passed
Erin, he going downstairs and she going up. They
didn't say a word. When he got to the kitchen, he
found Chris with her head resting in her arms on
the table. She looked up.

"What is it, David? You're white."

In his head a jumble of words struggled to arrange
themselves. He picked the ones that were easiest to say.

"I don't want to leave, Chris. Please don't make me."

And then she came to him, drawing him close so he
could feel her warmth. "Of course not, David. You're not
leaving." She pulled away and looked deep into his eyes.
"Have I ever lied to you?"

He shook his head.

"Well I don't intend to start now, David. No one will
ever make you leave here. Ever."

David still wasn't sure what had happened with Chris
and Neil and Erin upstairs, just as he wasn't sure what
had happened to him. The scene with Fletcher had skit-
tered in and out of his head so fast, he didn't know how
it got there or where it went. No matter how hard he
tried, he couldn't remember the scene ever happening.
Everyone was quiet at dinner. Afterwards when he and

Erin went to load the dishwasher, he finally said, "Tell me what happened this afternoon?"

"What makes you think something did?"

He shrugged. "Your father was spread-eagled out on the floor, you looked like you were ready to barf all over the place, and your mother was all upset. Other than that, things were fine."

"Let me think—which scene troubled you most?"

She didn't expect an answer so he didn't give her one.

"Actually it's quite simple," she said. "My father doesn't trust you as far as he can throw you, and my mother thinks the sun rises and sets on your empty little head. Quite a difference of opinion, I'd say. Of course I'm the only one who really knows you, David. I mean, really. What they probably need is a third opinion. You know, the kind that comes in as a tie-breaker."

"Meaning you?"

"Of course."

"But you won't."

"No, I won't."

"Because of the pictures?" He didn't mean it to come out a question, but it did. Erin poured in the powdered detergent, closed the dishwasher, and pressed the button to start it running, then looked up at him.

"What other reason could there possibly be, David?"

He had another question for Chris that night: "Do you ever lie?"

She thought about it for a minute before she answered. "I can't say that I've never lied, David. Sometimes, I suppose, it's more convenient—easier. But it's not something I feel at all comfortable about doing."

"I think it's more than just the convenience. Sometimes people have to tell lies."

She didn't disagree with him as he expected. Instead she said, "A person should do what he has to do. Just so long as he's willing to chance the consequences. And I don't mean his nose growing longer."

"What *do* you mean?"

"He's apt to forget what the truth really is."

"And lose it completely?"

"Yes."

"Forever?"

She frowned. "It doesn't have to be ...."

Then how do you get it back? His eyes asked her, and she answered. "You find the truth by searching, David. It's always there inside; it doesn't go away but it won't come out all on its own. Not unless you're willing to dig for it. And then the hardest part is facing up to it. That can sometimes be terrifying."

And then he knew they were talking about her. "What was the biggest truth you ever had to face?" he asked.

She took a deep breath. "That my son was dead. That I would never see him again. It took more than two years of therapy before I could face it. I had a nervous breakdown, David."

Her words hit him like a fist in his stomach. She must have been able to tell, because she took his hand. "It's all right, David. I can talk about it now."

"Chris ... What happens if a person never faces the truth? You know, just wants to leave things as they are?"

She smiled. "You mean, not make waves?"

He nodded.

"Well, you remember what you were studying, David. We all have choices. When a person chooses one thing, he gives up another. In this case, it seems to me, he would be choosing peace of mind, security, over his chance to really be in touch with himself and take charge of his own life."

David could hear Chris' and Erin's voices coming from the kitchen the next morning; when he walked in, they stopped. Chris quickly folded the sheet of paper she was holding and stuffed it into her pocket. He looked at both of them, wondering if he should run out and come back in. Finally, Chris spoke up. "David, we're going to have a Halloween party."

"A party?" was all he could say.

"Costumes and all."

He just stood there, looking and feeling dumb.

"You know, David, *dress-up*," Erin said.

"I know what costumes are. But what would I wear for one?"

Chris laughed. "That's entirely up to you. There's dozens of boxes of old clothes and props packed away in the cedar closet in the library. Maybe after school Erin can show you. I'm sure looking through them will inspire you."

"Is Neil going to do it?"

"He'll do it—if I have to dress him myself."

Erin laughed. "Do you think you'll have to?"

"I doubt it. I'm counting on his sense of adventure breaking through. There's a child down there somewhere, I remember it well. And I'm going to find it."

The more David thought about the idea of a party, the better it seemed. "You mean, I could be anything I want?"

"That's the fun of Halloween, David. For one night a year you get to put your fantasies into practice in front of the whole world. Be anything or anyone you'd like."

At work David thought of the party, hoping he'd come up with some respectable idea. He tried to think back to when he was little—was there anything he had really wanted to be? Once when he was young, he wanted to be a surfer, but that didn't last long. It was weird, but for as long as he could remember, he hadn't wanted to be David ... and he knew he couldn't be Kevin. Yet he never really fantasized who he'd like to be instead. The whole idea fascinated him; hundreds of possibilities now raced through his head, some of them making him laugh right out loud.

One of those times, Steel heard him and walked over, staring at him as if he had some screw loose. "See something funny?" he said, peeking into the frame of the stereo David was working on.

"No, nothing. I was just thinking."

"Yeah? Of what?"

"I'm going to a party."

"You party a lot, kid?"

It was the first time Steel had ever asked him anything personal. He shook his head—the truth was, never. "Not the kind you're thinking of," David said. "A costume party. You know, one of those deals where you dress up in weird clothes."

Steel screwed up his face in a you-gotta-be-kidding expression, and David dropped the little dial from the stereo. David bent down and reached under the table where it had rolled. He didn't know it then, but after thinking about it much later, he realized that's when the envelope holding Erin's negatives must have fallen out of his back pocket.

CHAPTER TWENTY-FOUR

hris took the opportunity to leave when Neil's therapist showed up at nine A.M. Craig was due to see Neil after his therapy session, which meant she had at least two hours to shop for the party the next night. At the supermarket she bought ingredients for the cake, and candy for any trick-or-treaters who might show up at the door; at a party store, orange and black Halloween decoration, cups and plates.

Finally, David's gift: she saved the pet store for last, feeling like a little kid herself as she walked down the long aisle, peeking into each cage lined up against the wall, each puppy as adorable as the one before. They all yelped with delight, some nuzzling their cool, wet noses against the bars of the cages, inviting her to reach in and touch. She felt like herding half a dozen of them into the car.

It wasn't until she reached the next-to-last cage that she spotted him: a sad-eyed collie, sitting with an air of dignity in the far corner of his cage, ignoring his littermates squealing and tumbling over each other in the sawdust. She stopped and stared at him. "What's-the-matter, fella? Won't they let you join in the fun?"

"That's Maverick," someone said. She turned slowly, a little embarrassed to be caught engaging in one-sided conversation with a dog, and faced the voice. The man was thin, balding, mustached.

"You name them?" she said, surprised.

"Usually not. But this one's different. Something of a snob."

She looked back at the puppy. "Do you really think so?"

"I know so. You never see him romping with the others. He sits in his corner like he's above it all."

"Maybe that's not it."

"What else, then?"

"I don't know ... Maybe he wants to play—and doesn't know how."

"I don't see anything stopping him. He's healthy enough." He pointed toward the other cages. "We've got a lot more playful ones here."

"There's something about this one, though ..."

"It's up to you, of course. But usually we suggest the friskier pups. They make better pets."

"This one *is* for sale, isn't it?"

"Sure."

"Then I'll take him. Who knows," she said, "maybe we can teach him how to play."

She picked up some dog food, a leash and collar, paid at the register and made arrangements to pick up the pup the next day. On David's birthday.

She walked into the house, loaded down with packages: Craig was just coming downstairs. "Here, let me help you, Mrs. Mathews." He took the two heaviest bundles from her arms and led the way into the kitchen, setting them on the table. "Looks like you've been busy."

"A little birthday celebration for David."

He put his hand to his tie, pulling the knot, loosening it around his neck.

"Neil told you that I saw your report. Didn't he, Craig?"

"He told me you weren't any too pleased with it. I know you think it wasn't called for, but Neil worries about you and Erin. He felt there was something not quite right about David. Or his story."

"And you agreed, of course."

"I have to say yes, I did agree. The boy seems troubled. Nothing you can easily put your finger on. He talked about becoming a psychiatrist . . ."

"So?"

"He carried on a pretty strange dialogue about mental illness. I don't know . . . he just seems very unsure of himself. Almost like he's groping around."

"Not everyone is sure of themselves, Craig. Not everyone's background is solid and secure."

"I'm aware of that. It wasn't that I didn't like the boy—I did. And he seemed to be trying very hard to fit in, particularly in front of Neil. But I do understand Neil's point of view. After all, look what goes on these days. You can't be too careful of who you befriend. Let alone whom you allow to live in your home."

"Craig, I'm not going to dignify your comments by telling you my reasons for believing in David. But I *do* believe in him—with all my heart. I've told Neil, and now I'm telling you. Don't interfere again. Whatever there is to know about David, I'll find out. From him—and in his own time."

Since she had left Craig with nothing to say, he left.

"A costume party?" Neil shook his head. "You've got to be joking."

"I couldn't be more serious."

"I don't suppose . . ."

"You'd better suppose you're coming, because you are."

"Just the four of us?"

"Would you rather I invited guests? It has been quite a while since we've entertained, and it's probably not a bad idea. It would give you a chance to make amends to friends you've boycotted these past few months."

"Why do I get the feeling I'm being outmanuevered here?"

"Not at all, Neil. It's your choice—guests or no guests?"

He sighed. "You win. Just the four of us."

"If you like, I could help you with your costume."

"What—and spoil my fun?"

She laughed, tossed a pillow at him and walked out, leaving him at his desk.

Downstairs, she glanced at the photographs on the mantel as she passed by. First Erin, then David, then Kevin. She stopped, her eyes going back to the pictures. Kevin had been blond and chubby; David was dark and very thin ... more like Erin. For the first time she did notice a slight similarity in the boy's facial structure: a strong Irish jaw. And the color of their eyes was the same. Except David's were bluer and much more intense.

Was there a definite likeness? Or was her mind inventing something that wasn't really there? She smiled—one way or the other, it was okay with her—and headed for the kitchen. She had a cake to bake.

After school, Erin counted out money from her savings and brought it downstairs. "I have ten dollars," she announced.

"You ought to be able to come up with something nice."

"Like what?"

"I don't know, what do you think David would like?"

"That's just it, mom. Other than photography—and he has everything when it comes to that—I can't think of one single thing he's interested in. You know him so much better than I do, what do *you* think?"

Chris turned toward her, wondering if the note of sarcasm in her voice was real or just her imagination. She couldn't tell by her expression. "It's your gift, Erin," she said finally. "You decide."

She started to leave, then stopped. "Did you ever read that report on David—the one dad had made up?"

"No, I didn't."

"Is David's father really alive?"

"I don't know, Erin. According to your father, he is."

"Maybe David ran away from him."

"I suppose that's possible."

"Or maybe he killed him, dug a hole and buried him so no one could find him."

"Erin! How could you say such a thing?"

She sighed. "Only kidding."

"That was hardly a joke."

"Sorry. That's how I meant it." She put on her jacket, slung her bag across her shoulder, and headed for the door. "Be back in a while," she called.

Chris watched her leave the yard, then went to the door, opened it again and took a deep breath, letting the cool air fill her lungs.

David came home a few minutes later. As usual, he headed first to the kitchen. He paused at the mantel on the way, studying the faces of Kevin and himself, then looked up to find Chris watching.

"How was school, David?"

"Good." He came into the kitchen, laid his books on the table, and leaned back against the wall with his hands tucked in his back pockets; Chris poured him a glass of milk and set it on the table along with some cookies. He looked at them as though he'd never laid eyes on an after-school snack, then said, "Do you believe in coincidence, Chris?"

"That depends on how it's meant. What kind of coincidence?"

"Like me coming here, to this house."

"I suppose I do believe there's some kind of . . ." She stopped because it was then that he began to slide his hands through his pockets, his mouth opening and his eyes narrowing; little beads of sweat dotting his upper lip. "What is it, David?" she said.

He continued his search, more agitated by the moment.

"Did you lose something?"

He looked at her as if startled to find she was there. "The envelope," he said. "I had an envelope."

"Maybe you dropped it in the car."

He ran off to go look, leaving the milk and cookies untouched on the table.

CHAPTER TWENTY-FIVE

t wasn't in the car. David searched his bedroom, and then he thought of the shop. He ran to the telephone in the upstairs hallway and dialed the number. "Tony's Repair," Steel answered.

"Steel, this is David. Did I leave an envelope in the shop?"

"What kind of envelope?"

"A yellow one. Not very big, maybe three by five."

"What was in it?"

"Nothing important."

"You're pretty shook-up over nothing."

He took a deep breath. "I'm not shook-up, I just need it."

"Let me go look." Steel dropped the receiver and David waited. Finally he came back. "Nothing here, kid. Must have dropped it someplace else."

"I thought maybe when I bent down on the floor . . ."

"You having trouble with your hearing? What did I just say?"

"It's not there."

Steel sighed. "There we go, kid. Sounds like we finally made a clear connection."

David hung up the receiver and ran back to his room...

He had been sitting on the floor in a yoga position for at least twenty minutes. He had no intention of using the pictures any more than people intend to collect on their hundred-thousand-dollar accident insurance policies. Which didn't stop them from taking out the policies and feeling good about it. Without the photographs, David felt like he was staggering on a brick ledge a dozen stories up in the sky. With nothing to hold onto.

Finally, it hit him—if Erin thought he still had the pictures, that was almost as good as having them. And he sure as hell wasn't about to let her know any different. So when she knocked on his door a little later, he managed to look halfway normal. "You want to look through the old clothes?" she asked.

He must have looked blank.

"Find a costume, David."

"Sure," he said. "Lead the way."

She led the way to the library, where she stopped in front of a closet and pulled open the door. The closet was more like a little room. David sniffed as he walked in. "Camphor balls," Erin said, pointing to the boxes lining the walls and shelves. "Well, here it is—happy hunting."

The first box he went to contained photographs, hundreds of them. He picked up a stack and started to look through them. "They're mostly of my brother," Erin said. "My dad made my mom store them up here."

"Why?"

"So she wouldn't keep looking at them all the time."

He stopped at one picture: the boy was sitting on a swing; David could almost feel the movement as it glided through the air. As if it were him swinging. One hand was hanging onto the thick steel chains; the other hand was raised ... He was wearing a red baseball cap way too big for his head. *The brim kept sliding, and he kept on pulling it forward. The big man was hunched over in front of him, holding a camera. "Daddy's over here—look over here, son!" The voice was not Fletcher's. The boy straightened the cap, then looked up, smiling. The camera clicked, and the man stood up. It was Neil.*

David gasped and dropped the pictures into the box. Erin turned and stared at him. "What's the matter?"

He felt hot. Real hot. He ran his sleeve over his forehead. "Nothing ... Where're the clothes?"

"You didn't expect to find them with the pictures, did you? Try another box."

He pulled another one off the shelf and set it in front of himself. Meanwhile Erin pulled out a long ball gown, billowing lace.

"Look David—this must have been my mother's."

"You going to wear that?"

She held it up against her, dancing around the closet. "Maybe." She put the dress over her arm. "I'm going to go try it on, anyway. Don't forget to close the door when you're through."

The minute she ran off, he looked at his box, which was labeled, "Kevin." He took off the cover and lifted out items of clothing, all neatly folded. Little outfits—different colors, short pants with suspenders, jerseys with pictures or lettering ... Dammit! These clothes weren't Kevin's at all—they were his!

But Kevin was dead. Kevin was dead ... He kept on saying that to himself, over and over. Then what was he doing with all *his* memories? He thought of a movie he saw once: a dead boy's spirit had invaded his best friend's body and eventually took it over, killing off the boy whose body it was. Only a movie, a dumb movie ...

He pushed that box aside and went through another, finding a high school baseball uniform and cap. He snatched it up and ran out of the closet, slamming the door as he went. Once he got back to his room, he threw the clothes on his bed, then stared at the red cap: it was the same one Kevin had worn in the picture. He picked it up carefully, almost like he expected it to move in his hands, and walked to the mirror. Then, very slowly, he lifted it to his head and put it on, waiting ... Twenty seconds, thirty seconds, a minute. Nothing happened.

He sank down onto the floor.

He had a question for Chris, but he didn't work up the courage to ask it till that night, right in the middle of her reading to him: "Chris, how did Kevin die?"

She closed the book and laid it down on his bed, her teeth nipping lightly at her bottom lip, like she was thinking, deciding. Finally she said, "I'm not quite sure, David."

"I don't understand," he said. "How could you not be?"

"You see, Kevin was kidnapped. I had taken him across to the park. He ran ahead of me—and then, suddenly, he was gone."

"Then how do you know—"

"Because we found him. It was much later, but we did find his body. No one could determine the cause of death." David didn't even know why he had asked her about him, but what she said next made him glad he had.

"This is a first, you might say. I've never been able to talk about this before without getting terribly tense. And here I am, telling you, and it feels good being able to do it." She looked at the book on the bed and picked it up. "You know, I sometimes wonder who these stories are for—me or you?"

"Maybe both of us."

She put her hand to his cheek, stroking it. "Whoever sent you to me, David—remind me to thank him."

He was running . . . running . . . running. Only once up on the monkey bars. The monkey bars were ahead of him. And he almost reached them—almost—when the voice called out, "Kevin." He stopped and turned, looking to find the voice. And then he did: the friend from daddy's office. Fletcher!

He ran up to him, smiling, but when he saw the look on Fletcher's face, his smile went away.

"I'm sure glad I found you, young man."

Had he been looking for him?

"Your daddy's been real worried."

But he went home with mommy. Didn't daddy know?

"You were supposed to stay with him, he was going to take you to the movies after work."

He couldn't remember . . . Did daddy say that?

"What are you doing here?"

He pointed back over his shoulder. "My mommy . . ."

"No, son, you've got it all wrong. You'd better come along with me right now, so's your daddy won't get mad, and—hey, where're you going?"

"To tell mommy."

"No need, son. I already told her. And she said to ske-daddle right down to meet your daddy."

And then he took his hand in his big one. And then he led him to his car. And then . . .

He jerked up in bed, clamping a hand over his mouth so he would stop screaming. He couldn't remember—had Chris told him all those things about Kevin? But how could even she know. . . ? Then, the next moment, she was in his room, her voice soothing him, then sitting there with him, her hand stroking his head until he fell back to sleep.

Chris greeted David the next morning with a cheery, "Happy Birthday" followed by a hug. David's mind was so muddled from last night's dream that he had almost forgotten. Chris, of course, picked right up on it.

"You're allowed to forget birthdays only after forty, David. Not before."

"I didn't forget the Halloween party, though."

"Better not!" She put a slice of french toast on his plate. "By the way, David, did you find whatever it was you lost yesterday?"

Erin looked up, suddenly interested. He shook his head.

"What was in the envelope?" Chris asked.

"Money," he said quickly, hating to lie. But what else could he say?

"If you need extra money—"

"Oh, no. I have enough. It was only a few dollars."

"All right, but you let me know if you do." She lifted the tray she had been setting for Neil and headed upstairs.

As soon as she was gone, Erin put down her fork and looked up at him. "Strange place to keep money, David."

He shrugged. "Not all that strange."

"What does the envelope look like? I'll look around for it."

"Don't bother."

"My, my—aren't we uptight. If I didn't know better, I'd think you lost something a lot more valuable than a measly few dollars." She scrunched up her face, thinking. "Now what could that be?"

She didn't know, she couldn't know ... She was only fishing, the way she always did. At least that's what he kept telling himself on the way to work. But he would have felt a lot better about it if those negatives were still in his pocket.

When David walked into the fix-it shop, Steel did something unusual—he smiled. That alone should have tipped him off, but it didn't, and it wasn't until he got to the back room that he found out what the smile was about ... He would have had to have been blind to miss the photograph—the one of Erin squatting on the floor—blown up to the size of a poster and scotchtaped to the wall. David sucked in his breath and wheeled around, almost touching noses with Steel.

"What'd you think of it, kid? A buddy of mine did it."

He didn't answer—he couldn't. He just stared at the picture.

"Come on, lighten up. I did you a favor. And here you are, acting so prissy. Costume parties, huh?" He started to laugh, his bad breath blowing in David's face.

David headed toward the wall, but one of Steel's hands, the weight of a bowling ball, fell onto his shoulder. "Hold it—what are you doing?"

"You had no right. Those negatives were mine!"

"Ever hear of sharing the wealth? You can always get more where they came from. Bring the little doll down, we can do it together. I'll even lend you the back room."

David looked down at the worktable in front of him, at the tools, at the wrench ... Then sighed. "Yeah, I guess you're right," he said finally, "I guess I am being selfish about it."

"Now you're making sense, kid."

He looked straight at Steel. "Why didn't you have your buddy do the rest of them?"

"Didn't get a chance." He walked over to the desk against the wall and pulled out the drawer, picking up the envelope of negatives. "Don't you worry, I'll get them made up. What I'd like to talk about now is getting some better ones. I'm not putting down your work, kid, but I see possibilities for improvement. You know, there's a big market for this stuff."

"You mean, we could make some money from this?"

"Big bucks." He drew out the words. "You supply the little girl and take the pictures and I'll supply the space and make the connections. And we split—fifty, fifty. Sound fair?"

David nodded, swallowing over the dryness in his throat. "You know, Steel, what surprises me is you didn't develop the best one. There's a way better one in that pile."

Steel walked to the window and held one of the negatives up to the light. With shaky fingers, David lifted the wrench ... Steel held up another negative. "Show me, kid," he said turning. But by that that time David was already behind him with the wrench lifted over his head and he brought it down hard.

As Steel's hands shot up, he dropped the envelope and negative to the floor. With one quick motion David bent and scooped them both in his hand. With another, he leapt toward the picture and tore it off the wall. Then he turned, but not fast enough ...

One of Steel's paws caught him and swung him around; the other pummeled him full in the face. Another punch was right behind. The force of the first threw David off-balance; the second knocked him off his feet. As he went down he grabbed for Steel's leg: then, with the pants leg held tightly in his fist, he pulled. Steel toppled over and David rolled on top of him, his hands going for and finding his neck ... He squeezed. Steel's face turned red and he squeezed even harder. He might have kept squeezing until all the breath was out of him had he not heard a customer call out, "Anybody here?" from the front of the shop.

He pulled his hands away, reached for the negatives and picture, stood up and tore off, almost knocking the customer over on his way out. David drove his car almost a mile before he pulled into an empty parking lot. He looked into the rearview mirror: his eye was already turning purple and his mouth was cut and bleeding. He pulled a rag from the glove compartment and wiped the blood away.

Then he looked down on the seat beside him and blew out a stream of air. He had them back. He picked up the picture of Erin, now torn, and looked at it for a few minutes before he ripped it ... and again into smaller pieces. Then he reached in the glove compartment and took out his jack-knife—and did something he never in a hundred years expected to do. One by one, he took out the negatives, and one by one he sliced them up until all that was left of them was a pile of gray confetti.

Finally he did the dumbest thing of all—he started to cry.

CHAPTER TWENTY-SIX

Chris bent down and placed the puppy on the carpet, then, with a tap on his backside, headed him into Neil's room. Neil turned and looked down from his desk, scowling. "Wrong house, buster." The puppy stopped in his tracks, a few feet from Neil. And Chris made her entrance.

"That's Maverick. I just picked him up. What do you think?"

"He's ours?"

"David's. For his birthday."

Neil reached down and scratched the back of the puppy's neck. "We going through with this charade tonight?"

"If you mean the party—of course."

"The costumes?"

"I take it that means you haven't come up with one yet."

A crooked smile. "Have you?"

She shook her head. "But I will. And you'd better too."

Neil's expression grew serious. "Craig called. We've found another man, and a child—no, *not* a child, a young man. Fourteen years old."

"When was he abducted?"

Neil shrugged. "Two, three years old."

Chris knelt down and picked up the puppy, almost wishing Neil wouldn't go on, but he did.

"The boy knows no other parents. Only the man." He raised his hands along with his voice. "The boy was violated by him, Chris. Yet he cried when we took him away!"

Chris shuddered and Maverick let out a short squeaky protest. "Maybe it would have been better ..." She stopped; she couldn't go on.

"Better what?"

"Nothing," she said.

Neil stared at her for a few moments, then stood up and grabbed his walker. "I've got a costume to find," he said.

Chris gathered a few worn blankets from the linen closet and took them, along with Maverick, to the cellar. She spread a dozen newspapers in the corner, hoping he'd figure out what to do with them. "Only until tonight, little guy," she said as she placed him on the makeshift bed. Back in the kitchen, she filled up the two stainless steel bowls she'd bought at the pet shop with food and water and brought them downstairs, setting them beside the puppy's bed. Finally she left, doing her best to ignore the outraged squeals of desertion.

Other than set up the party decor, which she wouldn't do till the last minute, she had nothing to do—that is, nothing except find herself a suitable costume. She headed back upstairs, looking in on Neil as she went by. "Well," she said, raising an eyebrow, "did you come up with something?"

He nodded. "Not just something—a sure prize winner."

Chris headed for the closet and opened the door. Judging by the muddle facing her, everyone had done their digging. She went to the box labeled "Kevin." Someone had been looking through it, maybe Neil. She lifted out a pair of red overalls—"I'm a-torney," stamped on the bib. Neil had bought them for Kevin. She smoothed the soft cotton material against her face, then folded them, placed them back in the box and put the box on the shelf. Now for the photographs—it had been so long. One by one she went through them, remembering a story for each and every photograph and silently reliving each and every story. Finally she packed them away. Kevin's birthday would have been in two days, but David's was today. And she was going to hold up just fine.

She pulled out an assortment of her own old clothing, rejecting each article until she came to the high school cheerleader's uniform—blue with a giant yellow school letter on the sweater. She held up the skirt, eyeing the elastic waistline. Would it make it over the extra inches? And surely she could come up with some bobby socks and a blue ribbon for her hair . . .

David came home earlier than usual, but Chris wouldn't have known it except that in passing the parlor window she spotted his car in the driveway. He always stopped to see her first, and she wondered immediately if something was wrong. She went upstairs to his room and knocked on the door. When he finally opened it, she blurted out. "What happened to you?"

"A fight."

She charged past him into the bathroom, soaked a washcloth in cold water, squeezed it out and said, "Sit down."

He sat on the toilet seat and let her put the cold compress on his eye. "Who did this to you?"

"Just a guy. I was at Kenmore Square between classes. He just came out of nowhere."

"What brought it on?"

"Nothing."

"David, it must have been something."

"Some of the guys have it in for the college kids. They hang around looking for trouble."

"Did you report it to the police?"

"It's no big deal, just a black eye."

"It makes me so angry. Someone like that ought to be locked up."

"It's all right—honest. It doesn't even hurt."

"Well, it hurts me just to look at it. And don't you dare tell me I should have seen the other guy."

He looked up at her and grinned.

She laughed. "Come on downstairs and I'll put some

ice on it." He watched her fill a plastic bag with ice cubes, then fold a towel around the bag. She brought it to him and put it against his bruised, swollen face. "Hold that there," she said, poured a glass of milk and set it with cookies in front of him. "I really think I ought to report this to the police."

"No, Chris . . . please. Don't do that."

"Do you think someone like that should be allowed to run around, beating people up?"

"No. But I just want to forget."

"Sometimes we can't, David. Sometimes it's important to remember and deal with whatever it is . . . and then put it to rest." She could see the familiar fear creep into his eyes; she put her hand to his hair and stroked it gently. "Today's your birthday, honey. Maybe we can talk about this tomorrow."

She went up to Neil with tea and bread sticks, leaving David in the kitchen to think about what she'd said. She hated to question or push him, never certain that he was strong enough to withstand the pressure. Especially from her. He had made *her* stronger, and in that uncanny way they had of picking up on each other's feelings she could even share his pain as he pushed to free himself of whatever it was that was crippling him. David counted on her to be always on his side, no matter what. And she was. But he had to be honest—at least with himself.

So she left it at that: they would talk about it tomorrow. She had no way of knowing then that by tomorrow, David would be gone.

CHAPTER TWENTY-SEVEN

D avid held the ice bag pressed over his tightly shut eye; yellow globules of light danced behind it, forming a chain that grew longer and longer. Just like his life—each lie was a link leading futher from the one big master link. *I am David Crane*: the original lie. But if he wasn't David Crane, who was he? And if he were to unravel the whole chain of lies, like Chris was suggesting, he'd be left holding that one . . .

He shivered, pulling the ice bag away, just as Erin opened the back door and came into the kitchen. She stopped short when she saw him. "Is that your costume, David? I must say it's realistic."

"Come over here and I'll let you try it on."

"I wouldn't think of it. I'd say it's perfect for you—almost like it was custom made." She set her books on the table. "Where'd you get it?"

"At the bottom of a box."

"Tell me. Where *did* you get it?"

"Does it really matter?"

She folded her arms across her chest. "Of course it does. If I can find out who did this to you, I can thank him personally."

David took a cookie off the plate and bit into it, hoping she'd leave. No such luck. "Did you find the envelope, David? You remember, the one with the money."

He nibbled the cookie, holding it with one hand and the ice bag with the other.

"Well, did you?"

Finally he looked at her. "As a matter of fact, I did."

"I'll bet." She picked up her books and strutted off. He would have laughed if his eye wasn't hurting so much. Here he was, telling her the honest-to-God truth for once, and she didn't believe a word of it.

At five o'clock, Chris told them all to put on their costumes. The doorbell had already rung several times—trick-or-treaters coming for their share of the goodies. Ghosts and goblins, witches and clowns. Fletcher had always discouraged them by keeping the lights off. And any kid who did approach the darkened house and ring the bell got no reward for bravery—Fletcher wouldn't even answer.

David put on the baseball uniform, which fit perfectly. Then he went to the mirror and tried on the hat. He frowned at his reflection; it struck him as better suited to a boxer than to a baseball player. In the hallway he met Erin, twirling around in her pink strapless gown, yards of filmy material swishing along with her.

"What do you think, David?"

"I think you'd better get a pair of suspenders or else you'll be wearing it around your ankles."

She ignored his remark and looked toward the stairwell: Chris was coming up, looking like a picture cut out of a teen magazine. "Oh mom," Erin squealed. "You look excellent! And it still fits you."

Chris grinned. "Actually, that's debatable. The skirt elastic is on its last breath. One sneeze and I've had it." She took Erin's hand and turned her around. "Absolutely sensational!" Then she turned toward David, touched the rim of his cap, and with a catch in her voice said, "David, you look so handsome."

Just then they heard a shout from Neil's room. "What about me?"

Chris laughed. "Come on, you guys." They headed into his room; when they reached the doorway they all started laughing. Neil had several yards of stiff shiny silver material wrapped around him, pinned tightly at his neck and falling full over the walker right down to the floor. A foot-long strip of white paper stuck out of his neckline.

"Well," he said, "say something!"

"What *is* it?" Chris said.

"Use some imagination!"

They walked in and studied him. "Give us a clue," Erin said.

Neil pointed to the white strip of paper at his neck. "Read the back of this."

Chris was first to make out the letters: H-e-r-s-h-e-y. "A candy kiss!" she cried out. Then she stepped back and examined the outfit again. "Neil, it's marvelous. Really."

The sides of Neil's mouth fell. "Then why didn't you guess?"

"Well ..." Chris threw up her hands. "We weren't expecting it. I mean, who would ever suspect you were *that* sweet!" They laughed again, Neil joining in this time. When the laughter died down, Chris stepped forward and raised her hand. "As much as I hate to do this, I give my vote for best costume to Neil."

"Good move," Neil said.

Erin and David followed suit, and it was decided right then and there—Neil had won. Chris pulled the prize out of her skirt pocket and handed it over: a figurine of a white elephant painting a billboard with a brush held in his trunk. The words on the billboard read: Creative Genius At Work.

As soon as they got downstairs, the doorbell rang, and Chris opened it: big black eyes and a bush of curly dark hair—no costume. The man's eyes grew even bigger as they took in their get-ups. Then he held forward a large flat box. "You ordered pizza?"

"Oh yes ... just a moment," Chris said. "I'll get my purse." She ran off, leaving them standing there as the man looked from Erin, to David—to Neil.

"Halloween party?" he said.

"Oh, no," Neil said. "Still in our work clothes." He gestured with his head toward Erin. "My daughter. Barnum and Bailey circus—rides wild horses." Then David. "My son—Red Sox rookie." A funny noise like a croak came out of David's throat, but Neil went right on . . . "My wife. The one coming in with the money. Cheerleader for the Dallas Cowboys."

The delivery man nodded. "And you?"

"Manufacturer of teflon ironing board covers."

The man looked lost, but they stood there like statues, their expressions set in granite.

"Here you are," Chris said, handing him the money.

He grabbed it and turned quickly to leave.

"Wait a minute—the pizza!"

He looked down at the box as if he had forgotten he was still holding it, then shoved it into Chris' arms. Shaking his head, he let himself out.

Chris turned to them. "What was that all about?"

Erin giggled.

"You are aware that we look . . ." Neil began.

"Eccentric," Chris finished.

Neil nodded. "Good word. Now—let's eat."

At first all David noticed was the orange and black streamers and crepe paper balls, then he saw the shiny black cardboard letters taped to the wall: "Happy Birthday, David." Suddenly Chris was bringing out a huge cake with brightly lit candles, and they were all singing. To him. The color of his face must have matched his red cap. He put his hands in his pockets, then took them out and fiddled with his sleeve, not knowing what to do with them. Finally the singing was through and they were all quiet, just waiting for him.

David looked down at the cake. Gum-drop eyes and nose, black licorice curled up into a smile on the orange frosting. A familiar smile. *Make a wish . . . blow out the candles.* Kevin's memories again. He pulled off the cap from his head, hoping the voice would stop, but he heard it again.

Louder: "Make a wish ... blow out the candles, David."

He looked up at Chris, startled.

She smiled. "Go ahead, they're starting to melt."

David turned back toward the cake, sucked in his breath and blew—there were nineteen candles. Eighteen and one for good luck. He blew them all out in one breath. The doorbell rang again; Erin grabbed a handful of candy bars and ran to answer it. David tried to think of something to say, a little speech, but when nothing came to mind, he just said, "thanks."

As Erin came back in the dining room, Chris said, "Before we eat, how about the presents? Erin, why don't you give David yours first."

Erin hesitated.

"Come on."

She went to the buffet and lifted a silver-wrapped package off the shelf, brought it back and handed it to him. David untied the ribbon and took off the paper. A book. He lifted it up and read the title: Grimm's Fairy Tales. He swallowed hard. Chris stared at Erin. He felt like running, but he couldn't do that to Chris. Or even Neil. It was so quiet, he was sure everyone could hear his heart thumping.

It was Neil who finally broke the silence. He directed his question to Erin. "Did I miss something?"

She didn't answer him.

"Well, what does the book mean?"

"Nothing, it was a joke. I guess it was kind of dumb."

Neil started to say something else, but David stopped him. "Actually, it's a pretty *good* joke. You see, I'm always teasing her, saying if she behaves herself I'll read her a fairy tale. Now I guess I'll be able to."

Erin nodded, licked her lips and sat down.

Chris stood up. "Neil and I have a presert or you, David. Now don't you move—I'll be right back." With that, she ran out of the room; they all sat and waited, not talking. Two minutes later she was back, carrying a furry, wriggly tan and white bundle. At first David wasn't even sure what it was, then she put it down on the floor, and it moved. For a minute, *he* couldn't—he just stared at it.

"It's for you, David," Chris said finally.

He got up and went to the puppy and knelt down next to him. His two front paws were shaking. "Oh, God, he's scared."

"Pick him up," Chris said.

David reached out, not quite sure where to touch first. Finally he put his hands around the puppy's belly, lifted him, and held him against his chest. The puppy squealed, and David jumped. Too tight. He loosened his hold, but the little thing started to skid down his chest so he tightened his hold again. He felt the pup's heart thumping away, against his, and when he looked down, he saw two big scared eyes looking at him. David nuzzled his face into the puppy's neck. Another squeal. He pulled away and just stared at him. He had never had anything as nice as this, never in his entire life. He wanted to say that to Chris. And Neil. But again the only word that come out of his mouth was: "Thanks."

Erin came over and stood beside him. "Can I pet him?"

"You'd better not. I don't think it's good for too many people to be handling him. You can tell how scared he is."

"I only want to pet him."

"Sure, *you* know that, but does he? For all he knows, everyone's an enemy. It looks to me like he's already been hurt, and it's going to take a while before he starts to trust."

"What about you? You're touching him," Erin argued.

"That's different. I'm going to be the one who teaches him."

A sigh. "Well, what are you going to name him?"

Chris opened her mouth to say something but stopped.

"I don't know," he said. "Names are important—I'll have to think about it."

"Can we eat now?" Neil said.

"Right now," Chris said. "David, I put down some blankets and newspapers for the puppy in the kitchen. He's already eaten. Why don't you leave him there while we have the pizza?"

David took him to the kitchen and settled him on the blankets, then set up a big barricade around the box so he couldn't wander around and get lost. Chris had fed him, but David put a couple handfuls of dry dog food into his dish anyway. Finally, David ran his hand over the pup's silky fur one more time just to make sure he was really there.

CHAPTER TWENTY-EIGHT

Chris had never seen David so happy. Twice during dinner he excused himself to go check on the dog. Though it was clear that David adored him, the puppy's reaction to his mothering was not so clear. More than once the puppy nipped at his fingers and squealed protests, but he reacted as if he'd been licked or kissed. As soon as dinner was over, he carted him into the living room with them, put him onto his lap, and never once let him down.

Chris had given up on the idea of bobbing for apples, so they settled for a game of Trivial Pursuit. They drew straws for teams; Erin and Chris got the short ones. Neil nudged David. "The men against the women—no contest."

"That's what you think," Erin said. "We'll show you two where the brains are." She pulled out two boxes of cards and set one in front of herself, the other box in front of David. David won the roll for first, and Erin read the first question: "What's the weight classification of a 159-pound boxer?"

"Well, what do you say, David?" Neil asked.

"Middleweight."

"I'll go with my partner."

The answer was correct, and David read the next question. An hour later, the guys had filled in their circles with all but one piece—green for Science. Erin and Chris had two pieces yet to go. David rolled the die and landed on green; Erin pulled out the next card and read it: "How long does it take the typical hen to lay nineteen dozen eggs?"

Neil sat forward, his forehead furrowing. "Now, you say the *typical* hen. Is that correct?"

"Yes," Erin said, giggling.

"Any other clues—normal feed, healthy fowl, extenuating circumstances?"

David laughed too, and Neil looked at him. "This is no time to fold on me, partner. What's your guess?"

He shrugged. "Maybe a dozen a month."

"Sounds reasonable." Neil turned to Erin. "We say nineteen months."

"Wrong!" she shouted. "One year."

David read the next question: "What does Wonder Woman have all over her blue shorts?" Chris immediately looked to Erin.

"That's easy. Stars."

David was just about to say "right" when Neil leaned over and peeked at the answer. "Please clarify," he said.

Erin shrugged. "Big stars?"

"Close but wrong," Neil said. "White stars."

"That's not fair. Stars are stars."

"Rules are rules."

Chris patted Erin's shoulder. "You know your father is a stickler for rules, particularly when they're in his favor. But let us not be petty—we'll win anyway."

Finally Chris and Erin filled in their circle. The guys still had not conquered Science, and Erin and she were heading to the center ring. Erin rolled the die and landed their circle right in the center. After a full minute of discussion, the guys decided to give them Geography—their very worst subject—as their final test. David pulled out the question: "What country would you be in if you whiled away time playing a didjeridoo in Wagga Wagga?"

Erin groaned. "Not to worry, David," Neil said. "This one they don't know."

"Let's try Australia, Erin," Chris said. Erin hesitated. "Go on, honey, I have a feeling about this one."

"All right." She turned to David and Neil. "We say Australia."

David looked down at the card, then at Neil. "They're *right.*"

"We win!" Erin shouted.

David pulled the puppy closer against his chest. "Not so loud, Erin. You made him jump a mile."

Neil sat forward. "You can tell me, Chris, what *is* a didjeridoo?"

"I don't believe I'm required to answer that. Of course if you'd like to check the rules . . .?"

Neil scowled.

"Can't you be a good loser, Neil?"

"Losers are losers. They're not good."

Chris laughed and kissed his cheek. "Come on, now. We're going to give you a chance to save your honor at charades."

Erin ran to put the game away. When she came back, she whispered in her mother's ear: "What *is* a didjeridoo?" Chris shrugged. "Then how did you know?"

She cupped her hands and whispered in Erin's ear. "Promise not to tell?" Erin nodded. "I had the same question last time."

Their game of charades had begun and David was just getting ready to act out a song title when the doorbell rang. Chris looked down at her watch. It was almost nine—late for trick-or-treaters.

"I'll get it." Erin jumped up and grabbed another handful of candy bars. She came back only a minute later, leading Craig into the living room. Neil stood up immediately, undoing the pin at his neck holding his costume and letting it fall to the floor.

"What is it, Craig?"

"News on Flannery. I just got it, and I wanted to deliver it in person."

Neil grabbed his walker. "The dining room," he said.

Chris followed behind, unnoticed. Craig hadn't even reached the dining room before he said, "We found him."

"You're sure?"

"Positive I.D."

"Dead or alive?" Neil asked.

"Alive. Very much so—in fact, he was apprehended in Connecticut, attempting to pick up a child."

"What about the boy?"

"There was no one, Neil. Flannery was living alone. His apartment was searched, and there was nothing to indicate that anyone had been living with him."

"What did he say?"

"So far, nothing. At least, that I know of."

"I want him brought here to Massachusetts. I want to do the questioning."

"The papers are being expedited now. He'll be here late tomorrow."

"Get me the files on Flannery, Craig. They're in my bedroom."

Craig rushed out of the room and Chris rushed in. "Neil," she said, "Please sit down. You look awful." He sank down in the chair and she knelt beside him. "What is it?"

"They found Flannery, but not the boy."

"I understand that. What I can't understand is the way you're taking it." She put her hands on his chest. "Look at you, you're sweating, your shirt is soaked."

"Dammit, Chris, a child is missing. I've got to find him!"

Craig came into the dining room, carrying the files and the black book. "Wait a minute!" Chris said, looking at Neil. "Be reasonable—there's nothing you can do right now. You must know those files backwards and forwards. And whatever it is you have to see can wait till tomorrow."

Neil stood up again and so did she. "Put the files on the table, Craig." Neil demanded. "Dammit, Chris, get out of here."

"I won't leave. I won't stand by and watch you do this to yourself." Chris looked at Craig. "Please . . . talk some sense into him." Instead, Craig put the files on the table and stepped back. Neil reached out to pick one up, and she pushed it away. As she did, the other file and book dropped to the floor, sections of the book falling loose. Chris immediately got down on her knees to pick them up; David and Erin, who were now behind her, stooped down to help. With one arm, David was holding the puppy against his chest.

"Get out of here—all of you!" Neil shouted.

David and Erin stood up, but Chris didn't. Craig took her arm. "Let me get those."

She pushed him away and picked up one of the magazine sections from the book. "What's wrong with you two, I can—" And that's when she saw the photograph. She stopped. For a few seconds she couldn't breathe: but once she could, a scream came out of her throat. Then, very slowly, she stood up, her eyes fixed on the picture in her hands.

"This is *Kevin!*"

Erin was at her side, pulling at her sleeve. "But it can't be, mom. Not with *that* man!"

"Stop it!" Chris pushed her hand away, then studied the boy's face again. He was about four or five years old. And he *was* Kevin. She looked at Neil. "You have to tell me—how is this possible?"

Tears were rolling down his cheeks, and he wasn't even bothering to brush them away.

"We buried our son, Neil. Together."

Silence.

She grabbed the collar of his shirt and pulled it; he didn't pull away. "Damn you—answer me! Tell me how this is possible!" Craig came over and loosened her hands from around Neil's collar, and Neil sank down in the chair.

"We never found him," he said finally.

"The funeral?"

"There was no body in the casket."

She leapt forward, this time going for his face. Still he didn't try to fight her off, but Craig again pulled her back.

"I wanted you to forget, Chris ... I wanted you well. I needed you, we needed you. I did it for all of us."

"*All of us?* Kevin—What about Kevin?"

"I was always looking. Always."

Suddenly it hit her. "And you think Flannery took Kevin—is that what you think?" She looked down at the picture again, and for the first time she saw the faceless man holding her son. Her stomach lurched and she hurled the magazine against the wall. She sank down onto her knees, her hands covering her face and her body rocking back and forth. "Oh my God, no ... I'd rather he be dead."

The last thing she heard before she went blank was running, a door slamming shut—and a puppy crying.

She remembered coming to ... Someone standing over her, a jab in her arm, then nothing. She didn't wake again until early afternoon the next day. When she opened her eyes, Erin was sitting on a chair by the bed, watching her. She started to sit up, then all the memories of the night before came flooding back, and she began to cry.

"Please don't do that," Erin said.

Chris reached out, took her daughter's hand and squeezed it.

Erin handed her some tissues and she wiped her eyes. Finally she sat up. "Why aren't you in school?"

"Dad told me to take care of you today."

"Where is he?"

"Downstairs with Craig."

"Is David home yet?"

Erin stood up. "You want me to get dad?"

"First I'd like to see David. Is he home yet?"

She didn't answer.

"Tell me, Erin. If something is wrong with David, I want to know about it."

"He's gone."

"What do you mean, gone?"

"He left last night, and he never came home."

Chris jumped out of bed, put on her robe and slippers and ran downstairs. Neil was fully dressed, sitting with Craig in the dining room; the telephone was in front of him on the table. The puppy was lying alone in the corner of the room. "What did you say to David to make him leave?" she demanded.

Neil looked up; his eyes had deep circles beneath them. He pulled out a chair. "Sit down, Chris."

"I want to know what you said!"

"Nothing."

"I don't believe you. He would never leave—not without saying goodbye, not without his puppy."

"He got scared. He just took off."

Then she remembered the running, the door slamming, the puppy crying. "Please, Neil. You've got to find him and bring him home."

"I'm trying, I have a man on it now."

"Where is he looking?"

He sighed. "Not at B.U. David doesn't go there."

"I know that."

"You ... how, Chris?"

"After your report, I checked."

"And never said a word?"

"It wasn't important, Neil."

"How can you still say that? Nearly everything he's told us is a lie."

"There are reasons for the lies. I don't know what they are, but I know they're good reasons. And I know when he trusts us enough, he'll tell us."

Craig stood up. "Mrs. Mathews, in spite of what you told me, I had some further investigating done for Neil. We learned that David works at a place over on Commonwealth Ave.—Tony's Fix-it Shop. We've sent a man over there."

She took a deep breath, sat down. "Neil, what about Kevin. Have the police questioned Flannery?"

"I'm going downtown to question him now," Neil said. "According to the Connecticut police, whom I spoke to this morning, Flannery said that when the boy and he parted company several months ago, the boy headed to the west coast."

She took a deep breath. "Then he *is* alive?"

"If Flannery's on the level. Chris ... please don't get your hopes up, not yet. I'll learn more when I question him."

"You won't forget Dav—" The phone rang, and Neil picked it up.

"This is Mathews ... All right, keep on it." He put down the receiver.

"Well, Neil?"

"David's left the job. A fight with the owner. I assume that accounts for the black eye."

"Can't you put out a missing-person's bulletin?"

"David's of age, Chris. He knows where we live. He left on his own accord."

"Then you're saying there's nothing we can do?"

"Not much, other than wait. Don't you understand— David is safe. Now we have to think about Kevin."

CHAPTER TWENTY-NINE

It had happened so fast, David didn't even see it coming. It was like an explosion in his brain; every cell split, spilling out the contents, then suddenly slammed back together again. Look Ma—no holes! Instead he was left with smoke, ashes, and a burning in his head, so hot he thought his brain might just melt away. Fletcher had only shown him the article, made him read it. But Neil had orchestrated his funeral as surely as if he'd killed him himself. And if David hadn't believed with his whole heart and soul that Kevin was dead, he never ever would have become David. He hadn't struck out at Neil—not then. Not yet . . .

Kevin Mathews. He had said the name so many times since leaving the house that it was beginning to feel natural. Not that it made a difference now. It was too late for Kevin—even Chris knew that. The proof was, she wanted him dead. He kept seeing the photograph lying on the carpet and Chris kneeling over it, horror in her eyes. He kept hearing her say, "I'd rather he be dead." It wasn't just Kevin's picture she had smashed against the wall—it was him! Now she could have neither of them. And the very worst part of all was, neither one of them could have *her*.

As soon as he'd pulled the car off the ramp onto the Mass. Pike last night, he floored the accelerator and watched the speedometer needle climb to eighty, then eighty-five. The old car shimmied like a crazed belly dancer, but he kept the needle more or less up there for three hours straight, stopping only twice for tolls. A game—something to keep him busy while his brain melted down.

He didn't even remember heading back to Massachusetts, but now he found himself circling Keeny Park. He pulled into the roadway that was the back entrance to the park, drove around until he came to the waterfall, then parked. He took his jackknife from the glove compartment, flipped it open and with quick, short strokes carved out K-e-v-i-n in the seat's plastic upholstery. Finally he went to the waterfall, sank down onto his knees, bent over, sucked in his breath, then dunked his head in the icy water. When he came up for air—nearly numb—he opened his eyes and there was Erin coming toward him.

She came down to the edge of the water. "What're you doing?" she said.

"Putting out a fire. It's fun—want to try it? Come on, I'll show you how."

He started to reach for her leg, but she backed away. "Don't!"

"There's nothing to be afraid of. I won't hold your head under long. The trick is to take a real deep breath—that way you might last as long as three minutes. If you're lucky, maybe even five."

Erin just stood there.

"Well, what do you want?" he said finally.

"Just to talk."

"How'd you know I was here?"

"I made a guess ... Can I sit down?"

"No. The park is mine, and you can't stay. Did you hear that, Erin? It has a ring to it—listen." He cupped his hands around his mouth and shouted: "The park is mine, and you can't stay!"

"Stop it. Please."

"Stop what?"

"Acting like this ..."

"Like what?"

"You know—funny."

"What's the matter, having trouble saying the word? It goes like this." He pronounced it real slow, dragging out the A. "Craaazy! Better watch out—I hear it can rub off from one person to another." Then he started to giggle and she just watched him, waiting till he stopped.

"I want to talk to you," she said.

"Go ahead—talk. Then get your ass out of here."

Now she sat down, careful to keep her distance. He waited for her to begin, but she didn't. Finally he said, "How's the puppy?"

"Lonely. He just sits in the corner all the time. Would you like me to bring him to you?"

He shook his head. "Let him stay ... He's better off there."

"Why?"

"Because it's too late for puppies."

"What's that supposed to mean?"

He shrugged. "Why did you really come here, Erin?"

"I had to see you."

He didn't say anything.

"Mom misses you."

He picked up a bunch of dried leaves and threw them into the wind.

"It's cold," she said.

"Yeah ..."

Then, very softly: "What should I call you?"

He looked up from the leaves in his lap. "What do you mean?"

She shrugged. "You know. Should I call you David ... or Kevin?"

He felt a prickling at the back of his neck. "How did you know?"

"The picture mom dropped on the floor. It was different from the one in your book. You looked older in the one I'd seen before, more like now."

The picture in his album was taken after Fletcher had smashed his nose, but he didn't say so, he just waited for Erin to go on.

"And in the picture on the floor you were blond."

"Then how *did* you—"

"That man, I could never forget him. Even with his face blocked .out, I knew him. The red heart on the inside of his wrist."

"That's when I knew, too. And then what Neil said."

Her eyes widened. "Really?"

"Really. Did you tell anyone—Chris or Neil?"

She shook her head. "I wanted to ask you first."

He took the jackknife out of his pocket, opened it and ran the sharp-edged blade along his finger. "I don't want them to know."

"Well, I'd still like to know what I should call you."

He thought about it for a minute or two. Then he said, "Kevin."

First she nodded her head, then said: "Are you ever going to come home, Kevin?"

"No."

"Why not?"

"I don't want to. And Chris doesn't want me to, either. You heard what she said."

"That's only because she doesn't know the whole truth. She'd change her mind if she did."

"But she *does* know the truth. She just doesn't know the bad one is David, not Kevin."

She tilted her chin up. "But David and Kevin are really the same person."

"In some ways maybe. But David's still the bad one."

"I don't think so."

He dropped his jackknife in the dirt and with both hands grabbed her tightly around the shoulders. "Don't lie to me!" he shouted. "Everyone always lies to me! You saw the pictures, and you thought I was bad—didn't you?"

He waited: nothing. He shook her again. "Answer me!"

"Yes . . . that's what I thought."

"And that's what anyone would think. David did terrible things—worse than you could even imagine."

She pressed her lips together and as she did, tears spilled down her face. "Oh, Kevin—I want to help you. I just don't know how." He let go of her shoulders, and she wiped her jacket sleeve on her cheeks, then stood up. "I better go now. I'm supposed to be staying with mom, she fell asleep."

He jumped up, too. "Don't hurt that puppy, Erin."

"Why would you say *that*? I would never do anything to hurt him."

He didn't answer.

"Are you going to be here later?"

He turned toward the water, then back to her. "I probably should stay near the water."

"Why?"

"Because of my head. It sometimes burns inside."

She opened her mouth, closed it, then opened it again. "Well, if you're going to be here, I'll try to sneak up later with some sandwiches. And some blankets."

"All right. Then I'll be here."

She stood staring.

"By the way, Erin, I cut up those negatives."

She nodded.

"Take care of your mother."

"She's your mother too, Kevin. Not just mine." And while that was sinking in, she said, "You know what else?"

"No, what?"

"You're my brother."

He thought about that as he watched her go down the hill.

She was back an hour later, out of breath, her arms full. He ran over and took the brown bag from her arm; she carried the two blankets the rest of the way to the car. He threw the blankets and bag of food into the back seat. "How's Chris?" he asked.

"She was up for a while, then fell back to sleep."

"Good. It's good to sleep. I haven't—not in a long time."

"Didn't you sleep last night?"

"No, I couldn't. I had to drive. Someone had to drive the car."

"Why couldn't you stop somewhere and sleep?"

"I don't know why. I don't remember."

"Oh . . . Maybe you should sleep now."

"Where's Neil?" he said.

"He's in Cambridge with Craig. At police headquarters. He went to question the man that kidnapped you. Louis Flannery."

"They have the wrong man."

"Why do you say that?"

"The man who took me was Fletcher Crane."

"Maybe he changed his name. Criminals do that all the time."

"No. It's not the right man. When Neil talks to him, he'll find that out."

"What makes you so sure?"

He walked over to a tree, took out his jackknife, opened it, and dug it into the bark. "Because the man that took me is dead. I killed him." He pulled the sharp blade out of the tree trunk and held it up. "I stabbed him with a knife. A lot bigger than this one."

He could see the color fade out of her face. He pointed the knife at her and stepped forward. "Don't pretend you don't think I could kill someone," he said.

"You're just trying to scare me, Kevin."

"Then if you're as smart as you think you are, you'll be scared, won't you?"

She didn't answer.

"Maybe you didn't hear me straight, Erin. I killed a man. For no reason at all."

"No. There had to be a reason. A good reason."

"Oh, yeah? Why's that?"

It took her a few moments to answer, and when she did, her voice was steady. "Because I finally know who you are, Kevin. And I realize that you wouldn't do something like that."

He raised his free hand to the knife, then with a quick motion made a two-inch slit along the side of his wrist. A fine line of blood rose to the surface and hung there, growing thicker, then spilled over, dribbling down his hand.

Erin gasped. "Why'd you do that?"

"Because you're too dumb to believe words. Maybe you'll believe this." He help up his hand so she could see the blood flowing onto the ground. "Now get out of here."

"Will you be all right?" She was still staring at his hand.

"I can take care of myself."

She still stood there, not moving.

"I don't want you to come back here, Erin. Not today, not tomorrow. Not ever."

"Why not?"

"Because I don't want you here! Are you so stupid, you can't understand that?"

She turned and started running. He watched her until she was only a speck, climbing the front stairs into the house. Then he looked down again at his hand: It was throbbing like the beat of a drum. He waited until the cut stopped bleeding all on its own—it took about an hour before he finally went down to the waterfall and washed it off.

In the brown bag, Erin had stuffed two tunafish sandwiches, an apple, two bananas, a quart of milk, and about a dozen cookies. He ate one of the sandwiches and drank half of the milk, then went to sleep.

It was dark when he woke up to a bright light shining in his eyes. He rubbed his eyes, trying to adjust them to the light. Finally he did—it was a cop.

"Get out of the car," he ordered.

He felt around for the door handle, found it and stepped out.

"Face the car, hands over your head and spread your legs." He turned and the cop pushed him against the car, patting him up and down to see if he was carrying a weapon.

It reminded David of the gangster movies he had seen. Except in the movies, the cop usually realizes when he has a killer staring him right in the face. This guy didn't. When he saw that all he had on him was a wallet, a rabbit's foot keyring, and a jackknife, he told him to turn around. Then the cop shined the flashlight on his clothes, down to his sneakers and back up to his face.

"What's your name, kid?"

"Kevin ... Kevin Mathews." As soon as he said it, he was sorry—suppose he asked to see his license. Instead, he said, "You didn't sound too sure of that."

"I guess I'm still half asleep."

"What are you doing here?"

"Nothing. I just like it here."

"Where do you live?"

"I'm a student. Boston University."

"You're pretty far from campus."

"I'm studying photography, I take a lot of pictures here."

"Well, you'd better get back where you belong."

The cop watched him as he got in the car, started the motor and drove off. He drove around for a while and then parked on a side street across from the park. An hour later he drove back in, this time parking off the road where the cop couldn't spot him if he passed by again. One thing he'd told him was the truth—he did like it here.

Finally, he fell asleep. He dreamt again of the beautiful lady calling to him. She kept telling him to turn around to see who was behind him. But even though he managed to turn his head some, he woke up again before he could see who it was. This time, Chris didn't come when he started to cry.

So he threw a blanket over his shoulders, got out of the car, walked to the top of the hill, and looked down at the house. It was pitch dark inside except for one light coming from Neil's window. He stared at the light for a very long time and was still staring at it when he heard the water begin ...

First quietly sloshing around his head, then suddenly pounding, whipping, roaring like a hurricane in his brain. He clamped his hands over his ears and raced through the darkness ... But the hurricane only gained momentum. Roaring louder. Oh, God, someone make it stop!

CHAPTER THIRTY

hris woke up when Erin walked into the room at six o'clock that evening. She sat up, still groggy. Then everything came back to her. "Has David come home?" she asked.

Erin shook her head and set a tray with a bowl of tomato soup and a tuna sandwich on the bedside stand. "Eat this, you'll feel better."

"I just wish I knew where he was."

Erin sat down in the chair across from her but didn't answer. Chris reached out and touched her hand to her daughter's face.

"Can you ever forgive me?"

"For what?"

"For not telling you what really happened to your brother."

"Sometimes you can't tell the truth. Even when you really want to."

"You've been a real help to me today."

"I didn't do that much."

"Sometimes there's not all that much you *can* do for other people, except be there for them. But that can mean an awful lot."

Erin thought about it, then, "Do you really think so?"

"Yes, honey, I know so. But tomorrow I want you to go to school. I'll be all right. Really, I will." Chris lifted the spoon from the tray and dipped it into the soup. "Is your father home yet?"

"No, but he called about an hour ago. He was still waiting to question Flannery. Flannery called in a lawyer."

Chris's hands started to shake, and she put down the spoon and clasped them in her lap. "Oh, dear God—I'm so frightened."

"Of what?"

"I guess ... of knowing. Never for one moment have I been able to forget your brother, and now there's a chance he might still be alive ..."

"I would think that would make you happy."

"Oh, it does—of course it does. But do you realize what it would mean if he *is* alive?" She didn't; Chris could tell by her face. "It's been so many years, Erin. He won't even remember me or your father. And the things he's been through ..." She stopped a moment, took a deep breath, then went on. "I don't know if I could help him. To forget."

"Of course you could. Because you love him."

Chris clenched her hands together and brought them up to her chin. "It's not always that simple. Of course we would love him, but would he love us? For all we know, he might not even want to come to us. He might prefer to live with ... that man."

"I know that can't be true. He wasn't living with him in Connecticut. That means Kevin left all on his own."

"Maybe ... *if* he's alive."

"He is, mom, I just know it. And maybe even at this very moment, he's out there looking for us."

"If that were only true ... But he was barely three years old, Erin. He would never remember."

"You remembered. And if you did, he will. Even little babies don't forget when someone loves them. If they did, why would everyone say it's so important to show them so much love?"

Chris got up from the bed, went over to Erin and put her arms around her, hugging her close. Then she heard a door slam and Neil call out: "Chris ... Erin!"

They rushed downstairs. In spite of his obvious exhaustion, Neil looked stronger. Over the weeks his steps had become surer and except for an occasional slowness, his speech was normal. "Get in the parlor and sit down," he said, already bouncing his walker ahead. Erin and she hurried into the parlor and sat.

"Well?" Chris said.

"I was right, Chris—it was Flannery ... And I think Kevin's alive."

"Where?"

"I only know he left on his own. To California, probably L.A. I already have a detective there working on it."

"When did he go?"

"Early summer."

"Where were they living before, Neil?"

"Flannery wouldn't say. He did have a post office box in Kingston, New Hampshire. I learned that from the publication records. But the police have been unable to turn up anything there."

"But he told you ... he told you Kevin was alive?"

"Yes."

"Then why wouldn't he tell you where they had lived?"

"Once he contacted counsel, his attorney instructed him to say nothing else—not until he had a chance to get the whole story first hand."

"And when will that be?"

"Tomorrow. I have an appointment to meet with Flannery and his lawyer at two o'clock. I'll get answers then."

All this time, Erin had not said a word. Now she asked her father, "How can you be sure this is the right man?"

"I knew him, Erin. I defended him once."

"But that doesn't mean he's the one—"

"I know. Trust me, it's him."

"Could anything have happened, dad? You know, when Kevin left him?"

"What do you mean?"

"I mean, could he have hurt Kevin? Or Kevin hurt him?"

Neil stared at Erin a moment. "It's possible he's lying, but I don't think so. As for Flannery, he hasn't yet had a physical, but he looks like he's in good enough health."

"Why do you ask that, Erin?" Chris said.

She bit her teeth into her bottom lip. "I don't know," she said. "I just thought maybe he was lying, that's all."

Then she did something that struck Chris as even odder than her question. She went to the front parlor window, pulled aside the draperies, and stared out into the darkness. Across to the park.

That night, Chris was tormented with dreams about both Kevin and David. In one, they were together—walking side by side, away from her. She ran after them and called their names. But even though their pace was so much slower than hers, she could never quite catch up. In another, she heard one of them crying out for her, but she couldn't tell whose voice it was or where it was coming from . . . Finally, at dawn, she fell into an untroubled sleep and didn't wake again until nine.

She went downstairs and found a note hanging on the bulletin board: *Mom: Fed the puppy and made a pot of coffee. See you after school, Love, Erin.* She took down the note; Erin was being unusually thoughtful, as if she'd grown up years in only the past few days. She poured herself a cup of coffee and sat down, trying to think where David might be, but she came up with nothing. Other than school—work, she should say—he was always home. And why would he have gotten so frightened? Was it because he thought if she found Kevin she would no longer want him? If *only* she could find David and tell him how wrong he was. She stood up, went to the phone directory and looked up the number she wanted.

"Tony's Repair," the voice answered.

"This is Chris Mathews. I'd like to know if David Crane has showed up for work today."

"Look, lady, I don't know who you are, but I told the cop yesterday—I don't expect him to show up here ever again. Not unless he wants his left eye to match his right one."

"What about his pay?"

Then he laughed. "If he's got the guts to face me, I'll double it for him. How's that?"

"It's very important that I find him. Have you any idea where he might be?"

"I mind my own business, lady, I don't ask questions. That way I don't get into trouble."

"What did he do to upset you?"

"Upset me? You gotta be joking, lady. That kid's a real screwball. He damned near killed me. He's dangerous!"

The phone clicked in her ear; she hung up the receiver and looked down at the puppy sitting alone in the corner...

Chris knew it was one o'clock when the telephone rang because she was staring at the clock, thinking that in just an hour Neil would be meeting with Flannery and his lawyer. She ran to the phone.

"Hello."

"May I please speak to Mrs. Mathews?"

"This is she."

"This is Rhoda Anderson, vice-principal at North Junior High."

"Oh, no. Is something wrong with Erin?"

A moment's pause, then, "I had hoped you could tell *me*, Mrs. Mathews. It's our policy to check on students who have been absent for more than one day."

"Erin was absent *only* one day—yesterday."

"I'm afraid not. I have her down for yesterday and today."

"You must be mistaken—she went to school today."

"I have the class attendance sheets right in front of me. Just a moment." Chris heard papers being shuffled, then, "She's been absent from all her classes until now. The children are now in fifth period."

"Except for Erin? That's impossible."

"I didn't mean to alarm you, Mrs. Mathews. This sort of thing happens fairly often. I suggest you contact her girlfriends. It sounds to me like a simple case of playing hookey. Any child—no matter how good a student, and of course Erin is one of our best—may decide to cut a day or two. They often—"

"Not Erin!"

And, Chris might have added, certainly not when she knew how anxious she was about Kevin and David. She thanked the vice-principal for calling, then dialed the DA's office; Neil's secretary answered. "Anne? This is Chris. Please let me speak to Neil."

"I'm sorry, but he's down at police headquarters."

"Contact him immediately, Anne, and tell him to call me. It's urgent."

She put down the phone and waited. When it finally rang, she snatched it up on the first ring. "Neil?"

"Chris—what's wrong?"

"It's Erin. She hasn't been to school today. I just got a call from the vice principal."

"Stay put, I'll be right home."

Twenty minutes later, he was there. "You've searched the house?" he asked.

"Of course. She left a note this morning." She handed him the paper from the bulletin board. "What are we going to do?"

"First of all—not panic. She could have played hookey."

"But why? And of all times, why now?"

"What time does she normally get home?"

"Three o'clock."

"That's what we're going to do."

"What?"

"Wait until three."

The hour and a half dragged by interminably. Neil asked Chris only one question during that time: "Why do you suppose Erin asked about Flannery or Kevin getting hurt?"

"I have no idea—why?"

"Because Flannery had a physical today."

"And?"

"There was a scar from a recent stab wound. On his stomach."

She stared at Neil, wondering what he was thinking but afraid to ask. Every so often she'd stand up, go to the window and look out, feeling as if this were just another part of another nightmare. At 3:05, Neil reached for the phone.

"What are you going to do?"

He didn't answer, he was already dialing the police.

Fifteen minutes later, Lieutenant Hanson from the Brookline police was at their door. Chris recognized him the moment she opened it—he looked only a little older than he had when she'd let him in that afternoon fifteen years ago. Then, as now, he immediately preceded her into the dining room where Neil was waiting.

"What's going on?" he asked.

"Sit down, Jack."

Lieutenant Hanson sat across from Neil, and Chris stood on the sidelines. "You don't think she's off with a friend—something like that?" he asked Neil.

"I think it's highly unlikely "

"What *can* you tell me?"

Neil turned to her. "Please go and get David's report. And Erin's and David's photographs."

"I don't understand. You said—"

"Please, Chris. Just get them."

She ran upstairs, took the report on David from Neil's nightstand, then went to the living room for the pictures. She stared at them for a moment, took them off the mantel and headed back to Neil, stopping at the archway.

"How old is he?" the lieutenant was scratching notes on a miniature pad.

"Eighteen yesterday. Dark hair, blue eyes—intense. Skinny but muscular. About five foot eleven."

Chris walked in. "Neil . . . Surely you can't be thinking—"

"I'm not thinking anything. But it's a possibility."

"No it's not!"

He turned back to Lieutenant Hanson. "The Fix-it Shop is at three-thirty Commonwealth. As I said, we checked it yesterday. But try again."

"David didn't show up there today," Chris said.

Neil turned. "How do you know that?"

"I called this morning."

"What did the guy say?"

She could feel her body suddenly go limp. The lieutenant jumped up, grabbed her arm, and eased her into a chair. Neil reached over and took her hand. "Tell me, Chris. This has gone beyond your blind faith in David. Erin is missing!"

"He said . . . he said David almost killed him."

Neil looked from her to the lieutenant. "Look, Jack, I don't know how reliable this guy is, but I do know the boy's got serious problems."

The lieutenant picked up the pictures and report from the table where she had placed them.

"I'll put out an APB right away," he said. "If you think of anything else, call the station and they'll get word to me. Try to think—any new names she's mentioned lately, someplace she's wanted to go, you know what I'm looking for." Then he turned to Chris. "Nine times out of ten, Mrs. Mathews, we find the kids good as new. What you hear about are the ones we don't . . ." He stopped, realizing how innappropriate his little speech sounded. He knew as well as she: Kevin had been the one in ten. Why should Erin be any different?

As soon as he left, her hands starting shaking. She tried to clasp them together, to control the movement, but the trembling only grew worse. Neil stood up and, using only one arm for his walker, headed to the down-stairs bathroom. He returned with a glass of water and a vial of Valium she hadn't touched in years, put the water on the coffee table, then shook two pills into his hand and handed them to her.

"You'd better take these."

"I don't want them, Neil."

"Please—just this once."

She took the pills. Within fifteen minutes, the shaking stopped; within thirty minutes, she felt numb. She leaned back on the sofa, waiting . . . Neil paced the floor in front of her, his walker thumping back and forth along the carpet.

It was close to eight o'clock when the doorbell rang again. She started to stand up.

"Stay put, Chris, I'll get it." Neil was already on his way to the door. She sat on the edge of the couch . . . She heard the sound of Neil's and the lieutenant's voices, but couldn't make out their words. She stood up and went to the foyer. As soon as she got there, the lieutenant stopped talking; he looked at her, then back at Neil. "Maybe alone, Neil."

"There's no news on Erin yet, Chris. Why don't you lie down upstairs?"

"No."

"I promise, if there's anything—anything at all—I'll tell you."

"She's my daughter too. I'm not leaving."

Neil sighed, then turned back to the lieutenant. "Go ahead—what were you about to say?"

"I doubt this has anything to do with the girl, but I just came up with something I think you ought to know."

"Let's have it."

"I had the boys at the department check out the usual. Strangers in the neighborhood, that kind of thing."

"And?"

"Late last night one of the patrol cops stopped a young boy—seventeen, eighteen—over in the park. Not really doing anything, just minding his own business. Still, you know anything like that we check out ..."

"Go on."

"The officer finally sent him on his way, told him he couldn't camp out there."

"What's the point, Jack?"

"The point is the kid's name. At least, the name he gave the officer."

"What was it?"

"Kevin Mathews."

Neil's expression froze as if the slightest movement would knock his concentration out of whack. Chris felt as if she were being suddenly swept into her dreams—and given a message delivered hundreds of times before.

Finally Neil turned to her. "Are you all right, Chris?"

She started to speak, but all she could manage was a nod.

"I'm going with Jack, we'll check out the park." He reached down and stroked her face. "Don't get your hopes up, Chris. Chances are it's some kind of misunderstanding, a mixup of names ..."

"I want to go, too."

"No, Chris, you can't. Erin is still missing—she might come home on her own. If she does, I want you here."

Neil was right, Chris knew. She had to be here for Erin. Besides, it was a misunderstanding ... a mixup of names. Neil put on his coat and went out with the lieutenant. She went into the parlor. She listened to the car door slamming, then to the police car starting up. She went to the window, pulled aside the draperies and watched as the white cruiser sped down the block toward the roadway to the park.

Chris stayed there for a long time, staring into the darkness ...

CHAPTER THIRTY-ONE

The first thing that penetrated his brain that morning wasn't water; it was a voice—Erin's voice—saying, "You all right, Kevin?" He opened his eyes, rolled over on the grass, and looked up, surprised to see her though he wasn't sure why. She had never listened to him before—what had made him think she'd start now? She carried a big brown bag and held it out to him like a peace offering. He sat up, took the bag from her and went through it: four bologna sandwiches, three blueberry muffins, a box of raisins, four cans of root beer, a carton of orange juice.

"I told you to stay away from here."

"I thought you'd be hungry."

"There's enough here to last me a week."

"I thought maybe I'd stay. And eat with you."

"What time is it?"

"Seven-thirty."

His lips turned up in a smile and he began to laugh. Erin just stood there, watching him. When he finally stopped, she asked, "What's so funny?"

He shrugged. "I don't know." And he really didn't. Except here he was, camping out in the park, not sure from one minute to the next if his brain would boil over or flood out, and Erin—of all people—wanted to have a picnic breakfast with him.

She knelt down on the ground next to him.

"Get away," he said. "Don't sit near me."

"Why not?"

"Because I said so—that's why."

She backed away and sat. "Where's the car, Kevin?"

He gestured toward the trees. "I hid it back there. A cop stopped here last night and told me to get out."

"But you aren't going to, are you?"

He took out his jackknife again and started to play with it. "I don't know. Suppose I do?"

"Then we'll never get to see each other again."

"So what? I don't know if I even want to see you again."

"What about mom and dad?"

"Don't talk to me about Neil."

"Why not?"

"Because he's the one who killed me."

"What do you mean by that?"

"The funeral for Kevin. He's the one who made everyone believe he was dead. Even me."

She didn't say anything.

"How would you feel if it were you?"

For once she didn't try to defend Neil, she just shrugged. Then, "What about mom? I know you want to see her."

He lifted the knife and again cut into his hand, this time working around to the other side of his wrist. A little puddle of blood formed, then dripped down onto a leaf.

"Don't do that, Kevin. Please!"

"I have to."

"Why?"

He looked up at Erin, trying to think what to tell her. He decided on the truth: "Because I have to hurt someone."

After a while they did eat, and by three o'clock they had finished most of the food. They talked a lot too, mostly about things they had done as kids. Of course Erin did most of the talking, and he did most of the listening. She resisted asking him to come home, but when three o'clock rolled around and he said, "You'd better go," she said, "I'm not leaving without you."

"You have to—your mother will worry."

She stood up and walked over to the edge of the hill and looked down. "I don't care," she said. "You won't let me tell her or dad you're here, so I'm going to do the next best thing. I'm going to stay with you."

"That's crazy."

"No crazier than you staying." She stared down at the playground, a thought forming. "Besides . . ."

"Besides what?"

"I never even told you the best story of all. And it's one I never ever told anybody before."

"Sounds like some story."

"It is. But you've got to promise not to laugh."

"Okay—I promise."

"Come over here," she said, gesturing with her hand. He went to the edge of the hill and stood next to her. Erin pointed down to the playground where two boys were riding bicycles. "See that boy—the big one with the red hair?"

"Yeah, I see him."

"When I was eight years old, when mom first let me come to the park alone, he used to really torture me."

"How old was he?"

"About eleven."

"What did he do to you?"

"All kinds of things."

He looked down at the ground, at his sneaker digging into the dirt. "Like what, Erin?"

"He'd never let me go on any of the rides. If I did get on something, he'd push me off. Once he pushed me into the duck pond. And he always made fun of me."

"About what?"

"Well, I'm not so bad now, but when I was little, I was really ugly. Of course, don't ever ask mom or dad if that was so, because they'd say it wasn't. But the truth is, I was awful to look at. I was little and skinny, with big buck teeth.

"And this kid used to call you names?"

"All the time."

"Why didn't you tell your mom about him?"

"Because if I did, she'd never let me come to the park alone again."

"So what finally happened?"

"So one day he and his friend dragged me into the woods." Kevin sank down on the ground, not sure he even wanted to hear any more, but of course Erin went on. "He tried to get me to pull down my panties . . ."

He looked up at her, knowing she was waiting for him to ask, so he did. "And did you?"

"No, I ran. He chased me and said if I ever came back to the park again he'd get me good."

"Did you tell your mother then?"

"No, I didn't have to."

"Why not?"

"Because I told my brother instead."

He stared at her.

"You see, I used to pretend that I had a big brother. And of course, he was you, Kevin."

A pause, then, "But you never even knew me."

"No, but I knew about you. Not a lot, because mom couldn't talk about you and dad wouldn't . . . Mostly I got to know you from the pictures in the storage closet. And even though you died—at least, I thought you died— before I was born, that didn't mean you weren't my brother." She stopped.

Kevin looked away. His eyes were wet. "How'd you get the kid to leave you alone?"

"That's the best part. I didn't really, you did."

"What do you mean?"

"I wrote him a letter, wrote it real slow so my handwriting looked grown-up, and I signed *your* name. And the next day in the park, I gave it to him."

"What did I say in the letter?"

"Just that you were going to break him into little pieces for picking on your kid sister. And that you'd meet him the next day at the duck pond after school to do it."

He smiled; he wanted to laugh, but he remembered his promise just in time. "Did he show up?" he asked her.

She shook her head. "Not that day and not the next. In fact, not for two whole weeks. And when he did finally show up, he stayed as far away from me and the duck pond as he could get."

He stared at Erin for a few minutes, then said. "Come on, let's go in the car. It's getting cold."

It was after eight o'clock, and Erin was asleep in the back of the car. He was sitting up front, trying to figure out how to get her to go home, when he heard a car engine.

He looked out the window, through the trees, but didn't see any lights. He listened again: still nothing. Finally he turned on the radio real low—a piano solo— then sat back and closed his eyes. That's when he heard the rustling of leaves. He jumped forward, looking out the window. This time, there was a light—a lantern, directed at him. He pushed the door open and jumped out, pulling Fletcher's hunting knife from under the driver's seat. He heard Erin getting up.

"Stay down," he said, hoping for once she'd listen.

Then, slowly, the light moved out of his face, and he could see Neil standing there.

"David?" was all he said.

Erin got out from the back seat and stood next to the car, near him. Neil's eyes shifted to Erin, and he took a deep breath. "Did David force you here, Erin?" he said finally.

"No, dad. I came on my own."

"For God's sake, why? We've been worried sick. The police are out hunting for you."

She just stood there.

"Answer me, Erin. Why?"

"Because he wouldn't come home."

"That's David's choice—not yours."

"But you don't understand."

A pause. "Okay, I'm listening. Tell me."

Erin turned to Kevin. "Please—oh, please, *you* tell him."

He shook his head.

Tears spilled over, down her face. "Then let me."

Again he shook his head, but this time, Neil shouted: "Whatever it is, Erin—say it. And say it now!"

She turned back to Neil and swallowed hard. "Dad, this isn't David. I mean, it is, but ..." She paused and all sound seemed to pause with her, until her thin voice cracked through: "This is my brother, Kevin."

He heard Neil's swift intake of breath, then the thump of the lantern onto the ground. Neil stood there without a move or a word, staring ... "But how—" he began, then his voice cracked and he was unable to go on.

But Erin knew the question. "The picture, dad ... the one with the man. He's got one just like it ... in his scrapbook. I even saw it."

Kevin waited for him to say more, but he didn't. He just stared at his face as if he had never seen one like it before. Finally Kevin held up the knife and walked to Neil, touching the blade to his chest.

"Don't, Kevin—*please* don't!" Erin cried.

First a twig snapped, then a shadow jumped from the bushes to the clearing. He looked to his left; the cop was pointing his gun at him.

"Drop the knife, kid."

He didn't, of course.

"This gun will go off before you have a chance to use it," the cop said. "Now you just—"

Still staring at Kevin, Neil finally spoke: "Put the gun away, Jack."

"I can't do that, Neil. Not until he gets rid of the knife."

Suddenly: "Get out of here!" Neil shouted. "And take Erin with you."

The cop went over and took Erin's arm; she pulled back, but he marched her off into the darkness. Kevin and Neil stood face to face.

"Kevin, I ..." A solitary tear streaked down Neil's cheek. "Can you ever forgive me?"

He didn't answer him—he didn't know if he could.

"I've been looking for you ... For so long."

Kevin pushed the tip of the knife back against Neil's chest. "Then why did you hold a funeral for me?"

Neil looked up, and Kevin waited. Finally his eyes came down and looked into Kevin's. "Your mother," he said. "I did it for your mother."

"My mother didn't want me dead. Not then."

"No, not ever. But I had a choice—it was your funeral or hers."

"What's that supposed to mean?"

"She needed so badly to grieve. But she couldn't, not the way it was."

"So you gave her a reason."

A sigh, then, "Do you know that your mother never sets foot in this park?"

Kevin nodded.

"And do you know why that is?"

"Because her little boy disappeared from here."

"That's not all there is to it. I would get calls from the police, two or three times a week. She'd be wandering around here, usually finding some little boy that—to her—looked like you. Finally she agreed to see a psychiatrist, and I thought it was helping. The calls stopped coming ..."

Kevin waited.

"One day, it was early April, you'd been missing then about fourteen, fifteen months ..."

"Go on."

"I'd left the office early, the weather forecast was for a late-season northeaster. When I got home, there was already three inches of snow on the ground. Your mother wasn't home. I looked everywhere, the police looked everywhere. She was missing for twelve hours, Kevin."

"Where was she?"

"She was here. Right here." He pointed toward the top of the hill. "She was lying on the ground with binoculars, keeping a lookout over the playground. She'd fallen asleep, fainted, something. When we found her, she was unconscious, nearly frozen to death. There was a bagful of your toys and books next to her."

A lump swelled in his throat, growing bigger and bigger.

"And when the doctors saved *her*, they saved another life too. Your sister's. Your mother was one month pregnant with Erin."

Kevin could feel his eyes filling up.

"Do you have any idea how she felt about you?" Neil's voice choked.

He nodded his head, and tears flickered down his cheeks.

"I wanted to keep her, Kevin. Not just for me or Erin, but for you. When you came home, I wanted her waiting."

Kevin's arm dropped and the knife rolled onto the ground, but Neil didn't even seem to notice.

"And you did come home. Right to our door." He shook his head. "How . . . how did you know?"

"The newspaper story about the funeral. When I was seven, Fletcher gave it to me."

Neil put out his hand to Kevin's chin and lifted his face up so he was almost eye-level. Now his own tears were skiing down his face. "And still I didn't guess," he said. "Only your mother felt it. She loved you like a son from the very first moment. She gave you *your* room."

"But that was before."

"And now?"

"Now it's too late. She knows . . ."

"I don't understand . . . knows what?"

"About me."

"Only what *you* know counts. What a person knows about himself."

"But David did things. Bad things."

Neil studied his face, then nodded his head. "What choice did you have?"

"People have choices. Always. And he was no different."

"How did he—how did you feel about what you did?"

Kevin didn't answer, just looked down at the ground,

digging his sneaker into the dirt.

"Don't you understand, you made your choice inside. The only place you had any control."

He thought about what Neil said, then stiffened, stepped back, and shook his head.

"What?"

"Fletcher. I killed him."

"No, Kevin, you didn't. His real name's Louis Flannery, and he's not dead."

"You're wrong, I stabbed him, I saw him lying there."

"He has a scar, a knife wound. But he didn't die."

"You're lying. I tell you I killed him!"

"Listen to me, Kevin—"

But he couldn't listen. He dropped to the ground and with his knees raised tighly to his chest and his hands covering his ears, he shouted, "No! No! No!"

Neil threw his walker aside, then sank down next to him and pushed himself over until his face was only a few inches from his. "What is it? Say it."

"I told you—I murdered!" He raised his arms and beat his fists against Neil's chest. "I hated him, God how I hated him! The bastard—I *wanted* him to die!"

Then as if his rage had suddenly exhausted itself, he collapsed against Neil's chest, crying. Father and son's arms intertwined and they cried together ... Finally Kevin pulled himself away. They didn't say a word for the next few minutes, just listened to the rustling of leaves blowing across the ground, the hum of cars cruising down below on the street. Neil reached out, grabbed hold of his walker, and stood up. Then held out his hand to Kevin. "What do you say, son—time to go home?"

They all drove back to the house in Kevin's car. Kevin helped Neil climb the front steps. Neil and Erin went inside, and he hung back on the porch. Neil turned and saw him, then came back out.

"What if she can't face me?" he said.

"The only thing in her whole life she ever couldn't face was losing you, Kevin. Don't you understand—having you back is all that matters to her. There's nothing you can tell her that would change that."

"But it took so long. So damned long . . ."

Neil sighed. "Yes it did, son."

"And now it's different. You know it as well as I do."

"Different how?"

"All those years. They're gone. We can't get them back no matter what we do. No matter how much we try."

Kevin stood there watching him, waiting for Neil to tell him he was wrong, but he didn't. Instead he reached out and took Kevin's hand in both of his. "Then what should we do?" he said finally. "Where do we go from here?"

He shrugged.

"Tell me, Kevin. Tell me what we can do, and we'll do it."

Again he shrugged.

"There's still today." He stopped a moment, then went on. "And there's still tomorrow. I'm not willing to throw *them* away too. Are you?"

Kevin shook his head, and Neil stepped back into the foyer with him following.

Neil and Erin headed for the parlor: Kevin waited by himself in the dining room. He heard Chris stand up and rush to Erin. "Thank God you're home! Where've you *been*, Erin?"

Erin didn't answer. Instead Kevin heard yelping—then, before he knew what was happening, the puppy scampered into the dining room and skidded to a stop in front of him. He bent down, picked up the puppy and held him against him.

Chris furrowed her brow. "Did you see that, Neil? Why do you suppose the puppy's so excited?"

Silence.

"I'd better fetch him."

"No, wait, Chris."

"What's going on? Your shirt, Neil—it's ripped."

"Nothing. Only a branch."

"But there is something, I can tell. Neil, your eyes, you've been—" She stopped, then. "Kevin?"

"Yes, Chris."

"You found him?"

"With Erin."

"But . . . I don't understand."

Suddenly Kevin wanted to back out—to run. It was only a fantasy. But it was already too late. He could hear the legs of Neil's walker thumping across the rug toward Chris. "He's here," Neil said. "We brought him home with us."

That's when the puppy and Kevin came through the archway. He was afraid even to look at her, afraid to see what he'd find in her eyes, but somehow he did look all the same. Her lips parted and her eyes got wide and so shiny he couldn't look away. She turned to Neil: "Kevin?" she whispered. He nodded his head and she turned back to him, raising her hands to her lips and sucking in her breath.

"Mom?"

"Oh, my dear God," she said. And he went to her because she was too stunned to come to him. Her shiny eyes stared up at him; she touched his face, brushing her cool familiar fingertips over his forehead and chin and cheeks, wiping his tears. Then she sighed and pulled him to her, puppy and all, wrapping her arms tightly around them.

CHAPTER EPILOGUE

Chris pulled open the curtain in the kitchen, then raised the window, letting in the warm spring air. Two robins flitted away together into the bush, then soared up: one flew with a worm in its beak to its nesting young; the other found a branch nearby, eager to make the trip once again. Not far from the branch were the beginnings of a garden: yesterday, Kevin and she had been outdoors with shovels and rakes, preparing the earth for planting. Rasputin—alias Maverick—slid around the kitchen floor, chasing his tail, until he finally went to the door and lay down to wait for Kevin.

Chris poured another cup of coffee and sat down. Neil had already left for work, Erin was in school, and Kevin had driven off to his weekly appointment with his psychiatrist, Dr. Margaret Stagler. Once a month, they all went for family therapy. At their last appointment, Kevin told her the dream that he still had occasionally.

"What do you think it means, Kevin?" Dr. Stagler asked.

"I think the beautiful lady calling me is my mother."

"And the guard?"

"I don't know about the guard."

"What about the silver tongue?"

Kevin looked over at Erin, then back at the doctor. "Maybe that represents my sister's braces. Or, for that matter, the aluminum walker my father had for so long."

She nodded. "And who do you suspect is behind you, Kevin?"

He looked down at his hands in his lap. "I expect to see a mirror, I expect to see myself looking back."

"Ah, and then once you face yourself, you must be ready to forgive yourself. But you are not quite ready to do that. Are you Kevin?

He shrugged.

Kevin had come a long way, but he still tended to separate David from Kevin. When he did something he was ashamed of, he often put it off on David. Or someone else—often quite unaware that this is what he had been doing. But Chris and he talked about it. And no matter what happened during the day, every night before he went to bed, they spent a while together alone. Sometimes she read to him, or he to her. Usually poetry. Kevin loved to discuss the meaning of a poem.

He didn't quite believe Flannery was alive until Neil and Chris took him down to pick him out of a police lineup. All the rest of that week, he was quiet, distant. Finally, at therapy, he admitted what it really was that bothered him: "My reason for wanting to kill him," he said. "Not really because of what he did to me or was trying to make me do. It was because he was going to leave me."

"Who else did you have, Kevin?" the doctor asked. "To you, good or bad he was the center of your universe. The only family that you knew. Children are abused by their parents every day and still, when asked who they want to live with, almost always choose their parents."

Neil and Kevin had been having discussions lately about Kevin's future. Kevin had already applied to several schools for the fall semester—all in Boston. None of them were ready for a separation yet. At the moment Kevin was doing photographic work, part time, for a local newspaper. Although he liked it, he was not yet sure of his course of study or career plans. Neil hoped he would choose law, but to his credit he hadn't pushed.

For a while Chris put more energy and time into her family than was good for them—or her. Then one night Neil slipped an article about an organization called

"Child Find" onto her nightstand. "They're doing some good work," he said. She read the article and called the Boston chapter the next day, volunteering her services several mornings a week.

Just last night as Neil and she were getting ready for bed, he said, "When I was lying there helpless after the stroke, all I knew was *I couldn't die yet.* There was something I had to do first. I couldn't remember seeing Kevin's photograph in that magazine, not then. Only when I came home and saw it again."

"How could you keep it all to yourself for so long?"

"Because I couldn't tell you until I found him. And there you went and found him yourself."

"No, Neil. We all played a part. But mostly, Kevin found us."

She leaned over and kissed him, then nuzzled close, her arm over his chest. And for maybe the hundredth time, she drifted off to sleep thinking how lucky she was. Everyone present and accounted for, safe and sound. Neil. Erin. And Kevin—her first born.